T0162737

A MESSAGE FROM GOD

A TRUE STORY

Rainy Sumner

authorHOUSE®

AuthorHouse™
1663 Liberty Drive
Bloomington, IN 47403
www.authorhouse.com
Phone: 1-800-839-8640

First published by AuthorHouse   11/24/2009

ISBN: 978-1-4490-4961-4 (e)
ISBN: 978-1-4490-4953-9 (sc)

Printed in the United States of America
Bloomington, Indiana

This book is printed on acid-free paper.

NOBODY WOULD LISTEN

A STORY ABOUT
GOD

I was born in a little country town outside of Utah . My earliest memories are of me outside Playing I remember living on a college campus. I remember people adoring me always complementing me. I remember playing outside by myself just talking. I pretended to be talking to people. When I got a doll, there were no words to express that feeling. I talked their heads off! I hugged them, I treated them with such care. I had a feeling that they needed to be taken care of. I don't have clear memories of being inside the apartment, it was always dark. All I can see is the man who fathered me, sitting in front of the T.V., with a beer. I'm trying to get his attention, but I never could. I remember the woman who had me, getting me ready to go somewhere, church, outside to play by myself, or to go to work with the man who fathered me. I remember being so impatient, busy body, ready to go. I love clothes. I love looking pretty. The man that fathered me, worked on the college campus, where we lived, and both parents attended. When he would take me to work with him, I WAS HAPPY! It was the people that I liked, because they liked me. Everybody was so nice, everybody was friendly, everybody wanted to take me with them, that was so much fun. I remember being picked up and thrown in the air. That scared me but I loved every minute of it. Sitting in the classrooms, I was given colors, pencil and paper to draw. I remember not liking my drawings. I remember the cafeteria, more than anything. It was so bright. There were no walls, or the walls were made of glass. I distinctly remember the cafeteria, because I loved running up and down that hallway, and by it being glass and so bright, I remember loving that place. When I was taken inside the cafeteria to eat, which was pretty often, that was the best thing. People were so nice! I remember that woman taking me with her to go and see that man. I Remember it didn't feel good. I remember playing outside, talking to myself. I remember discovering rocks that I could write with on the sidewalk. I remember getting a jump-rope which I loved so. Then out of nowhere, there was this man, white man. He would talk to me. I wasn't sure at first, but I remember that woman coming out to check on me. I remember her talking to him. I remember the conversation. I remember him saying nice things about me. After that, I remember him standing in the breezeway with this long camera, taking pictures of me. I became so shy at first. I remember sitting on the porch wanting to talk to myself, but now I remember worrying , thinking the strange man might here me. Whenever he would come out, I would shut down. I remember him asking that woman who had me, could I have candy, THAT DID IT! I wasn't shy anymore! I remember him taking pictures of me as I played. I loved that. I remember him holding conversations with me. He was so nice. I remember getting the pictures he had taken of me. I remember wanting to keep the pictures forever. I remember him not giving us all of them. I remember not liking that. I remember daydreaming into the ones he did leave, or let us have. I remember someone teaching me to draw a hop-scotch. I loved every minute of it. I remember learning the song "Banana nana foe fauna". I remember a lady brining a baby swing with a real baby, outside. I ALMOST DIED! I was so happy. I remember my mouth dropped wide open. I remember not hesitating to ask, can I play with her. I still have a picture of me with that baby, thanks to my friend the camera man. All of the pictures were black and white, and all of them turned out beautiful! That's when I began to notice a feeling I didn't like, I wanted my pictures. I remember actually being mad, my feelings were hurt. I remember turning that knob on that baby swing and making her laugh. I remember playing hide and seek with my big brother. I remember going with him to play in the woods. I remember trying to like it. I remember there was no sound. I remember the trees , the sun. I remember my brother having some type of hide away that he created. I always had a creepy feeling out there. I remember wondering, could I live out there. I remember wanting to give it a try. (my imagination)

I remember thinking if I actually tried that, that woman would fuss at me and make me come home. I remember hunger pains kicking in. I remember it lasting more than usual. I remember the camera man not being around anymore. I remember being sad, and mad, about "no more picture taking". I remember the baby was gone also. I remember it being cold. I remember not wanting to go outside to play in the cold. I remember that woman making my brother and I go outside and play in the cold anyway. I don't remember anything about the inside of the apartment we lived in. The only memories of the inside was when I was mad about not getting all of my pictures, and getting ready to go somewhere. All I can remember is being in what seem to be the hallway. I have very vague memories about the family members. I remember Easter! I remember my yellow and white NEW SUNDAY SUIT! I remember it had pleats all the way around. It was white at the top, with a yellow jacket. White ruffle socks , with black paten leather shoes. I remember feeling like a doll. I remember that woman taking me to church on campus in my beautiful outfit. I remember her holding my hand, standing in front of that church, talking to people. I remember getting loose and slowly sneaking off. I remember the church being new. It was big and beautiful, like a castle or chapel. I remember construction stuff around. I remember white mud everywhere, it had been raining. I remember getting further and further away. I remember ending up in the woods. There were tall trees all around me. I remember being scared and looking up at the sun, it was SO bright. I distinctly remember SOMETHING. SOMEBODY SAID SOMETHING! That voice came from the top of the trees! I distinctly remember the rain, but that was not THUNDER. I remember running for my LIFE! I remember running straight into that white mud, that I avoided so very carefully as I tipped into those woods. That same scary feeling is engraved in me. I remember shaking. I remember shaking that woman fussing at me. I remember the white mud all over my shoes. I remember her fussing , forcing me to be still, daring me to move. I remember not being able to go inside that new church with mud all over my shoes. I remember her going into the restroom to get paper towel, or napkins, there was none, so she had to ask people for tissue. I remember her fussing and cleaning my shoes and making me pretty again. I remember being scared as hell, from whatever that was in the woods. I remember her holding on to my hand very tight, and walking down the aisle in that chapel. I remember the new red carpet, the beautiful windows, and the ceiling being very high. I remember being scared and trying to get loose. I think I was antsy the whole time. I remember leaving, she had my hand, but I wasn't going anywhere, I was too scared. I remember thinking she was a pretty lady. I remember her clothes, her shoes, her hair. (early sixties) I remember looking at those Trees thinking, I'll never get near you again! I remember going to take pictures in my darling little yellow and white suit. I remember being scared and anxious. I remember the photographer playing with me, placing me in different poses. I remember him asking me how old I was. I remember saying the wrong age. I remember that woman correcting me. I remember the photographer told me to show him with my fingers how old I was. I was three, but I raised my whole hand, stating that I was five. That woman fussed at me, but I didn't care. She tried to make me hold up three fingers, I wouldn't. I didn't want to be three, I wanted to be five. That picture still hang on the wall in that woman's house. I began to remember a lot of fighting in that house. Those people who had me fought all the time. Things changed. I remember something about a baby. I remember being with that woman's sister. I remember when being with her , you had to behave. I remember spending the night with her, waking the next morning , putting on my clothes, eating breakfast, (wheat check, didn't like them then, don't like them now). I remember sitting on her couch being quite. I remember her apartment being full of light, bright , sun , daylight. There was a huge dark period, then out of the blue we had moved to a new neighborhood. I remember that house. I remember the neighborhood, it was beautiful. I remember really liking it. I remember the pretty houses and pretty yards. Low and behold, I remember my absolute, most favorite cousin living on that same street. I remember our house being dark all the time. I remember the room my brother and I shared. The bunk beds , and the plaid covers. I remember being cold, I needed more cover. I remember the kitchen very well. I remember the sun coming through the window. I remember the woman making fresh orange juice, cooking that man bacon and eggs. I remember drinking that orange juice. I remember that woman feeding me oatmeal. I remember GAGGING! I remember hating oatmeal and cream of wheat! I remember thinking of those hunger pains. I remember at the beginning I refused to eat. I remember getting some bacon and eggs. I remember that's all I wanted. I remember a woman who was supposed to be my god-mother. I remember she gave me a present, it was a present I couldn't play with.

I remember liking the gift, A cup, bowl and saucer, with my name on it. My name was spelled wrong. Of course I didn't know at the time. I just liked the gold letters. When I learned that my name was wrong, I was very uncomfortable with that. (I still have that dish set, and all I remember is GAGGING!) I remember being hungry. I remember going to bed hungry. I remember making my mind up to swallow that nasty stuff so I wouldn't be hungry. I hated that feeling. I don't remember the baby in the house, but low and behold I had a baby brother. I remember my high chair. I can still feel that woman squeezing that tray in my stomach. I remember the big gray pots with baby bottles in them on the stove, but I don't remember the baby that much. I remember one beautiful day she let me go outside. I remember sitting on the steps. I remember her bringing the baby outside, placing him in his walker. I stopped breathing. I couldn't believe it , she told me to watch him. I did just that. I guarded him with my life. I remember jumping and being happy! I was the best little three year old security guard anyone could have. I remember everyday being pretty. I remember pretty grass, pretty flowers. Wouldn't you know it, I LEARNED ABOUT COUSINS!

I thought it was CHRISTMAS! Cousin Henry and cousin PENNY! Henry was three years older, cousin Penny was only six months older than myself. I remember that man's mother lived with my cousins. Come to find out, cousin Penny's mother and that man that had me , were brother and sister, and of course, the mother was there for her daughter. It was July. I remember cousin Penny got a bike on her birthday. I remember she couldn't ride, neither could I. I remember cousin Henry talked me into letting him teach me to ride. I remember the training wheels, they were in the air. I remember him holding the bike while I paddled. Our house was on a hill. When you turned on our street, you were on a hill, then you would go down quick. The street was curved like an S. My cousins lived down the hill. I remember him giving me instructions. I remember trying to take it all in. I remember him letting that bike go. I remember being terrified, but I refused to fall. I refused to let go of those handle bars. I remember going down that hill, not being able to stop. I remember rolling into someone's beautiful yard, not being able to steer. I remember thinking we had better get out of this yard, but grass don't hurt like sidewalk. I remember letting them know I was through, DONE! I remember finally catching on. I remember everyday, I couldn't wait to go over their house. I remember clearly that , that man's mother had very little to do with me. I remember a lot of fighting going on at my house. I remember a milk carton flying across the room, knocking out a light bulb. I remember going to bed hungry on a regular basis. I remember running to my cousin house a lot, but there were times when I couldn't even get food there and they were my cousins. I remember watching that old lady in that pretty kitchen cooking. I remember the food smelled so GOOD! I remember daydreaming at those pretty pork chops. I remember having to go home. I remember I did not want to go. I remember my cousins walking me home, explaining to me who that woman was. I remember finally catching on to riding a bike. Simply HEAVEN! I remember that woman taking me to someone's house and leaving me. I remember being scared and hating her. The houses in the neighborhood were pretty, they looked like cottages. I remember a feeling I couldn't explain, as if something was wrong or not right. I remember listening to conversations about that man's mother dying. I remember the story about her being on the bus stop, waiting for the bus and dropped dead of a heart attack or a vain in her head burst. I remember that woman getting me ready for the funeral. I remember being scared and confused. I remember the church out in the country. I remember that woman picking me up to see the body. I remember being terrified! I remember that man not sitting with us. I remember trying to go to him, as if I hadn't seen him in a while. I remember seeing that man, his brother, and brother-in law standing in front of the casket, what seemed like a long time. I remember realizing he was sad. I remember wanting to go with him but I couldn't. I remember having to go to the restroom. I remember being told there were no restrooms. I remember that woman taking me outside to use the restroom behind a tree. I remember not wanting to, but I couldn't hold it. I remember her cleaning me with paper towels and leaves. Once again, there is this huge blank, as if everything just went totally dark. There is a huge gap. I have no memory of what happened after that funeral. A year a more past. I remember moving into a new place without that man. I remember hating that place, a shotgun house. You walk in, there was a room, you keep straight, there was another room, you keep straight, there was the kitchen, that was too little, even for me, you make another step and to your left there was the worst room of all, the bathroom. I remember the wooden floor. I remember it being cold and damp. I remember hating that place. I don't remember playing with my baby brother anymore.

There was a new addition to the family, a baby girl. I remember not having nothing to do with her. I remember acting like she didn't exist. I remember the milk man. I remember that woman leaving empty bottles outside for the milk man , and he would leave new bottles of milk. The bottles were glass with plastic red handles. I remember not liking that place at all. I remember the milk man began to leave a box of fresh doughnuts. I remember loving that. I remember the milk man began to leave vanilla bean ice cream. I remember trying to be happy, trying to get use to that place. I remember playing by myself out side. I remember a bird nest on the roof. I remember sitting on that porch and an egg fell from the nest. I remember the egg cracked open and there was a baby bird. I remember getting my big brother, showing him the baby bird. I remember him getting a shoe box and punching holes in it so the baby bird could breath. I remember the baby bird died. I remember waiting for another egg to fall. I remember practicing for a wedding. I was so scared to walk down that aisle. I remember going to my baby cousin's funeral, she was only months old. I remember her casket and everything around it was pink. I remember wanting to go home. I remember thinking why do we keep going to those places. I remember a little boy who lived next door. I remember his dog. I couldn't stand that dog. All he did was bark at people. The dog would chase us, but never did any harm. I remember the dog being pregnant, thinking, what is going on. I remember playing with the little boy next door. I remember us discovering a bee hive in that big old tree in the front yard. I remember us throwing rocks into the bee hive. I remember his mother and that woman caught us. I remember trembling, watching that woman pick a switch to whip me. I remember running with everything I had. I remember, no matter how fast I was running, she and that switch was right there. I remember knowing what I did was wrong. That was a feeling, it had nothing to do with being taught it was wrong. I remember going to another funeral. GOD, enough is enough! At the age of five, that was a bit too much. I remember thinking , why dose she keep taking me to those sad, scary things. I remember meeting the neighbors next door to us, it was a duplex. I remember the lady and her three sons. I remember being so unhappy. I remember the lady trying to be nice. (she looked like Endora from Bewitched) I remember her son trying to be nice. I remember the two older ones were nice, but something wasn't right. I remember the two older ones didn't live with her, they just came around. I remember the younger one, I didn't like him, he made me nervous. I remember more baby birds falling from the nest. I always got my brother to get a shoe box, punch holes in it, so the babies could live. I remember feeding the birds, trying to care for them. I remember thinking, if I took care of them, they would become strong and fly away. I remember each time, they died. I remember big rats in that place. I remember being too scared to walk around. I remember staying in the bed, if I couldn't go outside. I remember going to the doctor a lot, my baby brother had asthma bad. I remember not paying him any attention anymore. That woman tried to force that new baby on me, so I refused to play with either one. I remember the time came for me to start school. I remember wanting to go to school with my big brother, but I was five and my birthday fell in December, which meant I had to wait a year. I've heard that story all my life. It's funny, I don't remember any other schooling at all. I didn't like Head Start at all. I knew nothing. I remember hanging with cousin Penny at church, she was smart. She was the third child. She always asked me, what did I want to be when I grew up? I had no clue to what she was talking about. No one ever talk with me at home, it was just me, myself and I, with a POWERFUL imagination! Yet, I knew nothing. I remember the guy next door. I remember how he would come and try to talk to me. I remember I didn't like him. I remember my brother and I use to bath together. I remember not wanting to go in that bathroom by myself. I remember my brother and I had fun in the tub. I remember we use to sing out loud, laughing and having fun. My brother is five years older than I am. He was my brother and I was crazy about him. I was five, and knew nothing about people being naked, what are you talking about. I remember the guy next door coming over more often. I remember him asking me if I was hungry, and I would say yes. I was. Other older men had sat and talked with me and nothing happened. I remember him taking me by the hand. I remember my brother didn't like that.

I remember that woman not being around. I remember when leaving with that guy, the feeling I got. I remember him taking me to their place next door and sitting me on the couch. I remember him asking me if I were hungry, but once he got me over there, there was no food. I remember him putting his arm around me. I remember wanting to go home. I remember him going and getting me some very nasty food. His mother couldn't cook at all. I remember not eating at all. I remember that food was stinky and had an odor. I remember him trying to be nice to me. I remember wanting to go home. I remember his mother being in the next room. I remember thinking, she's going to come out in any second. I remember him unzipping his pants. I remember him trying to grab my hands. I remember him trying to get me to do things. I remember him touching me. I remember not knowing what to think. I remember him getting upset. I remember him making me stand and face him. I remember him taking my hands trying to force me to do things. I remember getting tired and sleepy. I remember thinking, I would never say I was hungry again. It came to me that I was being lied to. I was tricked. I never got a chance to go home that night. He kept me up all night. He knocked me around. He slapped me to the floor, then picked me up by hair. He kept asking me was I hungry. When I would say no, that was the wrong answer. He finally took me home. I wanted to just die. I remember that woman was nowhere around. I remember when she walked through that door, my brother told her, and she did nothing. She made me think it was me. I was totally confused, puzzled and scared out of my mind. I remember how my brother began to look at me when that monster would come and get me and bring me back. I remember being beaten to death, and coming home starving more than ever. I remember him beating me because I never told him what he wanted me to say. I remember being a hard headed child and for good reasons. I remember having to get up and attend Head Start. Out of the blue, that woman appears, she's home now. I remember my brother telling her about that monster, and what did she do? NOTHING. She get me ready for school. GOD, I hated that woman. I hated her hands. I hated everything about her. She would comb my hair, I would pull it out!!!! I remember being taught the alphabets and numbers. I had such a hard time. I remember trying hard to remember what letter came next. I remember having a terrible time with numbers. I remember not liking my hand writing. I remember thinking, hoping the teacher would see through me and take me with her. I remember that woman watching me walk to school as if she cared. I remember not wanting to go to that place that was supposed to be home. I remember that thing coming to get me again and again. He always asked if I was hungry, I finally learned what was really happening, but I was FIVE! He would grab me or pick me up and take me away. I remember him trying to give me bread pudding. Every time I hear those words, I want to kill. I remember not giving in to him. I remember he grabbed my hands and forced me. I remember a light on in the kitchen, but it was black dark every where else. I remember thinking, hoping his mother would come and save me, she never came out of that room. I remember being up all night with him. I remember crying, crying, crying, mostly from being so tired and hungry. I remember my hands being tired and wanting to go to bed. I remember that woman only being around in the mornings. I remember being more scared of her than the monster. I knew she was going to kill me once she found out. I remember we got a television, it was on a stand with wheels. I remember my brother got a record player. I remember the first Christmas there. Santa was very nice to me. The toys, and the clothes, and the mink coat. (In my head it was a mink coat). I remember the vanity the most. I remember sitting there for hours in another world. I remember my doll. I remember not HARMING her or ABUSING at all. I remember that being a good Christmas, but nothing could have made me happy. I remember sitting there at my vanity, and here comes the monster. By this time, he was just taking me. I remembered that my grandmother lived around the corner. We had gone there for Christmas, and of course I didn't want to go back to that place. My grandmother's house was always full of people, family. A couple of aunts, one uncle and cousins lived with her. I never understood. She was just around the corner. I remember the monster spoiling my happiness. He just started taking me against my will. He would keep me up all night. I remember being so tired when I got to school. (Head Start.) I remember not catching on, not learning or being praised, like the other children, I was to tired and sleepy. I remember the mail man flirting with that woman. I remember being scared of men now. I remember that woman and a man taking me with them to eat. I don't remember the food much, just the dessert. It was blueberry cobbler, I remember not chewing, only swallowing. I stuffed my face. I remember clearly, the man she was with, asking her, when was the last time I ate or even had food. I remember that same man bringing fried catfish to the house. I did it again. I swallowed without chewing, and choked on a bone. That woman beat me in my back until that bone came up. I remember thinking, why want she wake the others and feed them too. She always treated me different from the others, in a bad way. I remember her giving me bread and water after that bone came up. All the while she was fussing at me. I finally got a chance to find out what it was like to go to bed on a full stomach. I remember that monster's mother took me to the wrestling match. That was a big thing back then, but by now I was slowly loosing my mind.

That woman that had me and the monster's mother were friends. My big brother told what was happening, but no one did anything. I did not like being with that woman nor her son. I hated that feeling. The cobbler, the fish , the wrestling match, I was always the only child around. I remember after the wrestling match, I wondered was she going to take me to him. I remember always be tired and sleepy. I remember that thing coming after me again. I remember thinking hard, I'm not going!!!! I remembered I had rescued another baby bird, and had it under the bed. I remember the monster got it and threaten to kill it, if I didn't go. I remember being up all night, crying , just wanting to go to bed. I remember my brother and I covering the T.V. and stereo with clothes to hide those things we love from a robber or thief. I think the monster use to threaten us about taking those things. I remember we came home and the T.V. and stereo was gone. I remember being sick at the stomach and so scared. I remember hearing that it was the monster who took those items. I remember him being gone. I remember getting sleep. I remember still being hungry, but I would get up and go to Head Start for the graham crackers and orange juice. I remember the teacher had me draw a picture of my family. I remember drawing that woman, myself, and both brothers, not the girl. I remembered living in that house and the things that were going on and wanted so desperately to cry out loud, but I couldn't. I remember her talking to me about the drawing, but I don't remember a word she said. I remember going to church and seeing my cousin Penny again. I remember being happy about telling people we were cousins. I remember it seemed as though no one saw what was going on, not even the people I lived with. I remember my cousin talking my head off. She was so cool. She knew everything. She could write, spell, She knew what she wanted to be when she grew up. We were only five, going on six. I remember her asking me what did I want to be when I grew up. I remember saying I don't know. I remember never being asked such a thing. I remember her telling me we were going to be airline stewardess. I remember being confused but agreeing. She was my cousin and I loved her. I remember she even explained what a stewardess was. I thought that was so neat. I remember the feeling of not being smart around her. I remember not letting that stop me. I remember a lady and her daughters from church wanting to take me home with them. I remember going with them, but I was scared. I remember beginning to like them. I remember they lived in the projects. I remember they kept me a lot. I remember seeing a mentally challenged person for the first time. I remember asking a question in my mind, WHY? I remember the very sweet lady who began to take me in was always away at work, but her daughters were in High School, and I thought that was so cool, going to High School. I remember having to go home, not wanting to. I remember begging and pleading to go to school with them, but I couldn't. I remember wearing my hair down for the first time. It was super long, very, very thick, HOT and heavy. I remember Easter came again. This time I was dressed in a flower dress, with a hat. I remember liking it, but couldn't run and play. I remember being cautious of men. I remember my uncle and another man sitting on the parking lot complementing me. I remember my uncle picking me up, placing me on the hood of a car taking a picture of me, with that old fashion camera. I remember mostly being scared and nervous. I remember going home, and that woman taking that dress off of me. I was relieved. I remember trying to wear my yellow and white suit from when I was three. I loved that outfit more than anything. I was sick, when I realized I had to give it up. It was too little. I remember being so sad. I liked that style more than I liked flowers and ruffles. I remember Sesame Street. I remember Mr. Rodgers, and the Diane Carroll Show. I remember getting another T.V. and stereo. I remember my baby brother and I going to the hospital to have our tonsils removed. I remember my baby brother had to have more surgery than I did. He had asthma bad, plus he had to have tubs or plugs in his ears. I remember the instructions. NO WATER IN HIS EARS. I reminded him of that until we moved away from home. I remembered that woman taking me to the little shop in the hospital, to but me a rag doll. I remember waking up from that surgery, asking the SKY, what is wrong, and what is happening. I remember the pain in my throat and not being able to swallow. I remember thinking I couldn't help my little brother if I wanted to. I remember being so sick. I remember the only thing we could eat was ice cream, pop cycles and shakes. Wonderful! If only the pain went away. I remember that monster being around again. I remembered he started to come after me again. I remember that woman never being around, when he would come. I remember his mother fixing tea cakes, NASTY! I would throw them, like I was throwing rocks. I remember her fixing home made ice cream, SUPER NASTY!!!!! I remember it tasting like moth balls and salt. She, her son, and her house smelled like moth balls. I hate that smell! I remember IT starting again. I remember him coming to get me. I remember him telling me the same lies. I REMEMBER REFUSING! I remember him grabbing my hand and dragging me. I remember putting up a fight! I remember him knocking me upside my head. I remember my brother finally taking up for me. I remember scratching and screaming! I remember that thing snatching me up and taking me with me with him. I remember him snatching my clothes off and talking to me bad. I remember all the sick things that monster took me through. I remember thinking, please let the woman come and get me. She never did. I remember how he had to force me and beat me. I remember his smell. GOD HELP ME, PLEASE! I remember his breath. I remember it seemed as if it was forever. It always seemed as if it was forever. Where was that woman? Where was my big brother , my grandmother and other relatives who lived right around the corner. GOD, WHAT'S GOING ON?!!!!!!!! I remember totally loosing it. I remember fighting and kicking. I remember swinging. I remember throwing a tantrum. He hit me so hard, I couldn't move, I couldn't do anything, I couldn't even see. I remember him dressing me after not succeeding, and taking me home. I remember, but I was so out of it. I was drained, beaten and sore. My brother just looked at me, but did nothing. I remember Head Start, and falling asleep the moment I sat at the table. I remember that woman touching me, dressing me and combing my hair. I remember wanting her DEAD!. That feeling was worst than that thing. I remember that thing came again and got me out of bed. The more I refused, the more he beat me. He would slap me, and make me put my face in cold water. Then he locked me in that bathroom with those huge wood rats. They ran circles around me, and GOD KNOWS, I screamed and stumped for all the world to here, but no one heard or came to my rescue. He really tried to get me to do things. I WAS FIVE ! . How could no one know! He would let me out of the bathroom only to start all over again. Finally, he got tired and put me to bed. I remember the next night he came, but he walked right past me, and went and got my brother. Right till this day, I can not stand to hear my brother cry. It truly does something to my soul. I remember thinking I want fight anymore. I remember going to Head Start the next day, I was tired. I remember it was recess, time to play. I remember not liking the merry-go –round like I use to, do to the head injuries. I tried swinging, it was o.k. but playing wasn't the same anymore. I could barely get around. I remember going to the slide. I remember having a hard time going up the steps. I remember seeing that monster standing on the corner looking at me. When I got to the top of the slide, I don't remember what happened, but I fell off the slide head first on the concrete. I don't know why I'm still alive today. The teacher got me, put me in a room with a cripple boy who had braces on his legs, he could never play. My head ached. I can't explain the pain. But as I laid on that cot that cripple boy sang, "Sitting on the dock of the bay, watching the time roll away." GOD, I wanted him to shut up! I remember well, that was the night that monster succeeded. I remember he got me out of bed, as I slept. I remember him picking me up and caring me. I remember my eyes POPPED out of my head. I was a little girl no more. I remember clearly, it went on and on and on and on and on. I couldn't walk. I didn't talk. I couldn't function at all. I remember being around all types of adults,

NO ONE PAID ME ANY ATTENTION. That monster got the little boy next door and made him sleep with me. After that, I never saw that little boy again. I remember it happening night after night. I remember my big brother telling that woman all the time, it never stopped. By now, I'm in the first grade. I couldn't read, write, add or subtract. I couldn't do anything. I barely attended school. I COULDN"T WALK AT ALL! My left leg and hip were so out of whack. All of my organs were out of place. I remember my brother having nothing to do with me. I remember he wouldn't even walk with me to school. We attended the same school once I was of age. I remember always having to walk by myself. Slowly but surely I would make it. I was always late. I remember another thing that freaked me out. I HAD TO PASS MY GRANDMOTHER'S TO GET TO SCHOOL. Her door was always open. I couldn't walk at all. I walked so slow with a serious limp. I was totally ignored. I remember we went to CHURCH EVERY SUNDAY! But no one ever noticed me. ALL OF MY FAMILY WENT TO THE SAME CHURCH, NO ONE EVER NOTICED ME. That woman bathe me, comb my hair, dressed me, and the piece of ---- did nothing. I remember her calling me to come and get my hair comb. She sat in that chair and watched me limp all the way to her to get my hair comb. I CRIED OUT LOUD WITH ALL MY HEART AND SOUL, all she did was made me be still so she can finish combing my hair. I remember at that time, I HATED GOD AND ALL OF HIS PEOPLE. WHY DIDN"T I DIE!!!!!!!!!!!!!!!!

I remember running home with my report card. I remember I couldn't read, but I thought it was good. I remember my first grade teacher Mrs. High telling me to be sure and give it to my mother. I thought it was good. My first grade report card said; SHE NEEDS HELP. At the end of every six weeks, it had ; SHE NEEDS HELP. I didn't know. But I do remember the look on that woman's face every time I gave it to her. I remember not being able to take it back to school without that woman signing it. I remember that woman set me up for piano lessons, the worst thing ever. The teacher was a black male, and we were alone in a little room. I CRIED, I CRIED, I CRIED, I CRIED, I CRIED , I CRIED1!. That man fussed at me, and made me go back and forth to wash my face. He never touched me, but that was the only thing on my mind. That woman kept allowing me to go with men, strangers, alone. I cried so, I never had to take piano lessons again. I remember pulling my hair out on purpose. I thought if I had no hair, that woman wouldn't have a reason to touch me. I remember that monster bringing me home, and that little girl would crawl on me, trying to play with me, I knock a whole her head. I hit her so hard, her head hit the bed rail, and blood went every where. What did my big brother do, he hit me and pushed me to the floor. That's when I DIED FOR REAL. I remember after being up all night, I slept my heart out. But when I woke up, EVERYBODY was gone! My big brother, the little brother, that girl, and that woman was no where to be found. I CRIED, I WAS SO SHAKY! I WAS SO TIRED, I COULDN'T WALK AT ALL! ALL I THOUGHT ABOUT WAS THAT MAN COMING BACK FOR MORE AS USUAL. I was too scared to move. But I remember looking up and I know I saw my grandmother, the one who died on the bus stop, standing in the door way of that raggedy house. I remember putting on wrinkle clothes, I couldn't run, SO I PRAYED ALL THE WAY TO SCHOOL. There was a neighbor who lived across the street, she watched what happen to me on a regular basis, and this particular morning she watched me DRAG my left leg, as I forced myself to get out of that house. I remember talking to myself all the way to school. I imagined GOD HOLDING MY HAND, WALKING ME TO SCHOOL, THE WAY A PARENT SHOULD. It was spring. The morning was cool, the sun was bright, and the flowers were in full bloom. I could barely make it, but I was determined. I was terrified, because I know I saw that dead woman, and didn't want to see her again. I'm walking slowly, noticing all of the beautiful flowers, but now I had come to my grandmothers house , who lived around the corner, and her front door was opened. I wanted someone to notice, but then I was terrified of getting in trouble. It didn't matter what that monster did to me, I still got whippings. I got past her house. I had mixed feelings of being sad and happy. I finally made it to school. I was late as usual. I was the only one in the hall. I made it to class, I climbed in my seat, it was so hard then, the teacher called for group three. I hated being slow. I limped to the circle, the teacher called on me to read, it was Tip and Mitten. I began to read, then I came across a word I couldn't pronounce, island. I said is-land. The teacher grabbed my hand and hit me with that ruler. I CRIED, I CRIED, I CRIED!. She realized it wasn't the ruler that hurt me. She picked me up and held me so tight, no one has held me like that since. She held me and rocked me. She tried to put me down, but I wouldn't let her. She realized something was truly wrong and GOT ME SOME HELP!!!!!!! I remember waking up in the nurse's office, then a hospital. I never entered that old house again. I didn't see that family for a long time. I ended up with my mean grandmother who lived around the corner. But it was so weird, because she was never mean to me. I guess she couldn't be. I slept my life away. I never worried about eating again, I just wanted to sleep, and be left alone.

PHASE #2 LOST SOUL

I remember sleeping with my grandmother in that huge bed. I would sleep, and go to the bathroom. I remember the how everybody just stared at me. I remember the look people gave me. I couldn't walk, but eventually I got my left leg to work. All I remember was my grandmother's bed and the Price is Right. My grandmother cooked everyday, but the food was nasty. I was such a picky eater. I remember a lot of potatoe chips, Pepsi, and CANDY. Three of my cousins lived with my grandmother on a permanent basis, but at the time I was there, I don't remember being around them much. One of my cousins could play the piano, she was brilliant, but that brought back too many bad memories I was trying to erase. Time past, I got plenty of rest. So much rest, I can't remember much about that time. I do remember doctor appointment, after doctor appointment. I remember one doctor appointment. The doctor put me on a table, I turn my to the side and open my legs. I pretty sure that doctor QUIT his job after that. The next thing I knew, I was in an office that looked like a nursery. There were table and chairs, toys and stuffed animals everywhere. I remember a lady being nice to me. I remember her grabbing my hand, but I pulled away. I remember she kept trying to get me to talk, but a lump grew in my throat, like a frog, nothing would come out. That monster had proven to me what would happen if I talked. I remember not wanting anything to happen to my family. I remember thinking hard, that I had to save them, and the only way that could happen was to keep my mouth shut. I remember, the more I went to that doctor I realized what they were trying to get me to do, but I didn't TRUST anybody. I remember each time I left the doctor, I kept telling myself, next time I'm going to talk, but when that next time came, that lump in my throat grew bigger each time. I remember wanting to talk BAD, but IT wouldn't come out. I remember going through that ritual over and over and over again. I remember the songs that would take me back to that time, like the Beatles, "Hey Jude" don't be afraid. I can't stand to here it. I remember when living in that shack, watching Cinderella (Lesley Ann Warren) played the part. I remember disappearing into that movie. I remember talking to GOD, (whom I had NO clue about, no knowledge of) asking HIM, please let that be me. I remember thinking HE had come through, when I ended up in my grandmother's house.

I remember being so warn out, when it came to those doctors appointments I just wanted them to end. After what seemed to be a long period if time, that family appeared again. I remember nothing but SHAME on my part, total embarrassment. My whole family made me feel like that. I remember the time came for me to go back with them, that's when I maid a vow to talk, I never did. I remember so many blank periods at that time. I have flashes of memories, but not much. I remember moving back with that family, but now we lived in a new place, a bigger place. I remember we had all new furniture. I remember a new school was built. I remember sitting alone all the time, teaching myself, and talking to myself. I WORKED HARD! I wrote the alphabet some much, my hands ached. I remember how reading began to come natural. I remember thinking GOD IS REAL! I remember thinking I was actually surrounded by ANGELS! I FELT EVERY BIT OF IT!! I made a living off that feeling. I stayed to myself. I had an imagination out of this world. I couldn't stand my surroundings, but I knew secretly I was cared for. I remember starting a new school. I remember not wanting to be behind. I remember wanting so desperately to be in the second grade. I remember knowing what I had to do to get there. I don't know why I was placed in the second grade, but I was. I remember working my but off! I remember ALWAYS working alone. I hated that woman and her children and she knew it. I remember Mrs. Crabtree from church began to take me in more and more. Any time a holiday came up, or just the weekend, I was gone. I remember packing my bags in the middle of the week, preparing to leave. I remember, every time that woman mad me mad, I would vow to have her put away. I was never able to go through with it. I remember the night mares. I remember not being able to sleep. I remember, late at night, I would look out of the window, paranoid about that monster coming to get to get me. There were times I actually thought I saw him standing in the middle of the street. For years I made it off of very little sleep. I remember the highlight of my life was Mrs. Crabtree, Diana Ross, and the JACKSON 5, MICHAEL JACKSON! I remember , when I was with Mrs. Crabtree, which was all the time, she enforced chores, and when your chores were done, we took a trip downtown on the bus, went H&R Greens and I was able to buy all of the Right On books I could afford. She was the best! I kept every picture and poster of MICHAEL JACKSON. I WOULD KISS HIS PICTURE EVERY NIGHT, ON HIS LIPS. I HAD POSTERS OF MICHAEL AND HIS BROTHERS ALL OVER MY WALLS. AND I SLEPT WITH THE RIGHT-ON MAGAZINES I DIDN"T WANT TO CUT UP. MICHAEL AND HIS BROTHERS TOOK ME AWAY!!! Mrs. Crabtree, she was very FUNNY!, and she LOVED HER GOD!!!!!!!!! She always said, I don't know about your GOD, but MY GOD IS AWESOME!!!!!!!! Those were her favorite words. I never understood that as a child, but I knew DEEP inside what she meant. That was the same GOD I talked to when I was alone. I remember not having a choice. The PEOPLE around me treated me like Casper. It was strictly my imagination, but Mrs. Crabtree said it wasn't my imagination, she convinced me through the way she carried herself , that something about the belief in GOD was real! I remember slowly but surely becoming a little sneaky snake, a liar, and a thief. I remember never wanting to be at home with my family, and the more I was, the more I turned into a little monster. I remember HATING being poor. I remember how that woman never had any money. I remember once I learned how to write, I left her notes every morning asking for lunch money. I remember always being disappointed. I remember beginning to think the woman couldn't read either. I remember one day in the second grade, I had begged that woman for money to take school pictures, but she never came through. I hated her. This one particular day, I was coming from the restroom. My classroom was outside in the portables. One of my classmate's older brothers stopped me and asked if I would turn in his little brother's money for his school pictures. I immediately thought GOD had answered my prayers. I remember as I walked back to my classroom, I kept telling myself to do the right thing. I remember being scared and nervous, but I didn't won't to be the only one who didn't get to take pictures. I remember when I got to my teacher's desk, I told her that was MY MONEY, and that my aunt came up here and dropped it off. I remember for the next two weeks, I almost lost my MIND! I was scared and nervous! I couldn't come up with another lie to save my life! I was more terrified of the people I stole from. I remember thinking how they were going to hate me, and probably do some horrible things to me. I was a nervous wreck, but I played it so cool. The day came to take pictures. That woman never came off the money. My super plan didn't work. I was going to use the money she gave me, to pay for the person's pictures I stole from. I remember being nervous, but I made sure I was pretty. I went through with it. I got in line to go and take pictures, and the little boy was left behind. He was hot! No one ever confronted me about the situation until the pictures came back. I was happy when I got my pictures. I remember running home to show that woman. She asked how did I get a chance to take pictures, I came up with a brilliant lie. I told her, the children who received free lunch were able to take pictures for free. I remember not knowing where the HELL that lie came from, it wasn't my original lie, the one I practiced on for weeks. Before I knew it, she was called to the school immediately! I knew I was DEAD MEAT! I remember she had to pay my classmate's mother back every cent. That made me happy. I said to myself, next time I ask your (?) for some money, you need to cough it up. I never got in trouble for it. I wasn't punished or anything. I remember being scared as hell, that woman would whip me in a heart beat, but not this time. I didn't know what to do, but I was happy about my pictures. I went to school the next day, that teacher hated me. She began to treat me very mean. I was so nervous, I asked if I could go to the restroom, and she said yes. I didn't even think about running into my classmate's older brother, but when I did, I got my behind back in class. I remember entering the classroom, walking with my head up, looking at the ceiling, trying not to look at the person I stole from, low and behold, he tripped me, and I fell. My face hit the back of the desk, my lip hung onto the metal part of the chair. Blood shot every where, as if I had been shot. I looked like the elephant girl. I was rushed to the nurse's office, they called paramedics, then, they called my family. My grandmother came to pick me up. Once again, I had to stay with her until I healed. I remember believing with all my heart and soul that, that was GOD making me pay for my sins. I still believe that. What was worst, was people knowing what you did, Which brought on more stares, finger pointing, and WHISPERS. GOD, I HATED YOUR PEOPLE AT SUCH AN EARLY AGE. As I laid by myself and talked to myself, I asked GOD to make me pretty again. I looked like a walking monster. I remember the doctor trips started again. I remember beginning to go to the dentist. I remember the dentist saying there was nothing he could do for me, until my lip healed. I remember him saying it had to heal on its own. That's when the prayers began. They weren't really prayers. I would talk to GOD the same way I would talk to my dolls. In my mind, my dolls were real, and if you touched them, YOU DIED! I remember, every time I was alone, I WASN'T ALONE. There was something around me. I've had that feeling since I was three. I have never been alone. I remember not wanting to go back to that school and having to face those people. Once again, my WISH came true. The teacher said I had past to the second grade, it was the end of school, I could stay at home.

What a relief. I made a vow never to do anything like that again. I remember staying with my grandmother, watching her cook, clean, wash clothes in a big tub and hang them outside on the clothes line. Her house stayed clean and neat, and there was always food cooking on the stove. Then I remember going to Mrs. Crabtree's house, hanging out with her daughters, while she was at work. I remember there was some confusion about who would stay at home and keep me. Her daughters were in High School, and they were too close to graduation to miss school, so they decided to take a chance and take me with them. Boy, was I in HEAVEN! I was going to High School with the big kids. It was AWESOME! It had to be every bit of 1968 or 69. All I remember is the hair (afros) the clothes, (bell bottom jeans), the shoes (platforms), what a time to be alive! I remember the teacher saying it was o.k. for me to sit in class with them. I was given pencil, paper, and colors. I HAD A BALL! Everybody catered to me, just as those people did on that college campus we lived on. Everybody was super nice. I remember wanting to be grown so bad. The girls constantly said how cute I was, and the boys played with me. They thought I was a doll. I remember, one boy with the biggest fro I had ever seen, begin to chase me around that school building, I was in HEAVEN! There was nothing like running and playing. He chased me for a while. Then I came to a stairway, I was stuck. When turned that corner, I took a leap of faith, and JUMPED! I flew like a bird. I scared the CRAP out of everybody! I haven't had a feeling like that since. Mrs. Crabtree's daughters made him stop chasing me. I remember, he looked at me and smiled. I remember thinking, I burnt you, buddy. But then the PAIN THAT WENT THROUGH MY POOR LITTLE BODY. I had to walk down another flight of stairs, and thought I was going to DIE! My legs were weak and in so much PAIN! Mrs. Crabtree's daughters said, that's what I get. I wanted to sit down, but it was time to go home, and we had a long walk. I don't remember how I made it, but I did. When we got home, I laid down, never to wake up again, but I kept thinking about that JUMP, and how it made me feel like a star. That FELT GOOD!, but you can rest assure, I never took that leap of faith again. I remember staying with Mrs. Crabtree and her daughters the whole summer. I had forgotten about all the horrible things that had happen to me. Everything just WENT AWAY. The time came for me to go home, I didn't want to, but I had no choice. I had to go back to that school again. I remember talking to GOD, asking him, to make everybody FORGET what I had done the previous year. My lip began to look normal again, which made me believe GOD was on my side. The third grade was a big challenge. I'm not sure, but I think I was in a slow class the previous year. I hated being slow or dumb. But now the challenge was on. The teacher was pretty but mean and firm. She began to teach us to write in cursive handwriting. I remember thinking, I just learned how to print, now this! I remember working super hard, once again. Then my biggest fear came to light, READING OUT LOUD. All I could say was, GOD, WHERE ARE YOU! What did she do?, she picked me. I couldn't do it. I tried but I couldn't. I could read silently, but I couldn't read out loud. She picked me over and over again. I would stutter and clear my throat constantly. I did it some much she got the message, and left me alone. When I would turn my work in, she realized I could read. I made good grades. I was determined to succeed. I just had a serious problem reading out loud. I remember realizing the class next door had all the students who were really smart. My heart sank. But then I remember the rumors about that teacher and how hard she was, I eventually got over it, but I didn't stop pushing myself. I remember once again missing a lot of school, due to doctor and dentist appointments. I was a little liar. My aunt who would take me back and forth to my appointments always asked if I had missed lunch, and I told her, yes, my lunch is over. I was no good. Then she would ask me what did I want, and I said JACK-IN-THE-BOX! I remember during the drive, after leaving the doctor's office, how that LUMP would take forever to leave, and right when it was almost gone, the question would come up about me missing lunch, and there was that LUMP again. I could barely get the lie out, but I thought about how the students would be jealous of me, when they saw my JACK-IN-THE-BOX. I was right. They were jealous. (I knew nothing about jealousy, it was just a feeling)

I remember every time I made it back to the school, I was right on time for MY LUNCH. (smiling) I was a sneaky snake, and a liar. I knew I was wrong, but it would just come out of no where, I was amazed at myself. I remember learning the meaning of friendship. There was a little girl I paid attention to. She wore a fake ponytail and she was FUNNY! She reminded me of Carol Burnet. One day she asked me for some of my JACK-IN-THE-BOX, and I gave it to her. I couldn't eat, I had just come back from the dentist. GOD BLESSED ME WITH A BEST FRIEND. She was the only girl in the family, she had a younger brother. She ran the house! I was in amazement. We had FUN!!!!!!! She was the BEST! Her imagination made mine look stupid. I began to spend the night at her house EVERY WEEKEND! I remember that woman saying no a couple of times, but when I got through throwing a fit, rather she changed her mind or not, I was GONE! Then more friends began to appear. There was Stephie who was the only girl in her family, she was the baby. She was FUNNY and GOOFY too. I was at her house, when I wasn't with Paula or Mrs. Crabtree.

Then there was another friend, Samantha. She was older. She was the only girl and first born. Those girls saw NOTHING wrong with me. Around them, I was a normal human being, and that's all I ever WISHED for. I remember Mrs. Crabtree's older daughter getting married and became pregnant. Then the news came that she was having twins! Then, she ended up leaving her husband and moving back home. I remember asking GOD to blow up the school, so I wouldn't have to go. Finally, school was out! It was summer. My bags were packed that Spring. I loved babies. Now there were two at one time, and the mother needed all the help she could get. I worked my but off. I worked so hard, they promised to take me shopping for new school clothes, due to me being such a big help. I remember them taking me downtown to a nice dress shop, they had lay-away. I remember every outfit I tried on. They narrowed it down to five outfits. I was so thankful. I didn't know what to do with myself. I remember constantly working hard. I remember them going downtown to pay on my clothes each week. Then, I remember, it was time for school to start, and that meant it was time to get my clothes out of lay-away. Out of no where, I heard them talking. They were whispering. They weren't able to get my clothes out of lay-away. I became weak and sick. I pleaded with them, but it didn't do any good. I asked them if they could get at least two or three, and the answer was no. I called that woman to ask her, knowing all the while what that answer would be. I called my aunt who lived with my grandmother. She worked for a shoe store. I KNEW she would come through. The answer was no. I turned into a robot. I became EVIL! I began to focus on getting everybody back. I began to steal from Mrs. Crabtree and her daughters. I played it so smooth. I slowly but surely began to pack my bags, and stuffed them with every thing I could get my hands on. I stole records for my big brother, I stole the baby toys for my younger brother and that girl, I stole cleaning fluids and house spray for that woman, and I stole 20 dollars from Mrs. Crabtree for myself. Those people thought they were loosing their minds. I played so innocent. I carried on as if I didn't know what they were talking about. The time came for me to leave. All of us attended the same church. After church, I was going home with that family of mine.

I prayed that no one would ask to check my bags or help me with them, they didn't. We made it to church. I thought I was home free. I remember when Mrs. Crabtree and her daughters came to get me out of church. When we entered the hallway, my bags were on the floor, and everything was out on the floor, and I was SO BUSTED! I couldn't faint, I couldn't breath, I couldn't do NOTHING! PEOPLE WERE EVERY WHERE! NO ONE WAS IN CHURCH AT ALL! THEY WERE ALL IN THE HALLWAY! I wanted them to KILL

ME instead of walking me through that CROWD! Mrs. Crabtree grabbed my arm, took me in the restroom, and spanked me with a ruler. While that was happening, I knew she didn't want to spank me, it didn't hurt. I've watched Mrs. Crabtree BEAT THE CRAP OUT OF HER DAUGHTERS. They were grown women, but to Mrs. Crabtree, those were her children, and that was her house. So, I know for a fact, she didn't want to do what she did, but I needed to be taught a lesson. Once again I had to walk through that crowd, to go and get in the car. What really killed me was, having to face my cousins, Henry and Penny. It was like a funeral, when the men are walking with the casket. I had planned to kill myself, but I didn't know how. As my aunt drove us home, all she kept saying was, IT WASN'T HER FAULT! She told that woman, she shouldn't have allowed Mrs. Crabtree to whip me, IT WASN'T MY FAULT! I remember thinking, what in the HELL is she talking about, it wasn't my fault. What could she have possibly meant by that. I was lost, puzzled, and totally confused. I had no clue as to what she could have been talking about. I remember not being able to sleep that night. I remember having to get up and go to school. I remember wishing that, that woman would died on her way home from work, I was simply loosing my mind. I remember when that woman got home, she called me downstairs to talk to me. I hated her for real. She told me to come and sit by her, SO GROSS. She started talking to me, I HEARD NOTHING! I blocked it all out. I was playing the JACKSON 5 in my head. Dancing Machine was out, and I had to focus on getting my robot moves together. By this time, I had earned a reputation at school as being a dam good dancer. She finally finished and I left to go and throw up. I remember my aunt who drove us home, she immediately left that church for good. She ran and never looked back. I remember that woman telling me I was going back to that church. I never understood why I didn't kill her in her sleep. When she told me that, I made up my mind and heart to apologize to Mrs. Crabtree and her daughters. I realized, I really couldn't live with that woman. Mrs. Crabtree and her daughters forgave me, and immediately took me back in. I remember going back to that church, and having to face those people. The RUMORS, THE LOOKS, THE WHISPERS, I'm surprised I didn't get cancer and dic. I HATED PEOPLE, WITH ALL OF MY HEART AND SOUL. I was the talk of the town for a very long time. I didn't learn until later that, after that incident, everyone knew what I had gone through as a little girl. These are CHURCH FOLKS, GOD'S PEOPLE. I remember telling GOD out loud exactly what HE COULD DO WITH HIS PEOPLE. I remember making a vow to never steal again. I kept my promise this time. I did steal again, but, I ONLY STOLE FROM THAT WOMAN, NO ONE

ELSE! HUMILIATION IS NOT MY CUP OF TEA. I focused on school. I kept my grades up. I went on about my business. I graduated from the six grade, and entered Junior High. A scary, but fun change. Everyone seem to like me. I remember not having a problem that first year. My grades were wonderful, except for math. I made the drill team with no problem. Then I remember getting the news, that the school I was attending was going with all ninth graders the following year, which meant I had to attend another school again. I didn't want to go to the school I was assigned to, due to the gang fighting. I went any way. My grades were awesome. I stayed on the honor roll. I made the National Honor Society. I was with the smart group of people I've always wanted to be with. I had nothing to focus on. There were after school activities, but I didn't want to be around, due to a group of bad girls walking around beating up people for no reason. I was doing well in school. I had created my own style. I simply took care of me. I ran into my new best friend, Louise. She was a book worm! The people that she hung with, were so smart, they didn't have common sense. This was at a time when I discovered ENCYLOPEDIAS. I would disappear in them. There were things in those books, that school never taught. The moment I was given an assignment to do a paper on someone are something, I knew that was an easy A! I LOVE WRITING! When she began to talk to me, I was surprised and happy. We became best friends overnight. She was a good girl at school, but away from school, she was SUPER GOOFY! I love people who make me laugh out loud. Nothing on earth can compare to that feeling. The end of school came, and I got word, that I was on the bad girls hit list. I had a lot of friends. My classmates were pretty cool. I had hair like Chaka Khan, and the first thing I heard was, those bad girls were going to beat me, and hang me by my hair. That whole year, I stood back and watched them pick on the most helpless students, ever the mentally challenged. I hated them so much. So, when I got word, that they were coming after me, I kept my hair braided, and I wore a stocking cap, and a scarf tide tightly to my head. It was so tight, I couldn't think. I had never had a fight before, but no one, especially that trash, was going to whip me, and live to tell about it. They came after me, and I was ready. People began to come out of the wood works, wanting to help me. That was cool, I liked that feeling. I told them, don't let them jump me. I made it clear, I wanted the LEADER of the gang, no one else. I knew if I whipped her, I would never have a problem again. I didn't know at the time how messy kids could be, but I found out. Bottom line, I WHIPPED SOME ASS! I was throwing punching like a man. I whipped that leader so bad, her girls could do nothing but look with there mouth open. I knew nothing about KING DAVID at the time, but that had to be the same feeling. I never wanted to fight. That was low, and I hated it. I was suspended from school. I was exempt from all test. My grades and behavior were excellent that year. Word began to spread about me being able to fight, so there were other challenges. I WON THEM ALL, but that wasn't me. Finally, that woman decided it was time to move. I remember entering the ninth grade. I attended that school, with nothing but ninth graders, beautiful. That was my year. I felt it in the air. I had done something right. The people I whipped the previous year were there, but without their friends. Their friends had dropped out. Every time I saw them in the hall, I smiled. They could do nothing. That year, I won captain of the Drill Team, Freshman Princess, and Most Popular. I was in HEAVEN! I felt like a QUEEN. But of course that happiness was short lived. I ran into the love if my life. That boy made me forget everything I worked so hard for. I remember, sitting in my room, at the end of that school year, thinking about everything that had taken place, and noticed how I was beginning to fall off. That made me nervous. I didn't want to go back. I remember breaking it off. I remember that feeling. I wanted somebody to want me. I was sick. I was sad. My girl Louise tried to help, but she knew what I wanted her to say and do. I had a scrap book. I asked Louise to take it to him and let him sign it. The bastard wrote me a friendship letter. (laughing) Hannibal skoot over.

We had the same choir class. He sat in that class with his arm around another girl. Michael Myers didn't have a chance. I was not going to deal with that. That drove me PSYCHO! I broke that up, and the rest is history. I had a hard time in High School. I made the drill team there, but when you don't have transportation, why bother. When your family don't back you in anything, why waste time. It was a fun time I just didn't go to class anymore. I did what it took to get by. It was cool to know that I could miss class for a couple of days, show up and make an A. Not my first year. I failed English. That was IMPOSSIBLE. That's the subject of all subjects. That was my favorite. My mind was made up, I was never repeating anything. I stepped in that zone. I stole a check out of that woman's purse, made it out to the school for 33.00, signed it, and made an A. Having to get up that early in the summer and go to school was a lesson within itself. That woman wanted me dead. Old news. I remember my new girlfriend's parents, bought them both a car. They gave me orders. I was told that I was going to be picked up everyday at a certain time, and to be ready. I went to school. I graduated. I got a job. I bought a car. College was out of the question. I knew that was my ticket out, but they had math. I was tired of kissing but to get through math. My mind was already screwed, and those numbers didn't help. Louise and I went to different High Schools, then she went off to college. That friendship slowly ended. I was still hanging on to my High School sweetheart. We had plans to get married, and settle down. I knew all alone, I was not going to spend the rest of my life chasing him, and putting up with the naturally, messing around. I dated other guys, but he always broke it up. I thought that was signed of true love. I became pregnant with our first child. The moment I had my baby, something in me CHANGE. It was as if I hadn't done anything. I felt like I was wasting my life. Our plans were to move together. We did. I couldn't keep up with him, and I didn't want to be left at home alone. I became pregnant again. I went home. I remember when I went back home. Everybody was living their life. That woman and girl were going out of town. Baby brother was away at college. Big brother was getting married. I was at home alone with my son. Within a blink of an eye, someone broke in, held me at gunpoint, took me and my baby to the woods, and raped me. He hit my baby in the head with the handle of the gun, then, held his head face down in the ground. I knew I was dead, my babies too. Strange, those were the same woods, when I was a little girl, and the sky, the top of the trees, said something to me. The man shot the gun. I don't understand why I didn't die, faint, or have a heart attack. He told me not to look up, and I didn't. I had NO strength. But I began to realized, I'm terrified of the woods, and its animals. I SNATCHED GOD OUT OF THE SKY, AND DRUG HIM WITH ME! That's all I could do. There was a little shopping strip, but everything was closed. I saw somebody, and hid behind a soda machine. The first car that passed was a police car. I couldn't make a sound. I got my strength. I put my big baby on my pregnant hip, and went home. I will never be able to explain my mind at that time. I got home, and said to myself, I will never tell. I sat there, and I knew I was going to loose my mind. I called a neighbor. I tried to talk normal. My insides were about to explode! I just burst out and told her somebody raped me. She had the police at my house, almost quicker than GOD.(ALMOST.) That was a RELIEF! The police were great. They took their time. They were very patient and understanding. They actually wanted me to go back to that spot. I did, but I don't know how they got me there. That was the worst. They kept trying to calm me down, but I let them know, you can stay all you want, but I'm gone. We went straight to the hospital, to the emergency room.

I was o.k. My children were o.k. They got what they needed. Everybody was so nice. Everything seemed quite. I remember the nice guy, who kept me company, until the police took me back home. I remember crying hard, when I broke the news to my neighbor, who got me some help, but when I was with the police, and in the hospital, I didn't shed a tear. When I was sitting in the waiting room, flashes, pictures started appearing in my head. I had erased everything from my childhood. But instead of turning into a monster, I just dwelled on those flashes, and realized, that woman and my brother were very aware of what went on all of those years. The police took me back to my neighbor's house. By that time, everybody knew what had happened. My aunt and uncle came to pick me up. I ended up right back in my grandmother's house, just as I did, when I was rescued at the age of seven. Now, I was twenty-one. I told myself, not again. I began to remember everything. I sat in silence. I took care of my baby boy, and my soon to be, baby girl. Everybody catered to me again. I didn't eat my grandmother's food, so my aunt bought me Mc Donald's. That woman came home. I went home. That paranoid feeling kicked in strong, around all of my family members. By the time I got home, the RUMORS were out. It didn't bother me much, I knew people were EVIL. My big brother called me, he was on his honeymoon. I asked him about the things that happened in our childhood, he said he remembered, and said he wanted to kill that monster. Then, before I knew it, that woman shut him up. We never discussed it again. My High School sweetheart came to my rescue, but the rumors got to him, he dropped me like a hot potatoe. I got myself together. I prayed for a girl, I WAS BLESSED WITH A GIRL! I decided to move forward, and I did. That woman told me, I needed to get some help. In my mind, I said (? ?). In reality, I blew her off. I hated those words. I loved my babies. I became a big clown. I stopped going to that church that I was raised in. For years, I prayed that it would crumble, and it did. On a Sunday morning, there was shooting, killing, and people dropping dead of heart attacks. I said, thank you GOD. I actually saw, what goes around, comes around. That church was on the front page news. I began to go out. I didn't date. I just went out to have fun, and to forget. I noticed a change in my son. He would not talk. He just acted different. Something was wrong. I took him to the doctor, who sent me to another doctor. They ran test on him, and came to the conclusion, that he was autistic. I cried for weeks. I looked into the sun, and said, GOD, IF YOU ARE REAL, I NEED TO KNOW NOW! My son was immediately placed in school. I worked with him big time. I talked to him all the time, I never stopped. I knew it was my responsibility to care of him the best way I could, and I did. That situation began to make me stronger. I knew how special people were treated. They are placed in a closet and forgotten. I told GOD, I couldn't take anymore. I ran into someone else, who swept me off my feet. He spoiled me. That was a nice feeling. I could talk to him about anything. He took care of my babies, as if they were his own. Two years had past, and I hadn't dated anyone I didn't want to. Before I knew it, I was in love again. I became pregnant again.

My heart told me, my son needed a brother. I was right. Children are nothing like adults. After my baby boy was born, the night mare began again. A year past, my relationship with my new love went sour. He began to stay out later and later. He was messing around, and eventually got into drugs. I was living in total darkness. He would bring the drugs home. I joined him, but it didn't last. I lost sight of everything again. I was in total darkness. The rumors ran rampant once again, but no one knew, that all I wanted was that man that swept me off my feet, and took care of my babies, as if they were his, I wanted him back. I was use to rumors, and back stabbing, that was nothing. I had GOD in my heart, way before I met the man I was with. And I can rest assure, that GOD had me in the palm of his hands when the darkness took over. I looked at my babies, remembered my childhood and went home. I made a vow that my babies would have happy memories. At the time I was pregnant with my third child, my High School sweet heart's mother past away. That was so unbelievable. That woman loved her grandchildren. But I didn't want their father in their life period. When GOD called her home, it was very unexpected, but it made me wonder. I was caught up in a storm that had no ending. I didn't have any problems with their father, he never came around. He didn't have his mother around to tell him what to do. I decided to go back home. I wasn't wanted there, so what, I went anyway. I began to have dreams. The kind of dreams a person can't help but to remember. I had dreams when I was younger, but I didn't pay any attention to them. The moment I went back home, I had a dream. I was in my grandmother's house, and there were black cats every where. I couldn't move.(I hate cats.) I was standing in the middle of her bedroom, paranoid, stuck in one place. I looked up and there was my aunt standing at the back door. She opened the screen door, held her hand out to me, and told me, not to make a sound. I walked very softly, and very quietly. I finally got close enough to grab her hand, and she pulled me out of that place. For years, I thought that dream was about my friends who had stabbed me, and turned on me. Turns out, it was my family. For years, I've always had dreams of being in my grandmother's house. I thought it meant that I was in my safe haven. It probably did, at those times, but not this one. I remember telling my aunt about. That's when she really began to step up and help me no matter what. I don't know why I was glad to be back home, but I was. A long lost friend finally caught up with me. I gave him a hard time as usual. He always wanted to talk to me, but I would tell him, all we could be was friends. He would take me out to nice quiet places, where we did nothing but talk all night long. He listened to me. He made me laugh. He still wanted to be with me, and was willing to take care of my children. I was burnt out on that. I wanted nothing to do with that other side, the side that never shows in public. He treated me like a person. We had known each other for years. After graduation, he went off to college and did well for himself. It wasn't until I moved back home, when I found out, he had been calling the house asking about me, wanting to see me bad, but he was always one with patience. Once we started seeing each other again, it was magical. There was no sex, we were friends, and I was in love with that. That was priceless. He would make sure that woman would baby sit with no problem, then he would take me to romantic restaurants, and talk all night. Sometimes we would get take out, and go to his place, sit on the patio and just talk. I poured my heart out to him. Nothing would turn him away or make him think twice about me. He had heard every rumor there was about me, he only saw me. Most of our conversations were about people and their ways. We could talk about that all night. He was highly educated. I think he had read just about every book in the library. I love to listen to the stories he had to tell. He always tried to get me to read more, I would blow him off and tell him, one day. For every problem I had, he had a solution, a book that would help me. He really liked me, but I gave him the hardest time. I really began to fall for him. It was like a breath of fresh air. One night he came and got me, and took me to the lake. I was so paranoid at first. I don't like being outside at night, and especially sitting on a lake. That turned out to be one of the best nights of my life. The moon was bright. They stars were every where. We talked, and he held me. I could have stayed there forever. Then the sun began to peak, it was simply beautiful. He took me to get something to eat, and took me home. He never bothered me about sex. I guess he figured I had, had enough. That was love. I made sure I did nothing to spoil it. He would come over during the day when he got off from work and take the kids to the park, or out for ice cream. I didn't like that situation. He was from a wealthy family. He hated his step dad. The neighborhood they lived in was a dream to me. I met his family. His sister liked me. They were young. But I'm pretty sure his mother wasn't comfortable with her son being with a woman with three children, and they weren't his. I remember in High school, when I was mad at my sweetheart, my true love always showed up. His name was the same as my high school sweetheart, but I called him by his last name. I remember when we were in High School. I had tickets to see Cameo and the Deal, featuring Baby Face. I asked him at the last minute to go. His mother only let him go if he took his sister. I thought that was sweet. But I ended up getting mad at him. He was late picking me up, and we missed the Deal. They opened up the concert that night. I wanted to see the Deal more than I wanted to see Cameo. After that concert, the Deal broke up. That made me sad. They produced beautiful music. We had a real relationship. His mother raised a man. Her love was all over his apartment. There were plaques every where about a mother's love. I remember getting upset with him at times, and realizing how stupid I was. That last time he found me, nothing came between us. He was always my secret. It's rare to find someone who see YOU for who YOU are, and like YOU in spite of. He tried to get me to move with him. He wanted to be with me, but I refused. I didn't want anything to mess up what we had. I was in love in a different way. I wanted to hold on to that. My life was a living hell, but he became my quiet place, the calm after the storm.

PHASE #3 DREAMS

A year past, I got my own place. He was by my side. I had a hard time at first, but I was ready for a new life, my own life. No males aloud. I raised my children. I focused more on my autistic son. I never stop talking to him, face to face. I told him, you talked once, you will talk again. I worked part-time. I signed up for classes at the community college. I really wanted to be at home with my babies. Baby boy's father made that possible. I still worked off and on, but my baby's needed me in their life at that time. I'm a firm believer of mothers being at home with and for their children. My true love was there to ease the pressure. He would call and tell me to get the kids ready for that woman to baby sit, then take me to his place for rest and relaxation. That went on for the first two years I was in my new place. He became a policeman. I was shocked. That wasn't his character. That wasn't him at all. The moment he joined, he was chosen president of his class, and he shined like a star. I was never comfortable with his decision, but that was his decision, I had no choice in the matter. Now when he came to pick me up, he would drop me off at his house and went to work. He was a gentleman! Things began to change. There was something going on that was strange. I couldn't put my finger on it. He had just joined the police force, but when I went to his house things were leaving. Things he loved and had to have. When I began to notice that, I stopped going to his house. I told him, he had to come to my house. I would call, but he was always busy. That was normal, he was a policeman and he enjoyed it. One night I had a dream. A girlfriend of mind was standing in front of a tree, and someone shot her in the chest, and it left a huge hole. I jumped up out of my sleep. That dream stuck with me, it was so real. I didn't mention it to anyone. The next night, I had another dream.

I was in a church, getting ready to get married. I was standing at the alter in a wedding dress, with flowers in my hand. I was waiting for my future husband to come down the aisle. It was my High School sweetheart. As he began to come down the aisle, he turned around and broke out running. I woke up and asked what was happening. I couldn't dwell on it much, it was Halloween, a time for me and the children to HAVE FUN! I went to bed that night and had another dream. I was in a place with all of my classmates. I walked out of the place, and it was raining outside, light rain. No one had an umbrella. The rain was the furthest thing from everyone's mind. I walked around and ran into three of my classmates. I jumped up out of my sleep again. Now I'm scared. Something very weird was happening. That Friday, my true love called me and asked if he could come to my house and sleep. I said sure. He explained how he couldn't get any rest at his place. I told him he did not owe me an explanation. He came over. I made sure he was comfortable, baby boy and I went to my daughter's school to hang out with her, so my friend could rest. School was out, I walked my babies home, I had to get home to get my special one off the school bus. We sat in their room and worked on their home work. We ate junk food, Halloween had just past. My true love woke up around seven. He thanked me for being able to get some sleep. He hung out with the kids. He had presents in the car for them. All educational. He bought them a huge map, colors, and books to read. He told them, the next time he came over he was going to test them on the states and capitals. They were excited. They loved a challenge. They love to impress. He kissed me on the cheek and told me he would be back the next day. He was going to treat us to dinner. The next day came. I felt paranoid. I had a strong feeling, thinking my friend was going to let us down. I had been through that so much, I was burnt out. That was my reason for no more relationships. I could live a happy life without that burden. The day came and went, not a word from my friend. I played it off with the kids as usual. My friend was a policeman. I knew deep down, he would make it up. Sunday morning came, still no word from my friend. Something was heavy. Something wasn't right. I got a knock on the door. A neighborhood friend told me to turn it on the news. I began to get shaky. He said it's about my true love. I asked him, what was going on, what happened? He said, some teenagers KILLED him, SHOT A HOLE IN HIS CHEST. It didn't sink in right away. I figured I was still sleep. I forgot about my coffee, and went straight to the T.V. The story finally aired. A Utah Policeman was shot and killed at a crack house, by a group of teenagers. The tornado began to take form. The DREAMS. It was impossible, he was just here with me and the kids. He promised me he would be back. GOD, HEAVENLY FATHER, WHEN

IT HIT ME! MY SOUL SAID, SEE YA! I couldn't do anything for myself. I couldn't do nothing for my kids. I had never experienced anything like that. The only thing that ran through my mind was, LORD, PLEASE KILL ME. With all those emotions taking place, I began to have visions of my children being raised by my family. I couldn't do that to my babies, that thought drove me nuts. I don't how I got through that week. I don't know how my children got through that week. I thank GOD for having planting in them, a daily routine. During that week, the truth came out, about what really happened. I had come to the conclusion that it was a drug bust. When I found out, he was there to purchase drugs, and his intent was to scare the teenagers, …………

There are no words. GOD DIDN'T GIVE HIM A CHANCE. Now the emotions were worst than ever. I CRIED! I didn't know a human had some many tears. I noticed the burden my babies were caring. Lying in that bed, it was amazing seeing what they were capable of. My baby girl was strong. The funeral came. I wasn't going, but I knew I had to get that out of my system. I was gone. I cried, I cried, I cried. I had NO ONE. When my family, got word of what had happened, they came to the conclusion we were during drugs together. That gave me a back-bone. I saw myself bursting through a cement wall. I knew to slowly distant myself from them. I knew it would be hard, due to, not wanting to damage my children mentally. My oldest was six , which made he, his sister and brother babies. The funeral was packed. It rained all day that day. I wasn't going to the grave site, but I ended up there anyway. It was that last dream I had. People walking around in the rain not caring about getting wet. Everybody began to leave. I couldn't hold my head up for nothing. As I stood there in a daze, three of my classmates came up to me. It was the three friends in that dream. I dropped. My body was water. My friend girl caught me. They walked me to the car. I knew GOD WAS REAL!!!! But THE PAIN!!!! I wanted my bed! I got home, got my baby boy, and went to bed. The older ones made it to the house. My daughter came and sat with me in the bed. She was tired. I got up! I remembered every time I was totally stressed or under major pressure, I focused on house work, taking the kids out, doing things that would make me super tired, until I had no choice but to fall asleep when I hit the bed. I came up with an idea, that would take my children's burden away. A party! All the neighborhood kids were invited. We had so much stuff left from Halloween, so we put it to use. That following weekend, I had seventeen kids at my house. The only rule was, promise me you will tell your mother you had a GREAT TIME! I fixed hot dogs, chips and soda. I made everybody's face up. Everyone was a happy clown. Of course, one baby's face began to itch. I broke my neck, getting that make up off! I rather for GOD to come after me than a parent. We played, we laughed, we sang, we danced, we MADE NOISE!!!! ALL NIGHT LONG!!!! Every child slept hard, even with all of that candy in there system. I couldn't sleep. I couldn't get in that bed, with all of those kids in my house. I didn't want to go back into that shall. It took my strength. It left me helpless. I had promised everyone pancakes the next day. As I sat on that couch, and thought about that promise, I called myself a dumb ass. In reality, I didn't want that party to end. I felt better with a house full of kids. Morning came, they were up bright and early. I fulfilled me promise. Pancakes for everyone! The parents came over to offer help, I didn't want it. I had to do that by myself. I remember breaking down on one of the parents shoulders.The kids caught me, and I straightened up. I got the parents to leave. I finished cooking, making sure teeth were brushed, I combed hair, I talked they listened, they talked, I listened. Then I put them out. Go outside and play. Get out. I was too tired to think. I was talking to a couple of parents. I was honest about everything, but within that, I broke a promise. Some of the boys began to say bad words, in a funny way. I promised not to tell. The other kids began to tell on each other, and I told them, not tonight. This night is not about punishment. Well, one of the parents got upset. Let me have it. The child came to me in private, very hurt, because I broke that promise. I sank. I gave that baby some money to buy more junk, I don't think it helped but we did become friends again. The other parents stood up for me, and told that parent that they had a personal problem. I began to laugh, boy, did that hurt. I went in the house, looked around and noticed that I had no choice but to clean up. I took my time. I couldn't get in the bed, until my children were I the bed. The PAIN, The HEARTACHE, The MEMORIES. THE DREAMS! I went from sad to being pissed off! HOW COULD YOU GO OUT LIKE THAT?! AFTER EVERYTHING YOU TAUGHT ME, AND MADE ME SEE!. It took me a LONG time, but I got it together. My babies were HAPPY! My aunt told me something pretty deep. She said, GOD took him from YOU! Everyone else, like his family, just happened to be in the picture. I went into a deep zone, never to return. I began working on with my autistic child. I kept repeating to him, IF YOU START TALKING, YOU CAN GO TO SCHOOL WITH NED, HIS LITTLE BROTHER. The time was getting close for his little brother to start school. I made sure his brother and sister surrounded him. I made sure they played in his room, and stayed very close to him. They responded, telling me that, they couldn't get him to play with them. I told them in time, he would. I knew nothing of the sort. One day out of the blue, the two younger ones came running and screaming, saying momma he did it! He came and sat with us and started playing UNO, the card game. They explained, he didn't understand the part about waiting until it was his turn, but the important thing was, he joined them. My SOUL LEFT ME AGAIN. I talked to GOD IN PRIVATE EVERYDAY. I kept repeating to my child that, IF YOU START TALKING, YOU CAN GO TO SCHOOL WITH NED. One day, my autistic son came home with one of his drawings. His drawings were remarkable. He could look at something and put it on paper, as if he took a picture. This particular drawing was VERY DIFFERENT. At the top of the paper, he had taken a black crayon, and scrubbed that paper very hard, with that crayon. It was so thick, you could actually write a paragraph in it with your fingernail. Then, in the middle, underneath the black, there were the BEAUTIFUL COLORS. PURPLE, YELLOW, AND LIGHT BLUE. THAT WAS A SIGN. My stomach agreed. I didn't eat for days. His teacher called about that drawing. He tried to explain it, but I cut him off. I knew what it was. MY son was coming out of darkness, into the LIGHT! Nothing more. When I didn't want to hear something, I made it clear. It was Spring, I was preparing baby boy for school. He was so ready. From the time he was two years old, he tried to keep up, and out shine his older brother and sister. That third child is amazing. Very head strong. Out of the blue, my autistic child refused to go to school. Something was happening. It made me nervous. I couldn't get him on that bus for nothing. The bus driver came everyday. She wasn't supposed to, but she did. She knew something was wrong too. She was his bus driver for two years. My son never missed a day. His teacher started calling. I had no excuse. I told him, my son was sick. I had a dream. There was a snake in my house. I was comfortable with it. The snake crawled all over the house, like a normal pet. It was time for bed. My autistic son was sitting at the foot of my bed, facing the window. That was weird. He went from the baby bed, to his own bed, without a problem. He never slept with me, unless he was sick. The snake began to go after my son. It wrapped itself around my son. It raised its head, attempting to bite my baby, out of no where, a huge butcher knife appeared in my hand. I chopped that snake into pieces. The head of the snake kept making its way towards my baby. I took a deep breath and split the snake's head into. Blood was every where. On me the walls, and the bedroom door. The snake screamed out loud, like a woman. I thought I had killed someone. Then there was a knock on the door. It was that woman. I grabbed my house coat put it on to try and cover the blood. I closed the bedroom door, and answered the front door. That woman came in, looked at me, and said what have you done? She began to pass out animal crackers to the kids. I walked her to my bedroom. The blood had disappeared from the walls and door. I took my house coat off. The blood was gone. I jumped up out of that sleep. There was no one who could help me with that dream. His teacher called again. I told him what was on my heart, and what I had been praying for. I told him about my dream. That man PRAYED HIS HEART OUT! The tears rolled. He told me to get myself together. He told me it was time for my son's evaluation. He told me to come and STAND FIRM! He told me to snatch my baby and run! By now, I'm smoking cigarettes in my sleep. I was a nervous wreck. My son was very content at home. This was the same child who stood over me in my sleep, every morning at five o'clock, like clock work, ready to go to school. This was the same child who, I asked one morning, to go to a neighbor's house to get me some sugar. That neighbor called me and asked if I had sent my son to her house, I said yes. She told me he never made it. She told me my cup was sitting in the middle of the sidewalk, and that my son ran to that school bus, jumped on it, and was GONE! I laughed for an hour! That feeling was like, being able to fly! This was the same child, who had become content, sitting at home hanging out with his mother, watching T. V. It was time for the evaluation. I STOOD FIRM! I snatched my son out of special ed. His sister and brother were "normal" (whatever that is), special education was not his life. That was confusing. You're being taught one way at home, but at school it was a different story. He was in a class with children who were really bad off. He was picking up bad habits. I knew I was loose him forever if I kept him there. I began to strength from remembering that, that woman didn't give a dam about me. I wasn't going out like that. The people in that meeting hated me, and told me, I DIDN'T KNOW WHAT I WAS DOING! If I hadn't had the type of childhood that I had, I wouldn't have been able to cope. I looked at my son who was dressed like rain man, in his gray suit, and gray hat, (I added the hat) I took him by the hand, and we were HISTORY! When we made it home, I broke down! I remembered something my autistic son told me when he was four. One day he came home from school. I tried talking to him, asking how was his day. I got no response. He wouldn't talk. I called a friend, crying. My autistic son came in my room, walking in circles, SAYING OUT LOUD, DON"T WORRY ME, I'M GOING TO BE ALRIGHT. He said it three times. I almost checked myself into the crazy home. I hung up that phone, fell to my knees and tried to get him to say it again. I got nothing but a smile. I remembered how every Tuesday, he made me open the door to let him out so he could stand at the mailbox and wait on the postman. He knew on Tuesday's the T.V. Guide was coming. And of course, it came. He would get it, open it, look at each and every page, then pull me to the couch, made me sit down, he would crawl on lap, open that book that was in his lap, pronounce the days of the week, but his lips never move. I asked GOD WHAT IN ALL OF HELL IS HAPPENING! I was totally spaced out, and there were no drugs in site. I never taught him to read, HE WOULDN'T TALK! His teacher always provided tones of homework, but it was hard to get his attention. Everyday at three o'clock, he grabbed my hand, made me turn the T.V. on Jeopardy, and made it clear through that silence, to leave him alone. I tried to get him to read the days of the week in front of people. He made me look stupid. I told GOD, my family was going to call the WHITE VAN, to come and pick me up. It's that time. By that time I began to notice the hold my family had turned on me. What was worst, I had no control. That's the making of A MURDURER. I kept moving forward. It was time for school to start. Still, no word from my autistic son. It was the first day of school. I got my daughter ready, I GOT BABY BOY READY! Just as we began to walk out of that door, MY AUTISTIC SON SAID, YOU SAID IF I STARTED TALKING, I CAN GO TO SCHOOL WITH NED. My body said, FUCK IT! I GIVE UP!!! I stood in one place for thirty minutes. My Children were SHOCKED! The neighborhood kids were coming by the house one by one. EVERYBODY LIKED NED. I had transferred my daughter to a better school. I got her off to school first. I got the boys and we began to walk Ned to school. Ned was dragging. He was taking his time. He was crying. He didn't want me holding his hand. I stopped and reminded him of everything we had discussed the past eight months. Ned told me that wasn't his problem. He told me, his problem was me. I started looking around to see, who in the hell was talking. That was not coming from my baby. I asked him, what have I done. He said, his F R I E N D S were going to see his mother walking him to school. The neighborhood kids were on hush mode. Their mouths were wide open. The problem with that was my baby and I walked my daughter to school everyday. From the time she started Pre-K, until she was in the third grade. That boy was on my hip, in a stroller, and then he started walking. It was our daily routine, to get up every morning, and walk her to school. He remembered none of that. All he knew was, he wasn't walking to school with his momma. He was only five. The older boys stepped in and took over. They promised me nothing would ever happen to him. Nothing ever did. Nothing but ASS WHIPPINGS! I never laid a hand on my children, until NED. That boy didn't want me at the school. He didn't want me around in public period. But behind closed doors, he wanted to be my baby. I MADE IT VERY CLEAR TO HIM, THAT HIS FRIENDS WERE GOING TO GET HIM IN A WORLD OF TROUBLE! He didn't listen. I didn't stop whipping him. Before the whippings, I made sure we had a clear understanding.

I have every note his teachers sent home. From Pre-K, to TWELTH GRADE!!!!!!!!!!!!!!!!!! That's all the proof I need. He is intelligent beyond his years. OLD SOUL!!!!!! When I was nine months pregnant with that child, I went to the doctor for my regular check up. The doctor wouldn't say anything. She left the room. She came back and told me to turn on my side. I asked, what was going on? She wouldn't tell me at first, but she did. There was no heart beat. She asked when was the last time I felt the baby move. She looked at my face, and said, DON"T WORRY! Think of happy thoughts. I had my baby girl with me. The happy thoughts kicked in. All the while my insides were saying, GOD NO! GOD NO! PLEASE LET ME HAVE THIS BABY, PLEASE! The next thing I knew, I was in the back of an ambulance. The doctor was on the phone. He asked the paramedics could they get me there in five minutes, the paramedics said THREE MINUTES. The cord had wrapped around my baby's neck. That night my son was born! Alive and healthy! I PRAISED GOD EVERYDAY!!!!! I told people, I asked GOD for a boy, for my autistic son, and HE CAME THROUGH!!!!! I told that story so much, GOD'S PEOPLE GOT TIRED OF HEARING IT!!!!! I think about when GOD CALLED SAUL "A FOOL"! I wander what he would say now. Back to my baby boy, by the time he turned two, I began to tell people he was the devil. It's funny, but it's true.

I placed my autistic child in regular education. The teachers weren't ready for that. The teachers hated the thought of it. They had no choice. My autistic child and I have always communicated through letters and notes, thanks to his Special ed teacher. My son wouldn't talk, and he had a problem using his hands. But he could express himself, his feelings. Everyone around us thought that was amazing. He could spell like a champ, and never knew the meaning of studying or homework. On his first day of school, getting ready for regular ed., he came to me and said I'm scared. I thought to myself, only a normal person would say that. The first couple of months, his handwriting was so small, you could barely see it. My heart was right. I've always thought his problem had a lot to do with his SOUL. I felt like his soul was bald up in a knot, which left his body limp, but all the while his brain was sucking up everything without any effort. His new teacher had a hard time at first. Then there was the spelling test. He blew the whole school out of the water. All the students that teased him and talked about him were left feeling stupid. Finally he was accepted with open arms. Everybody mocked him, but it was out of love. He repeated the same thing over and over again. The he began to talk, his words left the paper. I wanted to keep communicating with him through notes, but when he would write, there were gaps. Every other word was missing. I would simply fill in the blanks, and eventually, it all came together.

Just when I started to fill like myself again I received some bad news. I got word that two of my cousins had Aids and were dying. Then my aunt, whom I loved dearly, had cancer, and it had spread all over her body. She was the one who made it clear to me that my children needed me at home, and stood behind me. I told GOD if you take her, what am I going to do? I began to think I was a puppet. No human could keep dealing with such horrible things alone. I had a dream that I had company. There were people in my house then the devil introduced me to a man. When I saw the man's face, I couldn't breath. I woke up not able to breath. I blew it off as just a dream. I tried to prepare myself for my aunt's passing. I tried to stay positive. I talk to GOD from my bedroom as I always have, but it was her time. The saddest thing about her passing was that she lived with her mother until she was 50 years old. She finally met man, got married, and was very happy. It only lasted for 5 years. My neighbors helped me, by getting my children from school and watching them until I got home. My aunt's husband bought her a house. It had wooden floors. It was a beautiful house, in a nice neighborhood. I caught the bus everyday to help take care of her and her new home. Her mother and sisters were the worst. I had never been around that much, now, I knew why. They were cold and very heartless. One weekend I put some meat on the grill and invited some friends over. I stepped right into that dream I had. One of my wild friends brought a friend over and introduced us. It made me weak. I told the person about my dream, but we came to the conclusion, that we were destined to meet. We dated. I needed support. He drove trucks for a leaving. The paychecks were nice. I introduced him to the kids, he took them on a shopping spree, and that did it, he was in. He was a provider. I was able to take care of my aunt and children without having to worry about money. Time past. The closer she go to death, the harder it became. I was always able to make her laugh. One weekend, I took the kids with me to her house. They loved her. She made sure their birthday's were exactly how they had imagined it. The cakes came from the best bakery in town, the best. That weekend, I told the kids to hold hands while I prayed for my aunt. It wasn't until I began to pray when I realized I didn't know the LORDS PRAYER. She LAUGHED FOR A LONG TIME! She told everybody, and they had a ball, laughing and talking about me. Slowly but surely I was loosing my strength. The more my aunt faded, so did I. One day as I cleaned her house, her mother and I got into it. That did it. I stopped going. That woman called me and told me she and her sisters had already predicted that would happen. I began to ask that woman about some cousins I hadn't seen since childhood. She told me, they were raised not to hang around girls like me. She said it so nice and sweet. I wanted to stab her in the face, but I realized it was better to never go around that family again. My aunt wanted me around during her last days. I didn't go. She passed and I LOST IT! But the weirdest thing happened that same night. My friend had to go to work. I was in my room CRYING! Balded up in a knot. Around 2 am the phone rang, I answered, it was nothing but static. I heard something in the background, I dropped the phone. I got up and hung the phone up. For some reason I began to feel different. I asked my aunt out loud, is that you? THE PHONE RANG AGAIN! I WANTED TO HEAR HER VOICE AGAIN! The static was loud, but I heard something in the background. I began to get nervous again. I hung up, and said if it's really you, I can't take it. I asked her to stop calling. The phone rang again, I didn't answer, I unplugged it. I got up TURNED ON ALL THE LIGHTS IN THE HOUSE AND, AND SLEPT ON THE FLOOR IN MY CHILDREN'S ROOM. I really didn't sleep. I've never been able to sleep in the dark anyway. (I sleep with the t.v. on every night, and I'm 46years old. No sound, I just NEED THE LIGHT.) My poor children. I didn't know what to think about GOD. My life was over. My new friend was a huge help. He was mean as hell. I took to my bed again. But it didn't last long. I kept remembering what my aunt would tell me about raising my children. Funny, she had no children, but she knew what she was talking about. I asked GOD why didn't you take those other mean witches. Why did you have to take the good one. For thirty years, there was not one funeral in that family. No sickness, nothing. And now, GOD took the good one, the one who was everybody's back bone. I remember when I moved on my own, and I made up my mind, to never go around them again. It was Thanksgiving. It was normal to go to my grandmother's house, or her oldest daughter's house. (she was the one who ran from that church when I was caught stealing.) My aunt (who past), called me and asked was I coming over. That lump that I hadn't felt since childhood tried to come back, but this time I didn't let it. I told her no. To my surprise, she understood, she was o.k. with my decision. I felt like Scooby when he didn't understand something. After my aunt's funeral, (no I didn't take the kids, I used my imagination to explain GOD and DEATH), I was no good. My new friend went to the store and made me bar-b-Q. That was my normal routine, to keep busy doing something when I'm totally depressed, but how did he know. I cooked and cleaned. The children were worried about me. They had begun to try to understand death. That was the second person in their young life to have past. But they were so happy about the new man in my life, who had a BMW, and plenty of money. That following week after my aunt's passing, I couldn't nor did I get out of bed. I HAD A DREAM. I was in bed. My baby girl was with me playing in my bed. MY AUNT APPEARED IN FULL BLOOM!!!!!

SHE HAD NEVER BEEN SICK!!! SHE WAS BEAUTIFUL AGAIN!!!

HER SMLE SHINED LIKE THE SUN!!!! THE SUN WAS HER BACKGROUND!!! IT WAS THE BRIGHTESS EVER!!!! I WAS HAPPY!!!!!! IT WAS HER, AND SHE WASN'T DEAD!!!!!! THEN SHE WAVED HER HAND, AND MY BED WAS COVERED WITH MONEY!!!!!!!! MONEY WAS EVERYWHERE!!!!!! MY BABY GIRL STARTED PLAYING WITH THE MONEY!!!! THEN MY AUNT SWOOPED THE MONEY UP IN HER HAND LIKE MAGIC!!!! AND PLACED IT IN MY CHEST!!!!!!!!!! HER HAND WAS ON MY CHEST!!!! SHE JUST SAT AT THE FOOT OF MY BED SMILING!!

I jumped up, got my ass out of bed, and told the world!!!! No one paid me any attention. I had convinced them even more, that I was crazy. I only have two words for them, (? ?) !!!!!! (Now, I had a <u>little</u> understanding of why GOD didn't <u>USE</u> those other mean witches, HE didn't like them.) (LAUGHING HARD!) No one could help me with that dream, not even the library. That woman told me, that was not what I thought it was, it meant something bad.(LORD, why didn't I kill her when I had a chance.) (smiling) I was happy! I had energy! I was a new person! I still had to deal with my aunt not being around. That was so weird and painful. All of a sudden, a person is erased, just GONE. My GOD! I told my children about my dream. I started TEACHING THEM ABOUT GOD ALMIGHT ABSOLUTLY EVERYDAY!!!!!!!! I can tell a story. My imagination has worked that way from the moment I was born. That dream excited them. From that point on, they wanted me to tell a story. They wanted to hear more. I didn't want to become this liar. Being a Sagittarius, the honesty came forward, but I didn't bite my tongue when it came to GOD! I was like a preacher who knew nothing, but you couldn't tell me different. NOT ME! I had a dream the following night. It was like watching a film. It was dark, and then there were Police lights flashing. I woke up. I was in deep thought about that dream, when I got a phone call. My new friend was in JAIL. TICKETS. I had to empty his bank account. (Dumb ?) I began to think, did my aunt give me that money for my friend? HELL NO! That didn't go together. That night after getting D.A. out of jail, I stopped for junk food, so the children and I could sit on the floor and watch a show about GOD and DREAMS. It took my breath away. My imagination took over. I talked so much, I had no idea the children had fallen asleep. (So funny) When the true love of my life passed, my aunt told me to read palms 23(I think it's 23. The LORD is my Shepard) I had no understanding. I tried, but it didn't make since. I stole the bible I had from the hospital. I just figured I would need it some day. Every time I opened it, nothing made sense. I was raised in church, but I WAS <u>NOT</u> TRYING HEAR NOTHING THEY HAD TO SAY, BUT, SEE YA NEXT SUNDAY. That woman forced me to go, but I was walking back and forth to Minyard's for candy. I couldn't stand those people! My aunt always gave me money for church. She knew what I was doing with it. She would test me. She'd ask, and I LIED. She ask again, I LIED AGAIN. In my mind, we could go on forever. Time past. I QUESTIONED that dream about my aunt, and that money. I was on a mission. That dream put me back on my feet! WHY ? I'm not supposed to have this good feeling inside when my aunt is gone. I had begun to ask GOD, if you are REALLY REAL, I NEED TO SEE YOU, I NEED TO KNOW.

THE DREAM OF ALL DREAMS !!!!!!!!!!!!!!!!!!!

I went to sleep, and had a DREAM. I walked into a school building. Then, I walked into a classroom. There was a HUGE eye, someone drew on the board. The classroom was empty, it was just me. I sat on the front row. The eye faded, and the sky appeared. It was dark. Words appeared. They were floating in mid air. They were going backwards, from right to left. I couldn't understand it. Then I began to float into THAT EYE. I WAS IN THE PUPIL OF THAT EYE! THERE IS NOTHING LIKE IT! THAT FEELING!!!!!! NOTHING IN LIFE MATTERED!!!!! NOTHING!!!! THE EYE began to fade. I began to feel bad. I ended up back in that seat on the front row. The board appeared again, with that EYE on it. I just sat there. I was mad. I DID NOT want to come back. I woke up HOT! PISSED! I knew exactly what that was! I thought about, how I didn't want to come back, and I didn't give a dam about my children! And I didn't even have a quilt trip. I told my kids about it. They were amazed and scared, so was I. I tried to make sense of those words going backwards, but I couldn't. I took a chance with the bible. The moment I opened that book, there it was.

I WILL INSTRUCT THEE AND TEACH THEE IN THE WAY WHICH THOU SHOULD GO. I WILL GUIDE THEE WITH MY EYE.

I dropped that bible as if it were on FIRE!

I PUT MY MUSIC ON!!!!!!!!!!!!!!!!!!!!!!

I've always been into Chaka khan. As a teenager, her music would take me away. Where ever it was it was total darkness, but it did something to me, it made me feel better. When the music stopped playing, I hated it. I didn't want to come back. I wanted to stay in that fantasy. There was one song I played over and over.

DON'T LET THEM, GET THE BEST, OF YOUR HEART, LEAVE THE REST OF YOUR LOVE, AND YOU'LL BE TAKEN CARE OF. TIME AND TIME AGAIN, YOU LISTEN TO A SMILE, NEVER KNOWING WHAT'S BEHIND IT, ALL THE WHILE. YOU GIVE YOURSELF AWAY UNTIL, LOVE IS GONE, AND DON'T CONSIDER THAT IT MIGHT BE DOING HARM.

POWERFUL! Yet, at that time in my life, I had no clue as to what it meant. My big brother had every album man ever put out. Young, old, black, white, you name it, he had it. And he knew when they had been touched. Of course, I didn't know what he was talking about. Nothing was going to stop me from going in that room, and disappearing into that music. When he left the house, I went into that room and VANISHED!

Just before my true love and my aunt past, Chaka came back with a new CD, <u>THE WOMAN I AM</u>!!!!!!!!!!!!!!! Once I learned every word, I played that CD over and over and over, until I became her. There are three songs on there that are strictly about GOD! <u>LOVE YOU ALL MY LIFE TIME</u>! <u>THIS TIME</u>! <u>THE WOMAN I AM</u>! After those DREAMS, when GOD CAME TO ME!!!!!!!! Everything came together! It was like she had me by the hand all along, but she had to wait until the time was right or GOD'S APPROVAL!!!!! I told everybody about that DREAM of being in GOD'S EYE!!! I didn't give a dam what no one thought anymore. <u>GOD IS REAL</u>! <u>GOD IS REAL</u>! <u>GOD IS REAL</u>!

<u>THROUGH THE FIRE</u>!!!!!!!!!!!!!! WHEN THAT WOMAN PUT THAT SONG OUT I KNEW THAT WAS AN ORDER FROM GOD!!!!!!

ONE DAY I'M ON THE HIGHWAY IN MY CAMARO LISTENING TO THE RADIO, LOW AND BEHOLD SHE DID A REMAKE OF THE JACKSON 5-MICHAEL JACKSON'S, <u>GOT TO BE THERE</u>!!!

THAT'S THE DAY MY LOVE DEEPENED FOR THAT WOMAN! EVERYTHING IS DONE FOR A REASON. GOD DOES THINGS ON PURPOSE!!!!!!!!!! Every Sunday morning, I LIISTEN TO HER CD. THAT'S

ALL THE CHURCH I NEED! JUST GOD AND MYSELF!!!!!!!!!!!!!!!!!!!
I'M GOING TO LISTEN TO THAT CD UNTIL I DIE! IF I LIVE TO
BE ONE-HUNDRED, YOU CAN REST ASSURE, IF IT'S SUNDAY
MORNING, I WILL BE IN MY BEDROOM, WITH GOD AND CHAKA,
SINGING MY HEART OUT !!!!!!!!

PRINCE played a HUGE part. I THANK GOD ALMIGHTY FOR ME
BEING A TEENAGER AT THAT TIME!!!!!!!!!! THE MEMORIES!

When I listen to KISS, my IMAGINATION TAKES ME TO
BEDROCK!!!!!!!!!!!!!!! When I listen to the rest of his music, I'm Serena from
Bewitched. A couple of years ago my children told me that BET was GOING
TO BE ALL ABOUT CHAKA. I COULDN'T WAIT!

WHEN THE CURTAINS OPENED AND THERE STOOD STEVIE
AND PRINCE, I THOUGHT I WAS DEAD!!!!! MY IMAGINATION
CAME TO LIFE!!!!!!!!!!!!!!!! I HAVE ALWAYS IMAGINED THEM
TOGETHER ON STAGE WHEN I'M IN CONCERT WITH
CHAKA!!!!!!!!!!!!!!! There is one thing I TRULY LOVE ABOUT PRINCE.
IT'S THE WAY HE LIVE HIS LIFE. <u>AWAY</u>!!!!!!!!!!!!!!!!!!!!!!

There WORLD was BEAUTIFUL in my eyes. Everything and everybody
was BEAUTIFUL! Happy times kicked in, everything was going great for
me and the kids. I pulled away from my family, but they forced themselves on
me. That's how I began to catch on to that HOLD they had on me. They were
EXCELLENT AT SHUTTING ME DOWN! MAKING ME FEEL LIKE
SHIT! THEY WERE GOOD! By now, the shaky feeling I had off and on as
a child, was in full bloom. MY FAMILY MADE ME NERVOUS! AWAY
FROM THEM, I WAS WHO I WANTED TO BE. WHEN THEY CAME
AROUND, I COULDN'T THINK FOR MYSELF, I WAS CLUMSY, I
WAS HYPED, AND CONSTANTLY TRYING TO PLEASE THEM.
That was hard for me to understand. (every time I think about it, I turn into
HANNIBAL) I knew what I had to do. I just didn't want to screw my kids up.
All they knew was those people were family. But I'm going to show you how
COLD GOD IS! I worked a part-time job at night. I would take my children
to that woman's house, so she could baby sit. One night after picking them up,
and going home, my daughter came to me and said, I don't want to go over there
again. I got weak and scared. I asked why? She said, she is mean, she treat the
boys bad, and that one time she washed my daughter's hair in pure hot water. (
I'm shocked, I never chopped this woman's head off). They never went over there

again, without me. I looked to the sky, and said O.K. AUNT BOB, I HERE YOU! YOU SAID, I NEED TO STAY AT HOME WITH MY KIDS! IT'S A DONE DEAL! I was nervous and upset for weeks. My family had a way of BREAKING ME DOWN! Which always left me, thinking I was about to loose my mind. I knew if I killed them that problem would disappear. I don't like being confined and locked up. I don't do rules at all. Shawshank was NOTHING! There is something in me that even I'm scared of. I stopped answering the phone. I never liked the phone anyway, still don't. I began to cut everybody, and it felt good. But when those people came around, I had no strength.

After having those DREAMS OF BEING WITH GOD, I WAS ON CLOUD NINE! Nothing could break me. I HAD A DREAM.

The devil was in my bedroom! He stood there as if he was deep thought. He was RED! A DEEP DARK RED! He was TALL! HIS HORNS WERE HUGE! HIS BODY IS HARD TO DESCRIBE. I was scared at first, but then, he began to walk across MY room! THE WALK! HE HAD LEGS LIKE A HORSE! HIS FEET WERE, HOOFS! IT WAS HIM! HE STOPPED IN THE MIDDLE OF THE FLOOR! I SAT UP! HE STARED AT ME!, I STARED AT HIM! HIS EYES!!!!!!!!!!!!!!!!

THEY WERE GLOWING!! THEY WERE LIGHT GREEN!!!!!!!!!!! THE MORE I STARED AT HIM!!!, THE STRONGER!!!, I GOT!!!

I WOKE UP! I had the courage to whip anybody that crossed my path!

I had an attitude with EVERYBODY, for no reason. I told my children and anybody who would listen, about that dream. The more I talked about it, the more I UNDERSTOOD! THAT BASTARD WAS NOT GOING TO TOUCH ME EVER AGAIN!!!!!!!!!!!!!!!!!!!!!!!!!!!!!!!!!

AND I MEANT THAT!!!!!!!!!!!!!!!!! I'M S-I-C-K OF HIM!!! DYING IS EASY! I'VE BEEN WISHING I WAS DEAD EVER SINCE I WAS FIVE!!!!!!!! __ __ __ __ ! THE DEVIL!!!!!!!!!!!!!!!!!!!!!!!!!!!!!!!!!!!!!!!

The next morning, the unbelievable happened. My daughter came in my room, and stood next to my bed. I woke up, and right when I was about to move I COULDN"T ! SOMETHING LEFT ME! AND SOMETHING TOOK OVER ME! I WAS STIFF AS A ROCK! I WAS VERY AWARE OF WHAT WAS GOING ON! BUT I COULDN'T MOVE! I THOUGHT I HAD A STROKE! MY BABY WAS ON HER KNEES, LOOKING ME IN MY FACE! THEN I BEGAN TO MOVE VERY SLOW ! I COULD MOVE AGAIN, BUT IT WASN'T ME! I MOVED MY NECK AND HEAD! I COULDN'T MOVE ANYTHING ELSE! I TURNED TO MY BABY, AND SAID, I USE TO BRUSH MY TEETH WITH PENCIL

SHARPENERS! THEN I HAD A DEEP URGE TO BITE MY BABY'S FACE OFF!!!!! I REMEMBER, A PART OF ME WOULDN'T LET ME! MY HEAD TURNED BACK SLOWLY, MY FACE, FACING THE CEILING! SOMETHING LEFT ME! AND MY SOUL RETURNED!!!!!! I WAS REALLY FREAKED OUT! I WAS TOO SCARED TO MOVE! I STARTED WITH MY FEET, THEN MY HANDS, THEN MY NECK. I LOOKED AT MY BABY, AND REMEMBERED WANTING TO BITE HER FACE OFF! SHE WASN'T SCARED AT ALL! I ASKED HER, WHAT JUST HAPPENED, SHE SAID, I SAID, I USE TO BRUSH MY TEETH WITH PENCIL SHARPENERS. I TOLD NO ONE ABOUT THAT! I KEPT TALKING TO MY DAUGHTER ABOUT, BUT THAT WAS A MISTAKE! MY BABY WAS SCARED! EVEN NOW AT 25 SHE DOES NOT WANT TO TALK ABOUT IT, BUT SHE REMEMBERS IT WELL!!!!! Normally, I wouldn't have stepped in that room again, due to being the scariest SOUL on earth, BUT I WAS FED UP WITH THAT PIECE OF __ __ __ __!!!!!!! My friend worked at night. I couldn't wait until he left. I went in that room, and cut the lights off! Cut the T.V. OFF! (which is definitely NOT NORMAL FOR ME!) I CLOSED that door, and said, SON OF A __ __ __ __ __ BRING IT ON!!!!!!! I went to sleep like a baby. Nothing happened. No dream, nothing. But after experiencing what I experienced, I've been CHOPPING UP ANY AND ALL THINGS THAT ARE EVIL!!!! I KNOW GOD GOT MY BACK!!!!!! AND I WALK AROUND, LIKE GOD GOT MY BACK! I'M TIRED OF THE DEVIL AND HIS POSSE!!!!!!! I'M TIRED!!!!

Life went on. The children were happy. I was walking AROUND IGNORANT! MY friend always told me, quit trying to figure life out. I ONLY HAD TWO WORDS FOR HIM! MY CHILDREN LAUGHED AT ME!!!!! They said I was SO FUNNY!! I'M GLAD THEY TOOK IT THAT WAY. My baby brother kept coming around. He was my heart and soul every since he was born, but things were changing. I will never forget what he did for my babies the first Christmas we were on our own. I was BROKE! I told no one. I took a deep breath and told the kids Santa might not come. They were so hurt. I promised them, that I would make it up, if Santa didn't come through. I didn't know how I was going to face them that next morning. HELL, I STILL BELIEVE IN HIM, AND I'M 46! IF I LIVED TO BE ONE-HUNDRED, I'M GOING TO BED EARLY, ON DECEMBER 24TH, I DON'T WANT HIM TO SPRINKLE PEPPER IN MY EYES! Christmas Eve, my brother called me. He asked if everything was o.k., THE TEARS ROLLED. I told him, I used the money I had to buy groceries. He said WHAT DO THEY WANT! EVERYTHING I NAMED, HE WENT TO THE MALL, THE NIGHT BEFORE CHRISTMAS AND GOT IT!! I CRIED, AND COOKED ALL NIGHT!! COOKING HAVE ALWAYS CALMED MY NERVES. HE MADE IT TO THE HOUSE AROUND 2 am, AND STUFFED MY LIVING WITH TOYS AND PRESENTS!! I HAD NEVER BEEN SO THANKFUL!!!!!! In return, I fixed him a plate with two turkey legs, ribs, greens, pasta salad, and MY SPECIALTY, CHOCOLATE CUPCAKES!!! MORE ICING THAN CAKE. (I didn't know how to fix dressing at the time, I do now) My babies woke up, ran in the living room, and started SCREAMING, HE CAME!! SANTA CAME!!!! They had toys, shoes, and clothes. My brother took the time to wrap the clothes and shoes. He really went all out. He called later that day, to see how things were going. All I had to do was hold the receiver in the air. It was very obvious. Then he asked if I had opened my present. I said what present. There is nothing else to open. He told me to look in the corner behind the stereo. There was a gift for me. Calvin had just come out with Escape. I cried, and I cried, and I cried. You can't repay someone for the HAPPY FEELINGS HE BROUGHT TO MY HOUSE THAT NIGHT, YOU JUST CAN'T.

My new friend would take the kids to his family reunions, and they would have so much fun. He got baby boy into football, he took my daughter to a modeling studio to attend classes, SUGAR AND SPICE, and for my autistic son, he spoiled him by taking all over Utah! All my baby wanted to do was ride, he love to see the sites and could recall every sign on every highway and building. He love maps, atlas. That child would look at those books forever. It was so funny, he could be outside sitting on the porch, and I would straighten his books up. HE WOULD COME RUNNING, PITCHING A FIT!! I LEARNED TO LEAVE HIS STUFF ALONE! The second year my friend was with us, Christmas came and he bought everybody in the house bikes, including the two of us. Baby boy couldn't ride his bike, but he played it off, he was so HARD. He was 5. Daughter could barely ride her bike. She just wanted everybody to see her with a bike. MY AUTISTIC SON, GOT ON HIS BIKE AND RODE IT, AS IF HE WERE SPEED RACER!!!!!!!!!!! THE CHILD ONLY HAD A TRICYCLE, AND HE NEVER TOUCHED IT! My friend thought he really needed to help my special one. I thought the child was just going to look at and keep going, NOT! That boy was turning corner, like he was in a race to win. I was too scared to be nervous. All I could say was, LORD, MY CHILD IS RIDING A TEN SPEED. My friend and I rode around with him. But we gave up. We couldn't keep up with him! The funny thing was, I was only 29, and my friend was 30. That's SAD. I told the other two they had better keep up with their older brother. I eventually got out there with them. I'm A CHILD AT HEART! And the thought of not being able to ride a mile, gave me sleepless nights. Once I got back in shape, I bought a volley ball net, and wore the neighbor kids OUT!!!!!! THAT'S WHO I AM! One day while the kids and I were out riding our bikes, there was a little boy working on his bike. I don't know how, but that bike was held together with shoe strings. He called out to us, and asked if he could join us. Of course I said yes. It was hard for him, but he kept up with us. He asked our names, I introduced everybody. He asked my name again, I said Alice, he said o.k. LIZ. The kids laughed, but he thought nothing of it. We had to stop at every other house, so he could work on his bike. He asked my name again, I said Alice he said, YO LIZ. My name became Liz. It felt comfortable. I said to myself that will become my name later on in life. Every time that baby saw me, he said, HEY LIZ. I said, hey PUMPKIN, WITH A SMILE.

The party began to end. My friend true colors began to show. Out of the blue, he started punching on me, as if I were a man. He would knock me out. I knew what I had to do, but I didn't want to be broke again, and have to leave my kids at home, to fend for themselves. I was so depressed. I had a dream. I saw my aunt who passed, but this time, she was in the hospital sick again, she looked like a skeleton. I woke up. I thought about that dream, and came to my senses. My children needed me. No more depression, just keep on moving. I dealt with it. He knew I was getting ready to take that leap of FAITH, and what did he do? He bought me a JEEP. Once again, I couldn't let the kids down, not to mention, momma was happy. The jealousy began to show from my neighbors. So stupid. I had a girlfriend who had Lupus. She had three beautiful daughters. I had always told her, to take care of herself for her babies, nothing else mattered. She never listened. Before my new friend came along, I had already started the cutting process. I dropped everybody I use to hang with. But with her, I just kept my distance, we still talked, and our children always played together. Her oldest daughter and my daughter were best friends. My daughter started selling candy for her own profit. Her friend wanted some candy for free. My daughter said no. That little girl ran home and told her mother. That woman came to my house, knocked on my door, talking trash. My daughter told me what happened, but I didn't take it that serious. When I opened the door, that woman was screaming at me then she burst through my door. I put her out. I didn't want to touch her. She was sick. She had Lupus. She kept talking loud, and putting her hand in my face. My mind went blank. Before I knew it I had the top of her head in my hand. I drug that away from my door. I didn't want to hit her, but she was trying to beat me down. I knocked her out. Then the neighborhood kids said, her sister is coming. I had my new Reebox on, nothing but grip. Her sister came. I climbed the outside of the stair rail with one hands, while I still had the top of her head in the other hand. I made sure my back was to no one. Everybody thought I had LOST my mind. Her sister didn't know what to do. She tried to come at me, I kicked her in the chest, then I lost my balance, all the while, I still had the top of her head in my hand. When I lost my balance, I almost fell, and the two sisters DUCKED for cover. Everybody was floored, including me. I started laughing out LOUD! Everyone called me a BIG KID! That's who I am. After I noticed how scared they were, I let the top of her head go. They walked away, I went in the House. I walked around my house, like Prince, in Purple Rain, when he was PISSED. I had energy to burn. I was SO HUMILIATED! My children were never to see that side of me. I grabbed my bike, I told my kids to grab their bikes, and we HIT THE STREETS. We rode our bikes until 10 pm that night. I was so mad with myself. I BEGGED GOD TO FORGIVE ME. While all of that was going on, my friend was in the bed sound asleep. When we got home, I had a long talk with my daughter, and got them ready for bed. I got on my knees, and talked to GOD OUT LOUD! I asked HIM to put a shield around me and my children, and GUARD US WITH ALL OF HIS MIGHT! I told my friend about what happened. So, the next day, he came home and said, let's wash the car OUTSIDE. I said NO, HE said YES. I went ahead, but I told my children to let me know if someone coming running up behind me! (Laughing) My friend told me to polish the rims, I did, I needed to make myself TIRED so I could rest. I don't know why, but I looked up at the sky. THERE WAS A HUGE WHITE CIRCLE! IN THE SKY!!!! The SHIELD THAT I PRAYED FOR!!!! I STARTED SCREAMING!!! I TURNED FLIPS!!! Everyone wanted to know why I was so HAPPY!!! I TOLD THEM TO LOOK AT THE SKY! I ASKED THEM, WHAT DID THEY SEE. THEY SAID A CIRCLE. I ASKED, HOW DID THAT CIRCLE GET THERE? I ASKED THEM, DID THEY SEE A PLANE? NO!!!! I ASKED DID YOU SEE ANYTHING IN THE SKY MAKING THAT CIRCLE. All I GOT WAS, NO. I WENT IN THE MIDDLE OF THE STREET, GOT ON MY KNEES IN FRONT OF EVERYBODY, AND THANKED GOD OUT LOUD!!

I didn't talk to anyone. I told my friend what he could do with his car and rims. HE LAUGHED. I WENT IN MY HOUSE, AND WENT TO BED!, WITH A SMILE!!!!!

My daughter and her friend made up, as children do. I hated that woman for taking me through that. She was sick, for real. I couldn't imagine her kids without her. I had a dream. I was in my house, but I kept leaving and coming back. I remember the children were sitting on the floor, playing. I remember one was hurt. I remember picking the child up and I took off running with the child in my hand. I remember bringing the child back to the house. I remember, there was a group of people with me when I brought the child back home. All of them had on white coats. As they left the house, the people in white coats went down the stairs. When they made it to the last step, the stairs disappeared. I remember watching them walk away they were talking and laughing with each other. I remember wanting to leave the house, but I couldn't, the stairs were gone. I remember thinking, how am I going to get out. When I woke up, I was puzzled. What did that dream mean? I went about my day as usual. I had to go to the store and get groceries, so I made the kids stay home and clean up. I took the microwave dish out, and told my daughter and baby boy clean the kitchen, wash dishes, and clean the microwave. I left. As I stood in line at the grocery store, I got sick at the stomach. I thought nothing of it. I paid for my groceries and left. When I got home, the house was quiet. I noticed the microwave dish was broke. I asked what happened. I got nothing. I asked where was baby boy and went to get him. He was in the bathroom, with his foot wrapped up with a towel. He was CRYING. I took the towel off, and the heel of his foot was hanging on by a thread. The towel was soaked in blood. I didn't say a word. I got a fresh towel, wrapped his foot up, picked him up, and flew to the car. 911 didn't cross my mind. I drove fast and ran every red light. I wanted the cops to stop me, that way I could have made it to the emergency room even faster. There was no cop in sight. We made it to the emergency room. A nurse took one look at his foot and took him straight to the back. That dream didn't cross my mind. I was told, I got him there in time. The doctors were able to save his foot. They had to deaden it, to stitch it back together. When I saw that needle, I couldn't move. Five doctors had to hold my baby down! They actually had to stick that needle on the inside of his foot. That raw flesh. They did it, and began the stitching. Twenty-ywo stitches, my poor baby. When I got home, my daughter was in her room with the door closed. I opened it, and told her, I did want to see her for a while. I couldn't touch her. I would have DAMAGED HER. All baby boy asked was, when is she going to get her whipping? I had no answer. I needed to take some time to think about that punishment. That year, his football career was over. I slept in his room, as if I had just had him. Boy, was I tired. At that time, I focused on the boys. I really had to stay away from my daughter. I finally asked how it happen. Baby boy said, they began to argue, they were fighting over that plate. They dropped it, and it broke. They cleaned the glass up, and put it in the trash. The trash was a plastic bag. They kept fighting, and she pushed him up against the trash bag. That THICK glass sliced the heel of his foot off! All the while, my friend was in the room sleep, and heard nothing. All I could think about was knowing baby boy was going to out grow her and remember what she did. As I hung out with him, I began to teach him, men don't hit women. They just don't. He understood, because his reply was, I would end up hurting her bad, and I said you are correct. I didn't know what to do. I had never had to punish her or lay my hands on her before. I told my special one to take care of his sister. I couldn't stand to look at her. He was more than happy to do it. Then I noticed how he wasn't able to use one of his hands. Just when he figured out how to use his hands, now he was back to just letting his hands hang again, as if there were no use in having them. When I asked him about it, he started walking backwards, shaking his head, as if to be saying, NO! I grabbed his hand, looked at it, and saw a big cut. There I was back at the doctor's office. The doctor said, it wasn't bad, and gave us some medicine for it, and told him to stay away from his sister. (laughing) I told the doctor I was going to take her skin off! He said, take something from her that would break her heart, and make her stay in her room. He began to tell me stories about what his sister and brothers did to him, when they were growing up, it was so funny, but he made it clear, it wasn't funny then. I felt a little better, but I still kept my distance from that child. I went in her room, and when I finished, there was NOTHING BUT A BED! NOTHING! She could only come out, to use the restroom. I told her, she better NOT enter my kitchen, or no other room. GOD STEPPED IN AND TOOK OVER. A week later, baby boy was getting around a little better than he had, ever since he cut foot. One morning I caught both boys sneaking in and out of her room. I thought nothing of it. I just figured they were trying to keep her from starving, because I didn't care. Then I saw the special one coming out of the bathroom with wet towels. I heard baby boy fussing at him, because water was dripping everywhere. I almost took that bedroom door off with one hand. I looked at her, and she was SICK AS A DOG! That girl had her brothers to sneak in the frig., and bring her a can of CHOCOLATE HERSHY'S SYRP! She drank the whole thing! I like the idea of them hanging together doing kid stuff, but dam! She threw her insides up! She was sick! I made her get up and sit at the dining room table, and I sat that can in front of her. She didn't what to do. She was sick, and then she was scared of me KNOCKING HER OUT! I wouldn't let her lay down for nothing. That DREAM finally hit me. I said THANK YOU GOD!!,

AND NEVER LET THEM OUT OF MY EYE SIGHT AGAIN! Before then, I thought I kept up with my children, I guess not. My bouts of depression made me miss quite a few things. Never again. Those boys really felt sorry for her. I said to myself, the <u>POWER OF LOVE</u>! When I finally started talking to her, and the answers I got from her, all I could think of was BAD SEED! (The original movie was a master piece! Another brilliant writer) Where did that come from, and when did it kick in, I have no I idea. But all the while <u>GOD HAD HIS EYE ON US</u>!!!!!, <u>WITHOUT A DOUBT</u>!!! At this time, I began to ask my children what did they want to be when they grew up. I figured my special one and I would be together always. My baby boy had football in his heart. My daughter had no clue. I remember when she was in the first grade, we were in her room, sitting at her little table and chair set, I asked her what did she want be when she grew up, and she said a PINK POWER RANGER. MY HEART STOPPED! It was so hard for me not to laugh. I took a deep breath, and told her, the POWER RANGERS WERE NOT REAL, but she was convinced that they were, and she went on to explain that she wanted to save people. I let it go, I went in my room, and laughed my heart out! I asked GOD to help my baby, knowing what the world had in store for her. I knew the older she got, that thought would change. That night I had a dream. In that dream, I heard my daughter in her room whining. I went to see what was wrong. I entered her room, and asked what was wrong. She said her big toe hurt. I looked at her foot then I slowly began to look at her body from her feet up. When I looked at her head/face, there was the head of a GOLF PRO on my baby's body, with a HUGE smile on his face. I woke up, didn't think twice, and went and bought a set of golf clubs for her. She had no clue what was going on. I told her about my dream, we went to the golf course, and it was magic! Her swing was unreal! People noticed her swing, and had all kind of advice for her. The people who came to her with advice were white men, fifty and up. They were super nice. But I said to myself, GOD YOU KNOW WE DON'T HAVE A DIME! I thanked them for their advice, time, and lessons. She said when she entered High School, she was going to join the golf team, and she did. I told her, I didn't know what that dream meant, but GOD HAD SOMETHING IN STORE FOR HER. We went out and got every book there was on TIGER WOODS. She watched every golf tournament there was to watch, rather Tiger played or not. At least she was focused on something. That was better than the PINK POWER RANGER. GOD was showing me HIS MAGIC every other night, so I decided to ask HIM, why did YOU allow those things to happen to me as a child, I just refused to believe GOD would let something so SICK happen to a baby. I HAD

A DREAM! In that dream, I had been shopping. I came home, and put the bags on the floor. I sat at the foot of the bed. I remember just sitting there looking around. I noticed I left the door open. I saw a man standing on the porch smoking a cigarette. All of a sudden I noticed it was that MONSTER who took my life! (the sun was shining around him, and I didn't like that at all) I ran to the door, he threw his cigarette down and came after me. We were fighting at in the doorway. I started pushing the door with everything I had! His arm and foot was stopping the door from closing. Out of nowhere, a key appeared in my hand, and I stabbed him in the leg with it! He fell back, and I SLAMMED the door the door with and locked it with that key. Once I locked the door, the key disappeared. I remember thinking, I GOT HIM!!!!I remember having a strong sense of being scared, but it left as quickly as it came. I remember I started cleaning up. I put the bags I had in the trash. I remember so VIVIDLY picking up the exact same rug that was in that house, when I was a little girl. I picked that rug up, shook it out, and put it in the trash. I remember going for the new rug I bought,(although I don't remember it being in my hands or arms, when I entered that house.) I remember, the new rug was over in the corner. I remember reaching for it, and when I did, I bumped into the t.v. stand. It rolled and brought my awareness to light!!! I remember beginning to unroll the new rug, then I looked up and around at the t.v. stand, and said, I'M IN MY HOUSE!!! I'M IN MY HOUSE!!! I woke up with an amazing feeling, knowing I had actually gone back in time! I WAS IN THAT OLD HOUSE! I ACTUALLY TOUCHED THE FURNITURE! I ACTUALLY HAD THAT FLIMSY RUG WE HAD IN MY HANDS!!!! IT WAS REAL!!!!! That stayed we ME! THE EMOTIONS!!! I remember being mad about the sun being around him. He COULD NOT BE HEAVEN! I wanted to go back, and finish what I was doing. I wanted to go and put my new rug down. The new rug was trimmed in black, with the most BEAUTIFUL on the inside. I remember YELLOW, LIGHT BLUE the most. I went to library in search for books on dreams. There, I met Sigmond Fraud! I fell in love with his books, but they didn't have exactly what I needed. But they were still very interesting. One sentence stuck with me. He believed that a person could cure themselves. I liked that. I returned those books, and went on about my business. I did learn I wasn't supposed to put that new rug down. Rugs are for people to WALK ON. I decided to write letters to my WHOLE FAMILY, TO LET THEM KNOW, I REMEMBERED EVERYTHING!!! I wrote the letters, and HAND DELIVERED THEM!! ABSOLUTELY NO ONE RESPONDED!! THE FEAR IN THEM RAN THICK!!! THEIR SILENCE SAID SO MUCH!! I ALMOST FELL OFF

TRACK, BUT SOME HOW I DIDN"T! MY DAUGHTER WAS WITH ME, AS I HAND DELIVERED THOSE LETTERS. I DON'T KNOW IF THAT WAS GOOD OR BAD, but she stood by my side. A couple of days later, I had another dream. I was outside in my neighborhood and there was a group of kids who had surrounded me. I remember falling, and the neighborhood kids were trying to help me in some way. I woke up. I thought about that dream, and came to the conclusion, that was going to get shot. So, I made my mind up, not to go outside. I tried to stop my kids from going outside, I thought about them having me as their mother, and figured, they really needed every chance they could get to get away for some fresh air. I watched them from the living room window. They were racing each other up and down the side walk in front of the house. One of my favorite teenagers came to race the little kids. He kept wining. That pissed me off! I couldn't take it anymore. I told GOD I didn't want to die, but I was taking a chance, and going outside anyway. I told that 14 year old teenager to come and race me! He said, come on OLD WOMAN! THAT DID IT! We raced and I BURNT HIS BEHIND!! I was running so fast, I tripped and fell and tore my knees UP! The neighborhood kids quickly came to my rescue. As I laid there in PAIN!, the teenage said, you don't want no more of this. I GOT UP and BURNT HIS ASS!!! That felt GOOD! I took my sore behind in the house, and that dream hit me. I knew GOD and I were really TRUE FRIENDS!! I continued to talk, not pray, just simply talk to HIM as I always have. I had a VERY unexpected dream. A shadow came woke me up, and took me by the hand. We were standing in the background, darkness. Then this wall opened up. It was a room full of guys having fun. There were drugs, and it was being passed around. There was this star sitting next to that opened wall. When the drugs got to him, he turned it down. Then the drugs ran low. Now, the star has changed his mind, and ended up hogging the drugs until it was gone. One of the guys got mad and a fight broke out. That DREAM was neat, because the SHADOW WOKE ME OUT OF MY SLEEP, AND TOOK ME TO THE PLACE WHILE IT WAS ACTALLY TAKING PLACE. It was like a HUGE MOVIE SCREEN, BUT IT WAS REAL. I REACHED OUT, AND THE SHADOW GRABBED MY ARM. IT FELT LIKE I COULD TOUCH THEM, OR THEY COULD SEE ME. The next day it was on the news. MY MOUTH DROPPED WIDE OPEN! I said TO MYSELF, I WAS THERE. The story was covered up. Now, my friend and I had been together for four years. The arguing was on, non stop. That's not me. I'm tired of being tired. He hit me, and my whole body was in the air, and I hit the floor, head first. He ran. He knew what he had done. I couldn't get out of bed for a week. He took the jeep with him. One night, I had a dream. The guy who introduced us appeared. HE WAS THE DEVIL. THE TOP PART OF HIS BODY WAS NORMAL, BUT THE BOTTOM WAS NOT! HE HAD THE LEGS AND FEET OF A HORSE! HE HAD HOOFS! THAT WALK IS THE CREEPIEST THING I'VE EVER SEEN! HE WAS SURROUNDED BY TWISTED WOMEN! THEY WERE STUCK TOGETHER AT THE TOP, BUT HAD ONE BOTTOM! THE LEGS AND FEET OF A HORSE!!!! AND THEIR MOVEMENT WERE……. I DON'T KNOW HOW TO DESCRIBE IT!!!! IT WAS SICK!!!! THEN, THE GUY WHO INTRODUCED US, WALKED UP TO ME WITH THAT WALK! I TOLD HIM, I WANTED MY CAR BACK! AND I WAS SCREAMING AT HIM!!! HE WAVED HIS HAND, AND MY RED JEEP APPEARED! HE SAID, IS THAT WHAT YOU WANT? AND I SAID, YES! I woke up. I knew it. I knew he was part of the devil's crew. I knew it. Before I got out of bed, my friend was at my door, ready to apologized, and wanted to get back together. I knew I wasn't supposed to, but I did. When he knocked on the door, the kids were hoping I got back with him. They wanted him back. They told me, hard times were better with him around. If they only knew. The things you would do for your children. Things got back to normal, but I held on to that DREAM. I never said a word, not even to my babies. It wasn't long before the fights started again. I had a talk with my children, after one of baby boy's football game. I told them, it wasn't good for me to stay with him. THEY TOLD ME IT WAS ME! Those words slapped the CRAP OUT OF ME! I shut my mouth, we went home, and never discussed it again. I made up my mind to stay in it for them. They didn't know any better, and I'm not one for having mind control over anybody. For the next three years, I dealt with the abuse. That was my SPECIALTY. One night, my daughter and I were on our way to the store, and past our neighbor, (the one I fought, for no reason). She was in the back seat of her mother's car. Her mother was rushing her to the hospital. DEATH WAS ALL OVER THAT GIRL. I HAVE NEVER SEEN THAT IN MY LIFE! MY DAUGHTER SAW IT TOO, AND SHE ASKED IF SHE COULD SLEEP WITH ME THAT NIGHT. THAT TRULY SCARED HER. I TOLD HER, GIRL YES, SHE KNEW I WAS SCARED TOO. We actually saw DEATH ON THAT WOMAN. I was nervous. All I thought about was that fight, and how I should have never opened my door. Two days later, that woman's sister came to my house and was beating on the door. It was after ten o'clock at night. I saw who it was, and opened the door. She told me her sister had passed. I was up all night. I cried. I didn't get any rest for a long time. They were from out of town, and they took her body back home. I was no good. I was scared. I didn't know what GOD thought about me, for fighting her, knowing she was sick. I finally fell asleep on the couch. I HAD A DREAM. That lady, my friend, came to me, took my hand, and we were FLYING!!!! I was trying to use my feet, I was trying to run, but there was no GROUND! I WAS SCARED AND YET, ON A NATURAL HIGH!!! WE WERE FLYING!!!!!!!! Then we came to a halt. (I'm SO GOOFY,) I FELL, (Aunt Clara on Bewitched) WE WERE GOING FAST, AND ALL OF A SUDDEN, I'M SUPPOSED TO KNOW TO STOP) I fell right into a pile of STICKER BUDS! THEY WERE EVERY WHERE, AND IT WAS SO DRY, I COULDN"T BREATH! SHE PULLED ME UP. SHE WAS SITTING ON A HUGE ROCK, AND SHE SAT ME NEXT TO HER.(I CAN"T STAND STICKER BUDS, HERE, ARE THERE.) I FELT SO GOOD SITTING THERE WITH HER, AND SHE WANTED ME TO STAY. WE JUST SAT ON A HUGE ROCK, NEXT TO EACH, IN THE MIDDLE OF NO WHERE. THE ONLY THING THAT WAS THERE WAS STICKER BUDS, AND NO AIR! I COULDN'T BREATH. I ATTEMPTED TO GET OFF THE ROCK, BUT THE STICKER BUDS RULED. I TOLD HER, I GOTTA GO. SHE WAS SAD. I WOKE UP. I told my daughter, but I never spoke about it again. I was already sad and hurting, behind her death, and that made it worst. For the next six months, I walked around like I was caring WET sand bags everywhere I went. My neighborhood knew I was over emotional, BUT THEY HAD NO CLUE. I questioned GOD. After experiencing that dream, once again, I was lost. I had a dream. In that dream, a woman gave me a book. I've wanted to write all my life, but at the time, I had no clue as to what I wanted to write about. I thought about that dream, and wondered what could it have meant. I ended up in the library. The kids and I have always gone to the library from the moment I had them. I like psychology, and there it was, Socrates. I have walked passed Socrates, and Plato for as long as I can remember. I thought those books were only for smart people. I checked out one of his book, went home, and began to read. The more I read that book, the more my wings grew. Everything made sense. As a child, I was always told, DO NOT QUESTION GOD. I knew the people that surrounded me in my childhood was hiding something, I knew they have always wanted me to shut up and keep my mouth closed, but dam, keeping that kind of information from a person is low. I remember that woman shutting me down. The more questions I had, the more she would TRY and shut me up. I remember clearly as a teenager, her control was slowly, slipping away. One day, when I was eighteen, she was fussing at me, and had the nerve to walk up on me. I don't know what happen to me, but remember that feeling of transforming into a witch. I turned around and got in her face and wanted to take her head off! She never walked up on me again. I went in my bedroom, thinking about what I had done, and if felt REMARKABLE! For once, I had CONTROL! Once I got a taste of Socrates, that was it, I knew what track I was on, and I haven't fallen since. I knew I wasn't talking to myself when I was alone. I knew someone was LISTENING TO ME !

GOD

Time past. I got closer to my children more than ever. I acted as if my friend wasn't around. He was seeing other women, and I didn't know what to do, I was a nervous wreck. I RAISED MY CHILDREN TO HAVE A SENSE OF HUMOR. They knew I love laughing, to me EVERYBODY IS FUNNY. Everyday my children came home from school they had something funny to tell me. They always wanted to know which one made me laugh the MOST. ALL OF MY CHILDREN ARE FUNNY! One day I was home cleaning up. My daughter left her favorite jacket for me to wash. I placed it on the back of a chair, and thought to myself, I would get it later. I ended up dropping the jacket in a bucket of FRESH PINE SOL WATER. I got it out, hung it up to dry, and told myself, I would wash the jacket by itself. Well I forgot about the jacket. The next day, my daughter grabbed her jacket and went to school. I never missed the jacket. When the kids got home, I asked as usual, how was your day. I had taken my daughter shopping for new clothes, so she was in HEAVEN. She began to tell me about her day. She said it was a beautiful day. (she was in the seventh grade) She said the school bus was fresh and clean. She said, all of her classrooms were SO CLEAN, AND SMELLED SO FRESH. She told me how she had a crush on an eight grader, and he finally made a move, and asked her if he could walk her to class. I could actually see the little hearts floating in the air. Then, she said the school bus was still fresh and clean after school. It HIT ME LIKE A TONE OF BRICKS! I grabbed her hand and held it tight, and asked her did she wear her favorite jacket to school, and she said YES. I fell on my knees, and said BABY, THE SCHOOL BUS, NOR THE SCHOOL WAS CLEAN. I DROPPED YOUR JACKET IN MY PINE SOL WATER YESTERDAY.

SHE WAS PARALIZED! SHE COULDN'T BREATH. THEN BABY BOY JUMPED UP AND SAID PINE SOL, BY CALVIN KLIEN !!!!!! I LAUGHED FOR A MONTH!!! My daughter stopped me from using Pine Sol ever again. My baby boy, that's the side his teachers loved and HATED. But it was that type of LAUGHTER THAT GOT ME THROUGH IT ALL. I had to let my daughter know, she was just like her momma. QUEEN OF HUMILIATION!!!! IF YOU CAN"T BEAT, JOIN EM. This time, I had a plan. My plan was to go back to work, while he was still there, and save money. I knew it was over, the moment I let him back. My two oldest kids began to see his evil side. NOT BABY BOY. My autistic son started calling him MANIAC. I was shocked. Every time that man came home from work, before he got out of the car, my autistic son would start saying, here comes that MANIAC. I tried HARD to get him to SHUT UP, but I couldn't, he would not stop. I did not talk about him to my children. They blamed me for the fighting, so I let it go. I have always allowed my children to speak their minds. If I could do it all over again, I would do the same thing.

One day, he heard my son calling him a MANIAC. That man went after my son. I said, LORD, if you don't STOP him, I WILL. He went in the boys room, he was fussing at him, I was right there. Then MY DAUGHTER CAME, AND CHARGED THAT MAN UP! SHE GOT IN HIS FACE AND TOLD HIM, YOU ARE NOT GOING TO TOUCH HIM!, THEN SHE TURNED TO ME AND SAID, YOU ARE NOT GOING TO LET HIM TOUCH HIM! MY SOUL WAS TURNING FLIPS WITH NO HANDS!!!!!! THAT WAS INSPIRATIONAL!!!!!!

GOD THAT FELT GOOD!!! But of course I got the short in of the stick. I had to listen to his CRAP. My mind was on, what I was going to for baby girl for being SO BOLD! I DIDN'T KNOW SHE HAD IT IN HER. THAT GIRL COULDN'T KILL A ROACH. BUT I MADE SURE I TOOK HER SHOPPING. THAT WAS A DONE DEAL. I LET HER KNOW I WAS P-R-O-U-D Of WHAT SHE DID! She broke his spirit. He knew there was nothing he could do. I WOULD HAVE KILLED HIM IN HIS SLEEP, BUT I REALLY WANTED TO SAVE THAT SIDE OF ME FOR MY FAMILY.

At this time, the two oldest were in Middle School, but I was Home Schooling my autistic child, the Middle schools in that area were not for him. I began to work part-time, gathering experience. I had been at home for a while. Baby boy was slowly falling off, acting up! He wasn't ready for the changes that were taking place, but at the time, I had no clue. He wouldn't talk to me anymore. I got a job at UPS as a loader. I loved that job. I have always had energy to burn. I like being too tired to think. One day I was standing on the parking lot, with a co-worker. She was giving me advice about other job possibilities. As we stood there talking, a man in a suit, with a briefcase was walking towards us. But there was this noise, and it was irritating. My co-worker and I stopped talking to see what that noise was. It was so neat. Behind that man was a soda can, and it was rolling behind the man as if it were following him like a puppy. Every turn that man took, the can was right there. When the man got close to us, we asked him was that his pet. He laughed and said how weird it was. Then I asked him if he had paid attention to the Miller Lite commercials, and he said yes. I told him that would be an excellent idea for a Miller Lite commercial. He stopped and came back over where we were standing. He said, you should really send that idea in. I said, that I would think about it. He said, no, you really should. He began to make me nervous, because I wanted to get out of my living situation, and that would have done it. I went ahead and told him I would. When that man got to his car, he turned around and said, send that idea in! I said, yes sir! I went home, told my daughter what happened. I went and got some Miller Lite, sat at the kitchen table, and wrote a commercial. I didn't get a paten, I couldn't afford it, and I refuse to let my friend know what I was trying to do. I wanted out. The commercial was about a man, a pimp walking down the sidewalk, there was this darling puppy, but instead of the people on the street falling for the puppy, they were in love with the can, petting the can that rolled and followed behind him. Miller Lite had some funny commercials going on at that time. After I put the idea on paper, I made sure my daughter proof read it, for any mistakes. I told her not to say a word. That was our secret. I gave it to GOD and mailed my idea to Miller Lite. I told my daughter to keep an eye I out for MY commercial. Miller Lite wrote me back, and said thank you, but they have a group of people who strictly work on their ideas for their commercials. They sent my letter back, my idea. A week after I mailed my letter, I HAD A DREAM. I was walking around my house, cleaning up, the T.V. was on. Something pulled me to the T.V. There was something playing, it wasn't clear. Then an A popped up at the top of the screen. Then another A. Then there was another A. I started screaming, running to get my babies. We sat in front of the T.V and, a man appeared. He was just standing there on the T.V. screen. Then he split in two, now there were two men. I said two men, two men. Then it hit me, TWO MILLION! I JUMPED OUT OF BED AND WOKE MY DAUGHTER UP, TO TELL HER ABOUT THAT DREAM! The summer passed. Now it was FALL. This particular day, I had errands on top of errands. My baby boy was at football practice. I left the two older ones at home, they were teenagers. Well my daughter left and went to a friend's house, and left the special one alone. He decided to cook himself something to eat. THE STOVE CAUGHT ON FIRE. MY AUTISTIC SON, WHO HATE SIRENS, POLICE CARS, FIRE TRUCKS, SMOKE ALARMS, *CALLED THE FIRE DEPARTMENT*! They came, there was no fire. The house was just smoked up. My son went and got our neighbor, and by the time the fire department got there, everything was under control. My autistic son explained to the firemen what happened, then he started walking in circles, repeating, please don't tell Alice, please don't tell Alice. When I got home, I knew nothing. I couldn't tell that someone had been in my house. My autistic son and daughter were in there room being very quiet. I thought nothing of it. My neighbor who took care of the problem, had gone out, she wasn't home. She returned around seven that night. She came over to let me know what happened. I was shocked. M y son and daughter were in there room shaking. But then, my daughter came running. She tried to get my attention, and I told her, not now. My neighbor was telling me how my special one had the firemen LAUGHING HARD! One firemen was had tears rolling. My neighbor told them that my son was autistic. The firemen were surprised. My son was 14 at the time and he was making great progress. The firemen aired my house out with that big fan, gave my special one a couple of tips, told to calm down, and assured him, he was going to be o.k. My son asked them, NOT TO LEAVE HIM. HE TOLD THEM I WAS GOING TO KILL HIM. That's when the laughter kicked in. My daughter didn't care how mad I was. She forced me to come watch T.V. During football season, all of my televisions are on football. There it was, MY COMMERCIAL! I can't explain all of the emotions that were running through me. It was a Monday night, New England and the Jets played, and My COMMERICAL was played on PRIME TIME TELEVISION! I wrote MILLER LITE AND LET THEM KNOW WHAT I THOUGHT! NO RESPONSE. I got a lawyer, paid him five-hundred dollars, he made a copy of my original letter, idea, and called MILLER LITE, had a conversation, then told me I needed ten-thousand dollars to go to court. I let it go. With all the PAIN inside me, I HAD NO CHOICE, but to move FORWARD. But that gave me SLEEPLESS NIGHTS. That five-hundred dollars was the money I had saved during the time I sent MY IDEA to MILLER LITE. I mailed it that summer, by now, it was Fall. Every morning I woke up, I was surprised, and would ask GOD, WHY. I didn't want to keep going. FOR WHAT? I did let my autistic son know he had done a GREAT JOB BY CALLING THE FIREMEN AND GETTING THE NEIGHBOR. I finally came to my senses and ask GOD, TO NOT ALLOW THE POLICE TO COME AND PICK ME UP FOR THAT INCIDENT. NO ONE EVER BOTHERED ME. Miller lite eventually SNATCHED the commercial off the air. By then it had aired, over and over again, PRIME TIME. I left UPS, in search for something better. I couldn't afford to let the medical and dental insurance go, but I did. THAT DROVE ME INSANE. FORGET THE KIDS, I NEEDED THE DENTAL BAD, but I told GOD, I KNEW HE WOULD TAKE CARE OF ME, AND LET THE JOB AND INSURANCE GO. There was a new company across town, paying the same as UPS, but more hours, and it was professional. An excuse to buy SUITS! I applied. I prayed. I HAD A DREAM. In that dream, a HAND handed me two cards. I woke up. The job called me. On the day of the interview, I over slept. I got up running. I ran into traffic. I gave up. I knew I didn't have a chance. When I got there, I felt so bad. I was no good for an interview, inspite of my new SUIT! I went in signed my name, knowing THAT SISTER WAS GOING TO SEND ME HOME, AND RIP UP MY APPLICATION. Instead, she said, we've been waiting for you, and walked me into an office. As I sat in that interview, my brain was identical to HOMER SIMPSON. After it was over, I blocked that interview OUT of my head. I don't want to remember the answers I had for those questions. SHE SAID, YOU"RE HIRED! LEFT THE OFFICE AND CAME BACK WITH T-W-O SECURITY CARDS! THE CARDS THAT HAND GAVE ME IN MY DREAM. I worked there for five maybe six months, but my boys were going though some changes, and the job didn't understand, plus there was TOO much favoritism, and that didn't mix with the baggage I was already caring. That was like pouring gasoline into the FIRE. But I hung in there for the children's sake.

One day, my friend needed me to come and pick him up, and drop him off at the Dealership to pick up his car. On my way back, a bird, CROW, flew straight into the car window, and died. That was nasty. My stomach told me something was taking place. As usual, I kept moving forward. I learned the hard way, I couldn't stop what I didn't have control of. That night, I HAD A DREAM. In that dream I was sitting in a church by myself. I woke up. Sunday came, I got up and got ready for church. My friend and my children thought I had lost it. My daughter came to me and asked, what was wrong. She knew how I felt about church. When the children and I moved on our own, we joined a church across the street from where we lived. It was a big church, but it only had ten people, including the preacher and the choir. That was perfect for me. Every time we went to church, the sermon was meant for me. That felt good. But at the time,

I was working part-time off and on and I would only go for the sermon. Well the people at the church caught on, and started the morning service earlier than usual, which made me miss everything. I stopped going. Maybe I'm tripping, but there were only TEN OF US ATTENDING THAT CHURCH. Anyway, I got ready for church that morning and left. I left everybody at home. I went to church and felt at peace. I went home, cooked dinner and relaxed. I was working at a department store part-time as a switchboard operator, and received a phone call. My friend's mother was killed by the hands of her grandson. That same week, the Columbine killings took place. That's the week of PASSOVER! People drop dead everyday, but that week, it's something different about that week. Man can put EASTER IN JANUARY IT WILL NEVER CHANGE OR STOP PASSOVER. <u>I LOVE GOD AND HIS SON</u>!, JESUS! I couldn't help my friend, although I TRIED! I HAD BEEN DOWN THAT ROAD, AND I LEARNED NO HUMAN CAN HELP YOU AT ALL!!!!!!! ONLY GOD AND TIME!!!!!!!!!!!!!!!!!!!!! In my heart and mind, I knew what was really happening. That was my way out of that relationship. When my friend's mother was alive, he couldn't go home, nor did his mother want him with me. Now she's out of the picture, and his father needed him. We didn't break up right away, but we did. If not I would have died, by his hands. That was so scary, but I KNEW GOD HAD ME! He went home to his father. I got three jobs at one time. I had a dream. In that dream, I had some money in my hand, and a man appeared, he was mean, then he snatched the money out of my hand, and I was so hurt. I woke up, and the kids told me the car was gone. My friend sent someone to come and get it. (I'm glad Secret Window wasn't out yet.)

PHASE #4

MY BOYS (AND MORE DREAMS)

When he left, I was SICK! I was truly a NERVUOS WRECK! Although he worked at night, it was so hard sleeping by my self again. I had a dream. In that dream my friend and his mother were standing together in my bedroom. He had on an Army uniform, and his mother was smiling as if to be proud. I woke up, called him, and told him about it. He knew about my dreams, and came running to hear it again. That was a mistake, the relationship was over. My emotions were a wreck. I didn't want him to leave. I guess I was just use to abuse, and didn't know better. As far as the money was concerned, we wasted it all the time. When his spells would kick in, he would destroy the house, then the next day, we were out shopping to replace everything. That DROVE ME CRAZY! I had another dream. In that dream, my soul entered his house. I remember it as if it just happened. I walked through that living room, through the kitchen, into the den. There he was sleeping on the couch, in front of the big screen T.V. I stood over him and felt his pain. I just stood there looking at him. Then I woke up. I had no strength, but I had no choice but to keep going. The last thing I wanted to do was leave my children at home, but my daughter convinced me she would take good care of the boys. By this time, she was a sophomore. The boys fell off IMMEDIATELY! Baby boy started skipping school. One morning he had breakfast with the Principal. That child could hold a conversation with ANYBODY! He was born questioning people. When he was two, I would tell him to go and get the green cup, he would ask, what's wrong with the blue one.

63

That's when I started calling him the devil's child. Anyway, after he had breakfast with the Principal, he went outside, and there were two boys who had been suspended from school. My child left school with them. Went to their house, and they call themselves cooking some corny dogs. The cup towels caught on fire. I'm not sure what happened after that, but I was called to the school. When they told me what happened, I didn't know what to do. I couldn't stay at home. I was not applying for welfare. I didn't whip him, but I put him on punishment. My friend had taken the jeep from me, so I had to go and get a piece of car. I was still working across town part-time, and I was working at a department store part-time. I took a chance on taking baby boy and his best friend with me on my second job, to help my daughter out. She was a straight "A" student and I wanted it to stay that way. One time she made a B, and the tears wouldn't stop rolling. I knew how that felt. I was like that in Middle School. I would give baby boy and his friend some money, and let them run around the mall. They only went in the mall for food. The Electronic section of the store had VIDEO GAMES. I could work in piece. I didn't take him everyday, but did what I had to, to keep him close to me. My autistic son started acting out. I never excepted medicine for him. I thought at a young age it would block his progress. When he was ten and younger, he never had a problem serious enough to even think about medicine. I didn't know what was going on. I found out later it was SCHIZOPHRENIA!, after all that PROGRESS. I was loosing it. I prayed to GOD, and TALKED to GOD about my boys and their problems. I never got an answer. I pushed forward. Baby boy had to attend summer school. He was kicked out two weeks before summer school ended. The Principal called me on my job, and told me to come and get him. I was across town, and my boss had no understanding. I left to go and pick him up. When I got to the school, the Principal told me not to bring him back. His grades were good enough. He had passed to the seventh grade. I knew she was full of crap, but there was nothing I could do. All my time was spent at work, I was never home. I knew I had to get my special one on some medication, and put him back in school. I knew I had to work close to home and keep an eye on Baby boy. It was the summer, and I had very little time. I told GOD, those jobs weren't bringing in the money I needed to take care of my children, and maintain a decent life. I had a dream. In that dream, I was in the department store where I worked, but it was empty. I was the only one there. Then I heard SOMETHING! I HEARD A VOICE!!!!!!!!!! The VOICE SAID, MY ORDER. GO TO JUNIOR HIGH AND HIGH SCHOOL. I was looking up at the ceiling and said, Junior High and High School ? I kept questioning the VOICE until I woke up. I woke up repeating, Junior High and High School. By the time I fixed my coffee, and poured a cup, IT HIT ME, AND I DROPPED THAT CUP OF COFFEE! I told my daughter. I quit that job across town. I kept the other two jobs I had. I didn't have to work everyday. I went to the Middle School my baby boy was getting ready to attend, I signed up to volunteer. I went to the High School to put my special one back in School, and it was on. I had another dream. In that dream, I received a phone call. It was my two older children's grandmother, who passed away, when they were only babies. There was loud music, and my baby boy was all over the place. I asked her to hold on, because I couldn't here her, because of the music. I got back on the phone, and she called me country. She heard me fussing at baby boy about his loud music. She began to tell me, that her son was going to pay. She said it twice. Then the phone went dead. I popped up out of my sleep. I knew exactly what that was. I TOLD MY DAUGHTER. I went downtown to get the process started, but had no information on their father. I was stuck. I ask GOD to HELP ME. I TOLD HIM, YOU ARE SHOWING ME THESE THINGS, BUT I DON"T KNOW WHICH WAY TO GO. One day I took the kids to the movies. (OUR FAVORITE OUTING.) When we got home, THERE WAS A NOTE ON THE DOOR! IT SAID, SORRY I MISSED YALL, HERE'S MY NUMBER, CALL ME! My hand was shaking so, I couldn't hold the note still. My special one remember his father well, but my daughter didn't. That made things worst for me with my special one. All I heard was my daddy. That BOTHERED ME! My poor daughter. GOD, I HAD NEVER FELT SO HELPLESS. YOU COULD SEE THE SADDNESS AND CONFUSION. They called him, he came by. I didn't want my children hurt by his lies, but they were teenagers and I had no control or strength at that time. I didn't discuss child support with him, I didn't want to fight. I knew it would have been hard trying to get the information I needed. My special one's 16th birthday came and their father came by with a card and sixteen dollars. My child was happy! It was hard, but I DIDN"T SAY A WORD!. My daughter's birthday came, and THE BASTARD DID NOT SHOW UP! She asked if he knew it was her birthday, and I said yes. I called him, and asked him, why didn't he come by for her birthday, he told me, he was broke. I GAVE MY DAUGHTER WHATEVER SHE WANTED, trying to make up for that pain. Her birthday was WONDERFUL! Her birthday falls on the first week of school. I allowed that party to continue until after 10 pm, only with the other parents permission. That next day, I got that note, that piece of crap left us, with his numbers on it, took it downtown, and it worked. (Clinton was President at the time!) I received a letter for a court date. I had to take the children for a blood test. I had no idea I had to take one, so what. We met in court. HE WAS HOT! He had no clue I could have killed him right there in the court house, but I knew I had to go home to my children. The child support started coming. His income tax was coming to our house too. But, it didn't last long. He simply stopped working. I had a dream. In that dream, it was pure WHITENESS!! IT WAS SO WHITE!. Then I was handed a box. I opened it, and it was a BEAUTIFUL PAIR OF PUPLE SHOES!!! THEY WERE COVERED IN DIAMONDS!! THEY WERE SHINY AND GLITTERY!!! THEY SPARLKLED!!! I TOOK ONE SHOE OUT, PUT IT ON MY RIGHT FOOT, AND SCREAMED OUT, I LOVE THEM!!!!! I SAID IT AGAIN, I LOVE THEM!!!!!!!!!!!!! AS I ADMIRED THAT SHOE ON MY FOOT, IT BEGAN TO TURN OLD AND RAGGADY! THE DREAM BEGAN TO FADE! I SAID NO! I WOKE UP! I STARTED CRYING!!!! I WANTED MY SHOES BACK!!!!!! I WAS MAD, AND HAD AN ATTITUDE WITH GOD! I WAS HURT!!!!!!!! I DIDN"T WANT TO GO TO WORK OR DO ANYTHING, BUT I DID. I CAME TO MY SENSES. I APOLOGIZED TO GOD OVER AND OVER AND OVER AGAIN!!!!! I THOUGHT ABOUT HIM LETTING ME GO, AND STRAIGHTEN THE HELL UP! I WAS STILL VERY HURT INSIDE, BUT I FIGURED, IF I KEEP GOING, HE WOULD GIVE THEM BACK.

By now, I'm working for the School District. It started out o.k. But the true colors began to show. I wasn't there for that, I was there, due to FOLLOWING AN ORDER, and for my babies. It was hell, but I managed. My house hold was FALLING APART! My boys were off the chain! Time past. Out of the blue, the singer Aaliyah died in an air plane crash. I sleep with my T.V. on, and I kept hearing her name, and my T.V. was turned down. It was five that morning, so I got up. When I learned what happened, I started screaming, NO!!!!!!!!!!!! She was the love of my daughter's life! That's all the boys and I ever heard. Aaliyah, Aaliyah, Aaliyah. I would practice my but off, trying hard to dance like her. Her video, ARE YOU THAT SOMEBODY, is my favorite. All of her videos are my favorite, but ARE YOU THAT SOMEBODY, had me trying to keep up with that girl. I had that dance down, and then I performed it for my children. THEY ARE STILL LAUGHING! AND IT"S BEEN YEARS, SINCE THAT SONG CAME OUT. Right till this very day, it's still in my heart to MASTER every video she put out. (Debbie where are you?) My children know, they can kiss my behind. (smiling)Aaliyah was a very BEAUTIFUL AND SEXY YOUNG WOMAN. I keep her DVD in my computer. I have her calendars with her pictures. I will keep them forever. My daughter was motionless. She was in shock, but didn't react. I prayed about that, knowing what could happen if she kept her feelings inside. She had to have her hair like Aaliyah's. She had to dress like Aaliyah, she even prayed to have legs like Aaliyah. I knew how GOD worked, so I let my baby pray on. That was horrible! No one wanted to believe it. I was working at two different schools, and the students took it HARD! Then, 911 HIT. My children and I were in the car headed for school. We heard it on the radio, but we thought it was a joke. It wasn't until we made it to school and found out, that it was REAL!!!!! I wanted to leave school, get my kids and go home, but I couldn't, I needed to stay at work. After school, I got my children, went home and locked the door! I told them we were NOT leaving the house. The next day, my children told me, they were going to school, I could only say, O.K. Time past. I asked GOD was there a connection. I HAD A DREAM! In the dream, I parked my car, and went in a grocery store. I remember the cars on the parking lot were the same. All of them were red. I remember going into the grocery store, and the moment I entered, there was Aaliyah. We bumped into each other. She smiled and was friendly. She had on a cute little red sweater top, with a red skirt, and tiny red purse. When we bumped each other, I touched her, as if to say excuse me. THAT'S WHEN I NOTICED WHO SHE WAS. I BROKE OUT RUNNING TO THE PARKING LOT, TO GET MY DAUGHTER!, BUT ALL THE CARS WERE THE SAME. THEY WERE ALL RED, AND I COULDN'T FIND MY CAR OR MY DAUGHTER! I WOKE UP!!

I told my daughter about the dream. She was so cold. I couldn't get her to open up. I asked her did she want to go to the movies without the boys. That made her smile. I sent the boys to a neighbor's house, and the two of us headed for the movies. Before we got too far, my daughter complained of having a bad headache. (holding her emotions in) I stopped at the neighborhood grocery store for some medicine. I walked into my answer. The only thing, Aaliyah wasn't there. There was a major take over. The stores, the gas stations, you name it, it was taken over. I was speechless. (*the devil*) I got the medicine and I left. I never went in that store again. I had a HORRILE FEELING. As I walked out of that store, I said GOD, PLEASE LET MY BABY AND MY CAR BE ON THE PARKING LOT. They were there. I made sure my baby felt better. We went out to eat before the movies. I didn't want her at the movies, sick. We had a great time. She was smiling again. At night, the boys would hear her crying softly, I told them to let her be. She will be ALRIGHT.

My baby boy was in the eight grade, he was doing well. It didn't make any difference with me working at the school, but at least no one had to call me. He played football and baseball. His baseball coach was his History Teacher. That man took time with my son. That teacher communicated with all of my son's teachers to keep his grades in check and of course to be able to play ball. My child did great that year. He played in all of the football games. They only won one game, the last game. That coach talked about my son that whole semester. (In a bad way) He decided to give my son control and allowed him to call the shots at the last game. They WON!!, They WON BIG!! Every time I past that coach in the hall, he would turn his. The baseball team had a big game coming up, and my baby was ready. The coach kept close contact with the teachers, so there wouldn't be any problems. He tutored his students three times a week. Out of the blue, He came to speak with me. He told me, he didn't know what was going on, but something wasn't right. One of the teacher's were trying to stop my baby from playing in that major game. I went to the teacher, with my son's previous report cards, and his CLASS FOLDER, FOR THAT SIX WEEKS. She was ignorant, for no reason. I went to the Dean. She said it didn't make since, my baby should be able to play. She pulled up better records than I had. The next day, that Dean acted as if she didn't know me. I went to the Principal. She was on the teacher's side, inspite of the grades that were on paper. (Sorority sisters, that's all well and dandy, but not at work, I could have sworn that they were EDUCATORS) My son missed the game. He CRIED HIS HEART OUT! I WAS HELPLESS! That was the day he GAVE UP! I got my baby and we went home. I went in my bedroom and told GOD, YOU SENT ME TO THAT PLACE, AND YOU ALLOWED THIS TO HAPPEN.

I HAD A DREAM! I was inside the school building. It was very dark. I went into the teacher's room who hurt my son. I had a feeling she could help me. When I walked in, she turned around, and had the same EYES OF THE DEVIL. They glowed. They were light green, and were very scary looking. I broke out running down a long dark hallway, and came to another room. I entered that room, and the teacher standing in that room had the EYES OF THE DEVIL ALSO! Her EYES were red, and they glowed. I broke out running again! I was running from MONSTERS!, but I couldn't seem to get away. I finally made it to the main office. I entered, thinking, I know somebody in here could help me. I burst in the Principal's office. I was standing there begging for help. There was a huge chair, facing the window. The Principal was sitting in that chair. The chair began to turn around slowly. The Principal was the HEAD MONSTER! HER EYES WERE THE BIGGEST OF ALL! SHE WAS GIGANTIC! I RAN FOR MY LIFE! I RAN OUT THE NEAREST EXIT!, WHICH WAS THE FRONT DOOR! Then I heard something. I turned around and saw HANDS putting a large chain on that door, as if to lock me out. I woke up. That dream was too easy. I never went near that building again.

When I would go to the grocery store or mall, I ran into the students and their parents, and was told about the bad things that came to those people. I didn't care. I wasn't ever stepping foot in that building again.

One day, I promised my special one that I would take him to the park, and I did. We were walking, enjoying the weather, and enjoyed being outside. There were people walking there dogs. My son is TERRIFIED of all dogs. I told him, let's go have a seat. We sat and talked. Then this man came our way. He had a ROTTWEILER. My son tried to leave, but the man told him not to run. Out of the blue, THAT DOG TOOK TO MY SON, AS IF SHE WERE HIS MOTHER. EVEN THE OWNER WAS SURPRISED. MY SON WAS SCARED, BUT THAT BIG HEALTHY DOG DID NOTHING. My son tipped to the swing, that dog followed him to the swing. My son sat down, the dog sat down. My son got up, the dog got up. My son tried to ease away, that dog barked, but it wasn't the, I'm going to get you bark, it was a protection bark. The man told my son to sit back down. When he did, the dog laid down. She even relaxed her ears. THAT WAS THE MOST AMAZING THING! That dog barked at me and everybody else who past her way. But when it came to my special one, SHE GUARDED HIM LIKE A SOLDIER! She walked up to my son, and took a sniff, and SHE KNEW HE WAS SPECIAL!!!!!! I told my son it was time to go. He got up. The dog got up and stayed very close to my baby. The owner said look like we are walking you guys to your car. That's how close that dog was to my baby. She walked my son to the car in SILENCE! The owner and I just looked at each, shook our heads, and said good bye. When my son closed the car door, that dog turned to her owner, and barked as if she really knew what was going on. She barked as if she had done a good job, and she had. All the way to the house, I asked GOD out loud, WHY AREN'T YOUR PEOPLE LIKE THAT! I imagined HIM saying, I WISH SOMEBODY WOULD TELL ME, (IN THAT DEEP VOICE)
I LOVE HIM SO MUCH !!!!!!

I was worried about how GOD felt about me not working at the Middle School any more. It was on my mind heavily. I went on as usual. I sent baby boy to a school across town. I caught up with his father, and we went to hang out with him. I needed help with baby boy, and I thought being with his father would help out big time. His father's parents were very helpful. They bought that boy everything he needed. But being with his dad was a lost cause. He was still on drugs, so that didn't work out. We went on about our business. He passed the Taks, and went on to the ninth grade. I transferred my special one to another school that was more equipped for autistic children. My daughter was on the golf team. Those boys had me going so much, it was like she didn't even exsist.

I talked to GOD, all day everyday. I wanted to stop working those part-time jobs, and be at home at night with my babies. I kept in touch with the High School Principal. I still worked there part-time, but I wanted to work there full-time. That way, everybody left the house together, and everybody came home together. I bugged that Principal on a daily basis. I bugged him so much, he HUMILIATED ME, IN FRONT OF A LOT OF PEOPLE! Was I embarrassed, NO! I was where I was supposed to be, and working there part-time meant I had to go home early to the peace and quiet and I didn't want to do that. I worked my five hours everyday and went home.

I HAD A DREAM!!!

In that dream, there was a pregnant lady standing in front of a desk, then, she disappeared. A shadow showed me a desk and a filing cabinet on wheels. Then THE VOICE SAID, YOU WILL MAKE TWENTY-THOUSAND DOLLARS. I WOKE UP!, AND BEFORE I COULD DWELL ON THAT DREAM, I GOT A PHONE CALL! IT WAS THE PRINCIPAL! HE SAID, I HAVE A FULL-TIME POSITION, AND IT'S YOURS, IF YOU STILL WANT IT!!!!!!!!!!! I have never got ready so fast in my life!!! When I got to the school, the Principal was waiting for me. We talked, and he told me, he didn't have to interview me, because I had already proven myself to him, and the employees. He told me, that there was a lot of paper that had to be cleared, and that I couldn't get paid until everything was clear. I asked him could I work for free, and he said, of course, but first I needed to go downtown and get the process started. I flew out of that building! When I got back, the Principal walked me to the office I would be working in. There it was. The desk and filing cabinet on wheels. I was so week. It got worst. He began to tell me about the lady who left. She was PREGNANT, and her husband wanted her at home, full-time. I took a seat. He asked was I all right, and I said, yes, I'm fine, just a little dizzy. I met the Assistant Principal's I was hired to work for, and went straight to work. I didn't care how long it took, for my paper work to clear. I KNEW WHAT WAS IN STORE FOR ME! I WAS HAPPY! I finally understood, DO WHAT YOU LOVE!, and that was IT! I catered to the whole school, and loved every minute of it! That was a WONDERFUL POSITION FOR ME! I received more good news, the school my special one was attending, got him a part-time job, and told me he could work on week-ends, if I would supply the transportation. I said, hell yes. She laughed and said, it's a done deal. But that party ended. One night, I decided to get up and check on the boys. I don't know why, but I did. I walked in their room, and baby boy had the window up sky high, with one leg out, and the other was on the way. I couldn't breath. I asked him, what in the hell are you doing? He was stuck! He couldn't move. I told him, to let that window down, and GO OUT THE FRONT DOOR!!!!!! I TOLD HIM TO LEAVE, AND NEVER COME BACK!!!!!! That boy slept in every piece of clothing he could find. He just knew I was going to KILL him. I knew when to stay away from my children, and that was one of those times. I couldn't figure out why he was acting out so much. It came to me. I was always at work away from home. But, my daughter started telling me things about him, when he was Elementary. She kept telling me, the boy was lying to me all the time. She wouldn't stop telling me that. Could I have actually done something about that??, I'll never know. I had a dream. In that dream, there was a group of boys at my son's window and he left with them anyway, inspite of what I would do to him. I woke up hurt. A month later, it was income tax time, and I MOVED! I had another dream. In it, I walked into a place, it was a funeral home. I remember signing my name in the book, on a stand. I remember signing my first name, but when I got to my last name, I signed another name. I remember viewing the body from a distance. And it turned out to be my aunt on that man's side, who had not died yet. She was sick, but still alive. She, (my aunt) was looking at me from the casket, along with her daughters, who were sitting at the casket with their mother. They just sat there starring at me. Then, they began to make me notice the signature. The last name I signed came up in yellow, neon light. I said, that's not my name. It was the name of a celebrity. I woke up. When I thought about that dream, all I could think about was, she's not going to be around much longer. I was sad, because, that was cousin Penny's mother. I had not seen my family since I wrote those letters and hand delivered them. I told my self, when my aunt died, it would best for me not to go. I had a dream. In that dream, I walked into the living room, to check on baby boy who was watching T.V. I saw his cover on the floor, but I didn't see him. I picked up the cover, and there were two snakes wrestling. I remember asking GOD, had the snakes taken over baby boy too. I remember it was daughter's SENIOR YEAR, and I refused to let ANYTHING get in the way. Her senior activities were coming up, and I was happy I had the money she needed, and a little extra. To everyone's surprise, she WON THREE GOLF TOUNAMENTS!!!!!! THE FIRST WIN, TOOK HER TO COMPETE FOR THE DISTRICT TITLE, AND SHE WON!!!!!!!! THAT TITLE TOOK HER TO CITY DISTRICT, AND

SHE WON!!!!!!!!!!!!!!!!!!!!!!!!!!!!!!!! That fourth round, she came in last place. That was quite all right. GOD PROMISED HER THE TITLES SHE WON, YEARS AGO!!!!!!!!!! AND WE DIDN"T HAVE THE MONEY FOR HER TO PRACTICE THE WAY SHE REALLY SHOULD HAVE. I HAD PLANS TO CELEBRATE BIG TIME!!!!!!!! I went home, checked the mail box, and got sick to my stomach out of nowhere. I knew my day was getting ready to spoil. The cable bill, 300 dollars. The phone bill, 300 dollars. Then, there was a letter for truancy. All baby boy. He was calling the 1-800 numbers, talking sex talk. He was watching dirty movies all night. And he continued to skip school. I had been to court with him, four times already. When my daughter got home, I couldn't get out of bed. I looked at her face, and got up. I showed her the bills. I told her we were going out, but without baby boy. When he got home, I TORE HIS ASS UP! Did it work?, NO! I paid those bills, and took his ASS to court for the last time. When we got back from court, I walked him in the school, took him to the office, and walked him to class. Before I left the parking lot, the Principal called me, and told me, my child was in back of the school SKIPPING!. I WHIPPED HIM AGAIN!!!!!!!!!! At the same time my special one is walking around the house, screaming his longs out, CURSING EVERY BODY OUT, LIKE THE EXERSIST! MY house hold was gone. There was no PEACE AT ALL!!! I KNEW GOD WAS STILL WITH ME. IF I HAD LET HIM GO!!..

I woke up at 4 or 5 am every morning. I put my coffee on,, and checked on the boys. The special one was sleep. Baby boy was in the living room. At least I THOUGHT he was. Something told me to pick that cover up. It was TWO PILLOWS! AND MY DOOR WAS UNLOCKED! We lived on the third floor. I thought that would stop him from going out of the window, or leaving the house period. He made it home, and the door was locked. I opened it, and BEAT HIS ASS!!!!!!!!!!!!!!!!!!!!!!!!!!!!!!! I was hitting myself in the process, but it didn't matter. I decided to sleep on a mattress in front of the front door. I HAD A DREAM. I was in this house, and I heard someone sniggling. I kept hearing this soft laughter. The house was very dark. Out of nowhere, three flying skeletons had me surrounded. I tried to scream, but I was too SCARED!!!! They kept flying in circles and laughing. One had on a red evening gown. The other had on a green evening gown, and the last one had on a black and white stripe evening gown. I kept trying to call for my daughter, but nothing would come out. When I woke up, I GOT OFF THAT FLOOR, I PUT MY MATTRESS BACK ON MY BED, AND NEVER DID THAT AGAIN!!!!!!!!! I found out later, Baby boy was leaving my house at 2 or 3 am, walking two miles to his girlfriend's house. The PUNCH LINE TO THAT STORY IS, THE GIRL'S MOTHER WAS AN IMPORTANT PERSON FOR THE DISTRICT I WORKED FOR! SHE WORE A BIG TITLE. Those ghost were that lady and her two daughters. I guess they were highly upset. I began to look through every person with a title that came my way. In the mean time, my two oldest children's father got married. It was time for my daughter to take her senior pictures. I paid 800 dollars for those pictures. She was worth every penny. When we went to pick the pictures up, her father's wife was there. Why, I don't know. She actually came over to us and asked for one of my baby's pictures. I BLEW THE CEILING OFF THE ROOF! I TOLD HER NO, AND I TOLD HER, I WISH HE WOULD DROP DEAD, SO THEY COULD GET HIS SOCIAL SECURITY! BEFORE I KNEW IT, PEOPLE, STRANGERS WERE CLAPPING AND PRAISING ME! I WAS NO GOOD. I WAS TIRED!!!!!!!!!!!! I apologized to my baby for making a scene, and took her out to eat. We were going out by ourselves a LOT!. At that time, my special one was off the change, and for some reason, he wanted his dad. We had to listen to that everyday. HIS DAD WAS COMING TO GET HIM. THAT'S ALL WE HEARD! The child was leaving the house, running away. He was collecting any and everything. I couldn't throw the news papers away, or he would go and get them out of the trash. All the junk food I bought him was stored in a closet or somewhere in the house where he thought I wouldn't look. He had a bad habit of putting his money in foil and hiding it everywhere. Our lives were CRAZY!!!!! It was the special one's birthday. Everybody's birthday is very special in my house. We dress up. Go to dinner and a movie or whatever it was they wanted to do. This particular birthday, he would not stop screaming. He would not stop talking about his father. He hated me, and wanted to go with his father. He went on and on and on. Finally, I decided to order take out. His sister and baby brother had NO INTENTIONS OF GOING ANY WHERE WITH HIM! I still don't understand why we were not evicted. Then, everything was quiet. I got scared. But then, I thought my special one was just tired and burnt out. HE BEGAN TO SPEAK IN HIS DADDY'S VOICE. HE SAID, (in his father's voice) JAMAAL, I'M COMING TO SEE YOU, BUT I'M ONLY COMING TO SAY GOOD BYE. I couldn't get off the side of that bed, for nothing in the world. Finally, I got up, and asked the other two did they hear what I heard, THEY SAID YES! Then, he laid down in the hallway and SLEPT HIS LIFE AWAY! I went and got us some food and took some sleeping pills, and went to sleep too. That boy didn't wake up until the next afternoon. I kept checking on him, and he was breathing. When he got up, I waited for a while, then, asked if he remembered anything from last night, he said no. He warmed his food, I made him bathe, and he went back to sleep. The next weekend, I heard my daughter calling me, in a soft voice. I got up, and my special one was standing over her with a knife at her chest. THAT DID IT! I noticed he was in a daze. I called his name, he didn't respond. I slowly took that knife out of his hands. Again, he walked to his, room and went to sleep. That Monday, I took him to the doctor. They wanted to up his medication and send him home. I told them, he wasn't going nowhere with me! I told them I was leaving him with them, and I meant every word. They kept him. I CRIED, AS IF HE DIED! THAT WAS THE MOST PAINFUL THING EVER! I CRIED!!!!!!!!!!! I went to see him every day, and before I knew it, he was back home. He ended up in another place. Within three days, he was back at home. Then my aunt died. I went to the funeral, although I said I wasn't going. MISTAKE! There were family members I hadn't seen since I was a little girl. I was a nervous wreck, and it showed. At the grave site, my family came after me. They had my baby brother to question me about those letters. Before I knew it, I asked him did his family have anything to say about those letters, and he said yes, all of that is in the past, get over it. I told him, you know what, you are correct. That was it, the children were grown, and I didn't give a DAM what they thought! My daughter wanted them at her graduation. She had been through enough. I gave them tickets. When the children and left the house, I forgot our tickets. I didn't realize it until we got to the convention center. I dropped her off and went back home. I was glad I did that, that way, I didn't have to sit with them. Afterwards, that family really acted as if we were a happy family. I snatched my kids and left. We had some celebrating to do. My daughter's golf coach DID NOT HELP HER WITH ANY TYPE OF SCHLARSHIP. SAD, all the athletes in that school, always ended up at a good school. My daughter got herself in school. All I had to do was sign the papers. She went off to college that Fall, and that felt SO GOOD! I was glad she got away from us. No, I had no money, but I sent her what I had. It was hard, but somehow we survived. Back at work, it was crazy but fun. My house was still out of control, but if I didn't make money, it would have been worst. One day there was one of my favorite 9th graders walking the halls, having fun. He peaked his head in the office I was working in. I told him to get his behind to class. He took off running. That was a Friday. Monday when I got to work, I got word that my favorite 9th grader was KILLED over the weekend. I BROKE DOWN!! My last words to him was, GO TO CLASS! And now he was GONE! THE PAIN!!! Quite a few kids were killed the first couple of years I worked there. I ASKED GOD WHY!!!!!! I HAD A DREAM!!! In that dream, I was in the school building, and the hallway was full of kids all dressed in white. THEY WERE HAPPY! As I walked down the hallway, THOSE CHILDREN WERE SMILING, HIGH FIVING ME, PATTING ME ON THE BACK, AND CLAPPING!!! I WOKE UP! I THOUGHT I WAS DYING!!! But the more I thought about that dream I began to believe that GOD WAS TELLING ME THAT THOSE CHILDREN WERE FINE!!!!!!! And to quit WORRYING! That was the saddest funeral. I began to just roll with the punches, when it came to baby boy. I began to pay more attention to how LIFE really goes on. One morning I made it to work and everything seemed to be o.k. The moment I pulled up on that parking lot, all of my home problems would disappear. I clocked in, went to my office, and got a phone call. My two oldest children's father DROPPED DEAD OF AN ANUISM! HE JUST DIED! I STARTED CRYING BEFORE I KNEW IT! BOY, DID I CRY! THEN, IT HIT ME! MY AUTISTIC SON HAD ALREADY WARNED US!!!!!!!!!!! I wasn't supposed to drive home that day, but I did. There was no WAY!, I was going to tell my autistic son, NO WAY! I went to baby boy's school to tell him. He started crying, knowing what it was going to do to his brother. I told him, don't worry, we were not going to tell him, we couldn't. (By the way, baby boy was in CLASS!) (STRANGE.) I called my daughter and told her. She was sad, but only for a MOMENT. I told her, I would be down there, to hang out with her, the moment I got the boys settled. Baby boy came HOME, I got my special one from school, got him settled and told them, I would be back. I HUGGED MY BABY GIRL, TOOK HER OUT TO EAT, AND OF COURSE TALKED ABOUT THE SCENE I MADE AT STUDIO, AND HER BROTHER SPEAKING IN HIS DAD'S VOICE!!!!! YES, I TOLD A FEW PEOPLE ABOUT WHAT WE EXPERIENCED, BUT NOT MANY. All I could do was sit back, think and TALK TO GOD!!!!!!!!!!!!! My Tears didn't last long. All the FUN memories, GOOD memories surfaced. I TRULY BLOCKED EVERYTHING OUT. I took some time from work, I really needed it. And as I sat around, I SMILED. We had some fun. I loved that boy's dirty drawls. And I had his children. But I don't think about him when I look at my babies. <u>THEY ARE MY BABIES</u>!!!!!!!! The way it all came about, just blocks everything out. I've always wanted that woman dead more than anything. She want die for nothing in the world, so I'm not going to say, be careful what you pray for. No I'm not. That boy really dropped dead. I wished it out loud, and his SOUL TOOK OVER MY BABY AND WARNED US, LONG BEFORE IT HAPPENED. <u>GOD WORKS IN MYSTERIOUS WAYS</u>!!!!!!!!!!!!!! (I thought about something that happened when my baby brother's daughter was born. That woman baby sat that precious child, and when she was three, she told my brother and her mother that that woman was mean. She kept saying it. That was STRIKE THREE, YOU'RE OUT!) I went to the funeral service, and I couldn't believe it was actually taking place. I had no tears, no hate, nothing. I saw my classmates. They looked awful. I thanked GOD for making me go to bed at 8pm every night. I went to the grave site. There were only 15 people there. To me, that's the saddest of all. When the true love of my life passed, there were people all over that cemetery. I told my children when I die, THERE WILL BE NO FUNERAL!! PUT ME IN THE OVEN, AND PLACE MY ASHES IN A BEAUTIFUL GOLD JAR. I DON'T WANT ANYBODY STANDING OVER ME CRYING AND FULL OF __ __ __ __. Baby boy slowed down a little. He LOVED his big brother, but living with him was a different story. That special one began to fall DEEPER AND DEEPER. HE WAS ACTING WORST THAN EVER. AT HOME, SCHOOL, AND WORK. Nobody wanted him around, and that HURT! We were surrounded by all type of people. Religious, educators, the HIGHLY EDUCATED, and not once did anyone attempt to help us. I felt like I was back at home, with my so-call family. There wasn't A DROP OF COMPASSION!!!!!!!!!!!!!!!!!!!!!!!!!!!!!!!!!!!!!!! I was talked about. My son was talked about. People pointed and laughed. They talked about us behind our backs and in our face. And there was nothing I could do but keep on moving. I held on to GOD!!!!! I TOLD HIM I HATE HIS PEOPLE!!!! One Sunday morning I was slowly waking up, and I heard this voice one T.V. Then I heard that voice and what he was saying, I began to think to myself, who is this person, and how do they know what I know. I'm supposed to be the only one who knows those things. It was Joel Osteen. That man can make a three year understand GOD and how he works. I've been watching the man ever since. One Saturday morning I was cleaning up and again I heard these PRECIOUS VOICES. I went in my room to see where those voices were coming from, and it was THE PROUD FAMILY! I sat on the floor with a bowl of Honey Combs and had a ball. One day I went to pick up the special one, and one of his teachers came to my car and told me out loud in front of my boys, that I FAILED TREMENDOUSLY AS A PARENT!! I said, YOU TALKING TO ME! SHE SAID IT AGAIN. SHE TOLD ME I FAILED TREMENDUOSLY AS A PARENT!!!! I told my special one to get in the car, and left. I went straight to the SUPERINTENDANT. SHE WAS ERASED. THEN I SAW HER HUSBAND OUT WITH ANOTHER WOMAN, AND TOLD HIM TO HAVE A BALL! Come to find out, she was already being replaced. She lost her office, she lost her authority. That was the day she came to my car and took it out on ME! That was nothing. My co-workers were quick to call me NOTHING and a NOBODY, TO MY FACE!! I held it. I held it TOGETHER. Only because, I KNEW GOD WAS ON MY SIDE!!!! I used to ask GOD, DO YOUR PEOPLE KNOW SOMETHING I DON'T. BECAUSE I'M BEING ATTACKED AT EVERY CORNER I TURN. I GO TO WORK. I GO HOME AND LOCK UP. That was my routine. Then the unthinkable happened. I had a dream. In that dream, I heard a knock on my bedroom door. I got up, opened the door, and there was the longest, thickest SNAKE I HAD EVER SEEN. But I wasn't scared. It felt like a pet. I felt comfortable with it. That snake led me to the door.   I opened it and the snake left. I went back to bed. Then, I woke up. I had been searching for help, and placement for my special one. That was the last thing I wanted to do. The other children were tired. I was tired, but that's MY SON!! A group home finally accepted him. The place was horrible. But I was told, once he was in the system, things would change. The date was set. I didn't eat for a week. I missed worked, far more than I needed to. The day came. That morning, I was mad I woke up. I could not get out of bed. I just laid there. I wanted to change my mind so bad. That would have given me strength, but for how long. There was a knock at my door. THE HEARTACHE! My special one called my name. I answered. He said, I'm READY TO GO! I FELL TO THE FLOOR! I got a phone call. It was the white van, they were down stairs. Two men came up to our apartment, we talked. THEY KNEW I NEEDED HELP, BUT THEY COULDN"T GO THERE. They asked my son was he ready, HE SMILED AND SAID YES. I walked him to the van. I DID NOT WANT TO LET HIM GO! They pulled off, MY SON SMILED AND WAVED. I WENT UPSTAIRS AND LET A SCREAM OUT, I HAD NO CONTROL OVER. I FELL TO THE FLOOR, AND JUST SCREAMED!!!!!!!! My co-workers, called to check on me, they just listen to me CRY! They kept saying, I thought that's what you wanted. I REMEMBERED NONE OF THAT!!. Baby boy came home. He looked at me, AND WE BOTH HIT THE FLOOR!!! IT HURT SO BAD, IT WAS HARD TO TRY AND HOLD EACH OTHER!!! WE CRIED OUR HEARTS OUT!!!!! GOD, THE HEARTACHE AND PAIN!!!!!!!!! Two days later, I got myself together. I needed to eat. We needed food in the house. I left and came back. I entered my house, and all I saw was sagging jeans, and shirts that were too big for a fat person. My son let his friends in my house, and they were smoking in his room. They had the window wide open to let the smoke out. I put baby boy out of my house. I didn't think he would actually leave, but he did. As he walked to the door to leave, I BROKE DOWN AND ASKED

HIM NOT TO GO!! WE CRIED OUR HEARTS OUT!!!!!! HE SAID, I'M JUST GOING TO LEAVE FOR A LITTLE WHILE!! I said o.k. I closed the door and HIT THE FLOOR SCREAMING AT GOD! ASKING HIM, WHAT HAVE I DONE SO WRONG!!!!!!!!!! I WAS THE WEAKEST!! I HAD EVER BEEN!!! The thought of baby boy having company and smoking, I couldn't take it. From the time my ex left, NO ONE WAS ALLOWED IN MY HOUSE! NO ONE! The more that SCHIZOPHRENIA kicked in, the more we SHUT THE WORLD OUT!! AND I WAS VERY COMFORTABLE WITH THAT!!!! Co-workers and students were calling me, wanting me to come back to work. I got it together, and went back to work. I wouldn't leave that building until seven or eight at night. When I made it home, I just wanted to fall asleep, without thinking. The Principal, that hired me was let go. That was sad. He was let go, because the children couldn't read write or do math. All I could think about was my favorite movie. TO SIR ,WITH LOVE. AIN'T A DAM THING CHANGED! I was hurt, because it felt like that man knew what I knew. My co-workers were mad, because now they have to work. So many had been there for 25 to 40 years, without a DROP of change. The Assistant Principal's I worked for were fired for being no good. It was horrible. The next year, the District brought in a child to run the school. A young buck. I had a dream. In that dream I was walking down the hallways of the school NAKED! I was walking, waving, smiling, and shaking hands, with no clothes on! I wasn't embarrassed at all. I remember walking to the front entrance of the building. The new Principal was leaving as if he were leaving for good. I attempted to walk out the door behind him, but I realized I was NAKED! Out of the blue, I grabbed my clothes that were fresh from the cleaners. They were hanging and covered in plastic. I really wanted to catch up with him. I tried to leave again, with those clothes hanging across my arms. But as I stepped out the door, I noticed I was still NAKED, and thought to myself that I couldn't go out like that. I remember him walking away. I remember waking up sad, but was very puzzled about being NAKED! I came to the conclusion he wouldn't be around long. The part about being NAKED was me not being able to hide my pain. In the blink of an eye, my boys were gone, and it wasn't a good thing. The true colors of the things that were going on in that building were coming out. I spoke my mind. And it was at that point, the plotting began. I had a dream. In that dream, I was in the school building walking down the halls. There were shadows clearing my path. Ever where I walked in that building, my path was cleared. I woke up that morning with a STRONG SENSE, THAT I COULD DO ANYTHING! I KNEW THAT WAS PROTECTION FROM GOD

ALMIGHTY!!!!!! I KNEW IT!!!!!!! I remember going to the movies, and as I sat there, I heard a voice. I got there early, just to seat and think. I WAS IN PAIN!!!! That voice. The more I heard it, I knew it was somebody I KNEW! It came on again, and this time I paid attention to the introduction. IT WAS CHAKA!!!!! TO SIR, WITH LOVE!!!!! I WAS AT BEST BUY THAT NEXT MORNING, AT 6 am!!!!! WHAT THAT SONG DID FOR MY SOUL!!!!!!!!!!!!!!!!!!!!!!!!!! Then, something else came over me. An ending. I began to ask GOD were those people at work going to succeed at getting rid of me. I began to drag again. That SONG!! At the very beginning of that song, I imagine GOD RISING WITH THE MOST BEAUTIFUL COLORS BEAMING FROM HIM!!!!!!!!!!!!!! HE'S SITTING ON HIS THRONE, ENJOYING LISTENING TO ME SING TO HIM!!!!!!!! THE LOVE!!!!!!!!!!!!!!!!!!!!!!!!!!! !!!!!!!!!!!! I had another dream. In that dream, both of my aunts were sitting together. I walked up to them, but went to my aunt from that man's side of the family, not my favorite aunt. I walked away sad. When I woke up, I thought about that dream and figured, at some point, I had come to realize that my favorite aunt knew the things about me, but kept her mouth closed. The other aunt, wasn't able to help at all, she had her own problems, but NOW SHE KNEW, AND WANTED TO HELP ME!!!! I was SAD about not going to my favorite aunt. I eventually shook it off. The drama was on at work! There were things I knew and there were people who wanted to HUSH ME UP!!!! They wore me out! But I HUNG IN THERE! I WALKED IN FAITH!! I DIDN"T KNOW WHY I WAS THERE, BUT I KNEW WHO SENT ME!!!!!!!!!!!!!!!!! I HAD A DREAM!!!!!!!!!!! In that dream, I was in the woods. Then I came to a dirt road. I was standing in the middle of the dirt road, and out of nowhere, THREE BLACK HORSES WERE RUNNING FAST, HARD, STRONG, AND FULL FORCE!!!!!! I remember very clearly, when they were about to TRAMPLE ME DOWN, A HUGE KNIFE APPEARED IN MY HAND!! I RAISED IT AS FAR AS I COULD AND CHOPPED THE FIRST BLACK HORSE HEAD OFF!!!!!!!!!!!!!!!!!!!! THEN, I CHOPPED THE NEXT BLACK HORSE HEAD OFF!!!!!!!!!!!! I REMEMBER DROPPING TO MY KNEES IN ALL OF THAT BLOOD, STARRING INTO THE HORSE EYE WITH PURE HATE!!!!!!!!!!!!!!!!!!!! I REMEMBER SAYING OUT LOUD, I GOT YOU!!!!!!!!!!!!!!! I REMEMBER THE HATE I HAD IN ME!!!!!!!!!!!!!!!!!! I REMEMBER THAT LAST BLACK HORSE COMING AFTER ME!!!!!!I REMEMER NOT HAVING MUCH STRENGHT ANYMORE! I REMEMBER SAYING TO GOD OUT LOUD!!!!!!, GOD THEY CAN'T HAVE ME!!!!!!!!!!!!!!!!!!!!! THEN I RAISED THAT KNIFE

AND CHOPPED THAT LAST HORSE LEGS OFF!!!!!!!!!!!!!!! ALL FOUR!!!!!!!!!! I REMEMBER VERY CLEARLY STILL BEING ON MY KNEES, IN THE DEAD HORSES BLOOD!!!!!!! THEN, THAT LAST HORSE WHOSE LEGS I CHOPPED OFF, WAS STILL TRYING TO GET TO ME!!!!!!!! AND ON MY KNEES, I CHOPPED THAT HORSE'S HEAD OFF!! I REMEMBER HOW TIRED I WAS IN THAT DREAM, BUT I GOT THEM ALL!!!!!!!!!!!!!!!!!!!! I REMEMBER BEING COVERED IN BLOOD!!!!!!!!!!!!!!!!!!!!!!!!!! I woke up. I thought about that dream, and called in sick. Out of the blue, they were erased. No one ever figured out why. Time passed. My daughter and I were in a car wreck. I broke my hand. I didn't know it at the time, but the more I tried to use it, I couldn't. IT HURT! I called 911. They asked was anyone hurt, and I told them no. (Police should go to any and all accidents.) I had no money for the doctors, but I needed help! That next day, my hand was SWOLLEN! I was very well taken care of. At this time, I was praying, asking GOD could I move. I really needed a change of scenery. That apartment had too many BAD AND PAINFUL MEMORIES! I had a dream. In that dream, there was a SOUL guiding me showing me things, different scenes. The first scene, I was in a casket, and that woman was standing over me, just looking at my dead body. She was the only one there. When I noticed the person in the casket was me, I RAN!!! The next scene was a very small wooded shack. It looked like a dog house. Then a group of people popped out of that shack, SINGING LIKE ANGELS!!!!!!!!! IT WAS A BEAUTIFUL SOUND!!!!!!!!! Then, there was SNOW. It covered the shack, and the people that were singing. IT WAS PURE WHITE!!!!! IT COVERED EVERYTHING!! THERE WERE PILES OF IT! Then the snow melted, and a GATE appeared. Behind that gate was A BEAUTIFUL NEIGHBORHOOD!!!!!!! I REMEMBER VERY CLEARLY SAYING TO THE SOUL, I LOVE IT! IT IS BEAUTIFUL!!!!!!!!!!!!!!! When I woke up, I JUST KNEW I WAS DEAD! I began to drag. I talked to GOD and asked him, what's going to HAPPEN to my CHILDREN!!!! I told my daughter NOTHING! She was away at school, doing good, I let it be. When I did talk to her, we discussed moving. I knocked her ideas of moving to a smaller place. That was totally erasing my boys! I had to go to another doctor, to remove that first cast, and have it replaced with cement. (smiling) I drove though the neighborhood site seeing, because I wasn't familiar with the area. I saw HEAVEN FROM A DISTANCE! I MADE A WISH! My daughter came home for Spring break. We went apartment hunting. I showed her HEAVEN! She said lets try. I was so nervous. We went the office and got some information. I didn't want that to be the only place I tried, so we told the lady we would be back. Every where we went, we kept talking about the first place we looked at. I went against my will. I worried about not making enough money. I filled out the paper work and let it go. I PRAYED! Within that waiting period, it was April, and IT SNOWED!!!!!!!!!! IT WAS UNBELIEVABLE!!!!!! SNOW IN UTAH IN APRIL!!!!!!!!!!! School was closed, which made my nerves worst, because I had nothing to do. I finally got that cast off of my hand, so I was cautious about using my right hand. The SNOW MELTED. I WENT TO WORK. I GOT A PHONE CALL. IT WAS THE LADY FROM THOSE APARTMENTS. SHE SAID I WAS APPROVED!!!!!!!!!!!!!!!!!!!!!!!! I CALLED MY DAUGHTER SCREAMING!!!!!!!!!!!!!! WE BOTH SCREAMED!!! It wasn't until I got home, and crawled in the bed, and realized THAT DREAM!!!! I WASN'T DYING!!! ME LYING IN THAT CASKET WAS, ME CUTTING THAT RELATIOSHIP!!!!!! I WAS DEAD TO THAT WOMAN AND THAT WOMAN ONLY!!!! THAT SHACK, AND THOSE ANGELS SINGING!!!!! GOD HEARD MY CRY!!! !!!!!!!!!!!!!!!!!!!!! THE SNOW, IT HAD TO BE THE BEGINNING OF SOMETHING NEW! AND IT WAS!!!! WHEN I PULLED UP TO THAT GATE, THAT WAS THE LAST PART OF THAT MAGIFICENT DREAM!!!! I COULDN"T EAT THAT WHOLE WEEKEND!!!! THAT DREAM CAME WHEN I WAS AT MY LOWEST!! I finally got myself together. All my children were gone, and I had no one to help me move. THAT WAS EXACTLY WHAT I NEEDED!!!!!!! CLEANING AND THROWING STUFF AWAY, BOXING STUFF UP, HELPED MY MIND, BODY AND SOUL IN EVERY WAY!!!!!!!!! AND WENT TO WORK EVERYDAY ON CLOUD NINE!!!!!!!!!!!!! That young buck ran after one year. I KNEW IT! I said he had too much to hide, but he was gone the moment he was hired. One thing I liked about that man was, he called me a SOLDIER! THAT FELT GOOD! I liked that. Somebody had to stand up. There was too much crap going on for that to be a school. I had become the KING OF THE BLACK PANTHERS. NOT QUEEN, KING! That third year finally, a man who put it all back together. School was school again. In the mean time, I'm having the neatess dreams. In one of the dreams, I was in that church I was raised in. There was a dead body lying on a table, sitting up high. I realized where I was, then I noticed the dead body (female) had a big smile on her face. I thought that was weird. The dead woman's sister stood up to view the body. When she moved, I had a deep sense of knowing her. I followed her to view the body. I remember saying, she's just smiling. I woke up and thought about it, and figured someone was getting ready to die. When I went to work, that would erase anything. I forgot my name on a regular basis. It was Parent-Conference night. Of course I'm at baby boy's school acting as his shadow. I ran into an old classmate and we began to talk. She was giving me the update on some old classmates. She bought up the GANG LEADER FROM THE EIGHT GRADE, THE ONE I WHIPPED. She went on to tell me that the girl was buried the day before. I fell into the lockers. My classmate thought I was sad about that girl passing. SO WRONG! I never said a word. THE DEAD GIRL WAS HAPPY! A singer died very unxexpectantly. To me it was unexpected. I was home when I got the news. I SCREAMED NO!!!!! GOD NO!!!!!!!!!!!!!!!! I CAN'T IMAGINE NEVER ATTENDING ONE OF HIS CONCERTS EVER AGAIN!!!!!!! The world was sad. At that time I was living off of BUTTER PECAN ICE CREAM. Every night I went to bed, I had a pint of ice cream in my hand. I HAD A DREAM! I walked into this pool house. Sitting in a lounge chair holding a DAIQUIRI LAYING BACK was the PERSON THAT HAD PASSED! I KNOW THAT SMLIE ANY WHERE! I walked up to him and he told me TO PUT THAT ICE CREAM DOWN AND TO GET ME SOME RED WINE. I said o.k., then a woman came through a door and saw me talking to him, then I POPPED UP! I knew who that was, and I took HEED! I stopped the ice cream, and when I did the headaches went away. I tried to red wine, but I'm not a drinker. Time passed, and I had another DREAM! I was in this Victorian Home. It was old fashion, but beautiful, very well kept. This shadow appeared and began to give me a tour of the house. Every bed room was big. Every bed room had queen/king beds. All beds were dripped in linen. Linen everything. I remember the sheets the most. It was as if the shadow was trying to get it to sink in my head. Then the shadow turned and went into this room, it was small, more like a nice size closet. The shadow was reaching for something on a top shelf. Then, A ROLL OF THREAD FELL AND HIT ME, THEN IT HIT THE FLOOR AND ROLLED! I CHASED THE ROLL OF THREAD AND PICKED IT UP. I WENT BACK OVER TO THE SHADOW, AND SHE HAD GOTTEN AN OLD SEWING MACHINE DOWN OFF THE SHELF AND WAS SHOWING IT TO ME! THEN I NOTICE THERE WERE OTHER SEWING MACHINES, BUT THEY WERE MORE UP TO DATE. I woke up and said to myself, where was I, Whose house was I in. I thought maybe my grandmother's house, but that wasn't it. I KNOW THAT HOUSE. I got my coffee, set on the bed and turned on the news, AND I SAID, I'LL BE ALL OF DAMED!!!!! That's the day I began to tell people, IF YOU DIE BEFORE I DO, I PROMISE

YOU'RE COMING TO SEE ME! I HELD MY CHEST HIGH WHEN I MADE THAT COMMENT! I AIN'T GOING OUT LIKE JOAN OF ARK. Back at work everything ran so SMOOTH! But the people were still after me. One day that new Principal called me in the office and said, Ms. Willaby these people HATE YOU!!!!!!!! I SMILED AND ASKED HIM WHAT WAS NEW! HE LOOKED AT ME AND SAID YOU ARE DOING A GREAT JOB! HE ASKED IF I BELIEVED IN GOD, AND I SAID YES!, BUT I DON'T GO TO CHURCH. HE LAUGHED AND SENT ME ABOUT MY WAY. I had a dream. In that dream, I woke up and got out of bed. I heard something in my kitchen. I went into the living room. I saw this woman cooking and cleaning my kitchen. I remembered the feeling of knowing who that was and knowing that person was DEAD! I called out her name as she washed and dried the dishes. I looked at her from her feet to her head. She had on white girl tennis shoes with white socks. Her dress was green. Her hair was thick and pretty. It was in a flip. That sixties hair do. Her smile was big and white. When I called her name, she turned and smiled. Then I noticed she was FLOATING! I looked at her feet again. She was STANDING ON AIR!!!!! Then she FLEW AWAY! She went through a doorway head first! When I woke up, and remembered that dream, IT SCARED THE LIVING DAY LIGHTS OUT OF ME!!! There was so much going on at that time. I threw myself into my work, and the people kept me loaded with work. All the while, I needed it. My baby brother and that family were once again trying to get me to accept a child that was not my brother's. A couple of years ago, my brother's wife came home PREGNANT, WITH SOME OTHER MAN'S BABY! Before the information got to me, I HAD A DREAM. My brother was standing outside my house CRYING HARD!!!!!!!!!!!!!!!!!!!!!! THEN HE CALLED ME AND TOLD ME THE NEWS!!!!!!!!!!!! I just knew he would leave and take his daughter, but HE WENT BACK!!!! I KNEW I WASN"T GOING TO BE AROUND HIM MUCH LONGER!!! THAT WAS MY MAIN PROBLEM! THAT WOMAN COMING PREGNANT WITH SOME OTHER MAN'S CHILD!!!! THAT'S WHEN WE ENDED UP IN THAT SHACK!!!!!!!!!!!!!!!!!!!!!!!!!!!!!! I had moved to a BEAUTIFUL PLACE! I HAD A JOB THAT I LOVED! There was constant DRAMA at work, but GOD HAD THAT COVERED!!!!!!! I HELD ON TO THAT DREAM OF GOD TELLING ME TO GO TO THOSE SCHOOLS. I HELD ON TO THAT DREAM WITH ALL MY MIGHT!!!!!!!!!!!!!!!!! Now that family was TRULY TRYING TO FORCE ME TO ACCEPT IT, AND K-E-E-P M-Y M-O-U-T-H C-L-O-S-E-D!!!!!!!!!!!!!!!!!! That WEIGHED HEAVILY ON ME!!!!!!!!!!!! NO MORE LIES! NO MORE

SECRETS!!!!!!!!!!!!!!!!!!!!!!!!!!!!!!!!!! That Principal was removed. The school was on its last leg when it came to the Taks Testing. The children didn't pass. The graduation the year before, and the graduation that was coming up was pretty painful. I had been around those kids since they were in the ninth grade. (whoever wrote To Sir, With Love, was a brilliant person.)(Another favorite movie of mine was Valley of the Dolls. It was something about that MUSIC! And the actors were AWESOME! Whoever wrote that movie was brilliant too.) By now everyone who had come after me was GONE! They just vanished. I had a dream. In that dream, I HEARD A VOICE SAYING IT IS 808 TIME. I woke up repeating it. The more I thought about it, the more I couldn't make since of it. A new group of people came in, and it was obvious the school was closing. There was a new female Assistant Principal. And she had an agenda for ME! It all stemmed from past gossip. She threatened me and threatened me. Then the write ups came. I HAD A DREAM! I was in the Principal's Office, and this black cat came after me in FULL FORCE! Out of no where, a huge ANGRY DOG SWALLOWED THE BLACK CAT UP!!!!! But one of her PAWS were still in my face, and it was hard, but I held that PAW from scratching my FACE! When I woke up, I IMMEDIATELY KNEW SHE WAS GONE!!!!!! Within that week, she was gone. I got word that my great aunt was dying of cancer, and she didn't have long. I really liked that woman. When I was little, doing that horrible time, and afterwards, we would go to her house, and there were THE MOST FRIENDLIEST PEOPLE ANYONE COULD EVER MEET! There were people always sitting on the porch. My great-great grandmother would be sitting in the swing that was on the porch. (I remember when she died. I was taken to the FUNERAL! That was at the beginning of the horrible times. I was the only child taken to those frightening things) There was always smoke coming from the grill. There was always a group of people on the side of the house smoking. My great aunt was always in the kitchen cooking. She never sat down. (she was a Sagittarius) Her husband would come home and empty his pocket, giving all the kids some change. That screen door never stopped swinging open. I always had a BALL at her house. It was SO COLOR PURPLE. Well she passed, and I went to the funeral, grave site, and back to her house. ABSOLUTLY NOTHING HAD CHANGED AT ALL!!!!!! IT WAS EXACTLY THE SAME!!!!!! THE PEOPLE ON THE PORCH. It was another house, but the porch was the same. THE GRILL WAS GOING. CHILDREN WERE EVERY WHERE PLAYING! THERE WAS A GROUP OF PEOPLE ON THE SIDE OF THE HOUSE SMOKING. IT WAS EXACTLY LIKE I KNEW IT WOULD BE. THAT WOMAN WAS FULL OF LOVE AND

SHE LEFT HER MARK!!!!! HER CHILDREN WERE IN PAIN, BUT WE HAD FUN ANYWAY!! WE TALKED AND LAUGHED ALL NIGHT!!!! I DID NOT WANT TO LEAVE. BEING THERE BROUGHT BACK BEAUTIFUL MEMORIES!!!! Then the conversation came up about that man that fathered me. I WISHED OUT LOUD THAT HE WAS DEAD!! ONE OF MY AUNTS STARTED FUSSING AT ME, SAYING THAT WAS THAT WOMAN'S FIRST LOVE, AND THAT SHE DIDN'T KNOCK WHAT THAT WOMAN FELT. (She is that woman's baby sister.) THAT CHANGED EVERYTHING IN ME! I TOLD HER I DIDN'T GIVE A DAM!, I WANTED HIM DEAD!!! THE COURAGE TOOK OVER! I STOOD FIRM AND SAID I HAVE SOME QUESTIONS AND I NEED SOME ANSWERS! MY AUNT IMMEDIATELY SAID I DON'T KNOW NOTHING. SHE DEFLATED! MY OTHER AUNT, THE ONE WHO ALWAYS TOOK ME TO JACK-IN-THE-BOX TOOK OFF RUNNING! SHE WAS GONE FOR A MOMENT, THEN CAME BACK WITH THAT WOMAN. THEY PLAYED ME! THEY HAD SOMEONE TO CALL ME AWAY, TO DISTRACT ME, WHILE THEY DISCUSSED WHAT HAD TAKEN PLACE!! THE EVIL WITCHES!! I DIDN'T PUT THAT TOGETHER UNTIL MUCH LATER. ATFTER I WAS DISTRACTED, MY DAUGHTER CALLED ME AND TOLD ME TO COME HOME. SHE WAS HUNGRY. She WAS 22! (laughing) I HAD A WONDERFUL TIME! I TALKED ABOUT THAT NIGHT FOR A WHILE. I KNEW I WASN'T SUPPOSED TO GO, BUT I'M GLAD I DID. I GOT MY ANSWER, WHEN MY AUNT BROKE OUT WALKING FAST! THE ONLY ONE WHO HAD FORGOTTEN WAS <u>ME</u>. I had no dreams for the next battle. GOD LET ME TAKE CARE OF IT ON MY OWN!! AND I DID!!!!!! I STOOD SO FIRM!!!!!! All Principals and the Dean were fired before the year was up! Every adult in that building could not come to TERMS of WHY Ms. WILLABY WAS NOT FIRED!!! THE TALK WAS THICK!!!!!! AND PEOPLE STOOPED TO THE LOWEST TO TRY AND BREAK MY SPIRIT!!!!!! (Aristotle wrote about it BEST. People in the work place.) (I read somewhere else, that a man's greatest WEAKNESS was, DOUBT, FEAR, NOT BELEIVING, AND NO FAITH! The senior class had a picnic and I attended. I was in HEAVEN! The students and Teachers covered that park. I was the guard. I sat at the entrance. I knew who to let in and who to send away. Something told me to look around and when I did I saw seven students coming after me with water balloons! I BROKE OUT RUNNING! I RAN FOR MY LIFE! One student was on me, but I was running down a hill then I hit a curb and left him by a mile. That was the picnic of the century. The students I BURNT were athletes. Football and track, male and female. (I had just turned "40" the MOST BEAUTIFUL AGE) When I went back to work, I bragged about what I had done. I had FUN! Then those same students pulled me to the side and told me they had smoked weed that day. I LET OUT A LAUGH SO LOUD GOD PUT HIS HANDS OVER HIS EARS! THAT WAS FUNNY! I didn't believe them. I wanted to BELIEVE I BURNT them for REAL! One day as I was walking out of the school building, a little old man said, Willaby YOU HAVE DONE SOMETHING RIGHT! I DON'T KNOW WHAT IT IS, OR HOW TO EXPLAIN IT, BUT, ALL I KNOW IS THAT YOU HAVE DONE SOMETHING RIGHT! I COULDN'T SAY ANYTHING. I talked about GOD to EVRYBODY! But the people were all LIES! I just walked to my car, got in, and sat there. The next month the test scores came in and the school was closed. NOTHING HAS CHANGED ABOUT THE SCHOOLS IN THE HOOD. NOTHING. That summer passed, the District mailed out letters that August, and then it hit me. 808 TIME. IT WAS OVER. MY WORK WAS DONE. I SLAYED THE DRAGONS!!!

PHASE #5

NOTES FROM MY JOURNALS
AND MORE DREAMS

When I received that letter from the District I lost all DIGNITY. But as quick as it left it came right back. I said to myself, go the to another school. I got the internet, and applied to other schools. I got an interview. I went to that interview. And the principal said she would call. I had a dream. In that dream, there was a HUGE CROWD OF PEOPLE. THEY WERE RUNNING OVER EACH OTHER, TRAMPLING EACH OTHER, FIGHTING, AND BEATING EACH OTHER UP!!!!!!! IT WAS A HORRIBLE SCE NE!!!!!!!!!!!!!!!!!!!!!!!!!!! I woke up, and thought about it. I turned it on the news, and there it was. THE BIGGEST LAY OFF!! THAT DISTRICT GOT RID OF EVERYBODY!!!!!!!!!!!!!!!!!!!!!!!!! So I knew that was out of the question. That was GOD'S WAY OF TELLING ME NO!!!!!!!!! THAT'S MY FATHER!!!!!!!!!!!!!!!!!!!!!!!! I began to sink. What was I going to do, I had some money saved, but I wanted a house. That dream went out the window. I needed to stay exactly where I was. I walked around LOST. I filed for unemployment, and it was approved, but I didn't get it. I used the money in my savings. I ached. The more I tried to hold on to my strength, the more I lost it. I tried to act normal, but I ached to bad. Then the tears came. Thinking of having to start over from scratch. I gave in to the PAIN!!! I HAD TO! I WANTED IT OUT OF MY SYSTEM, SO I COULD BE STRONG AGAIN, AND DO

WHAT I HAD TO DO!!!! I CRIED ON MY DAUGHTER'S SHOULDER, I HAD NO CHOICE! She told me I had become one of those people who are DEFINED BY THEIR JOB TITLE. I SAID DAM! WHERE DID YOU GET THAT FROM? I'M THE ONE WHO READ BOOKS AROUND THIS HOUSE! THAT STRAIGHTENED MY BACK BONE UP!!!!!!!!!! I let it sink in. Then I thought to myself, that I needed a BREAK! I was no good for an interview. That thought took a load off. So I began to rest. But I couldn't. I WAS SCARED AS HELL! When I went to bed, I had no choice but to imagine I was LYING IN GOD'S ARMS, AND HE WAS HOLDIN ME TIGHT!!!!!!!!!!!!!!! I WENT THERE! AND IT COMFORTED ME, BUT MY MIND AND BODY ACHED!!!!!!!!!!!!!!!!! THE DREAMS KICKED IN! ONE AFTER THE OTHER!!

The first dream, I was inside a High School where I had that interview. I remember waiting in a line for a school shirt. The school shirts were green. I had a pant suit on. I had folders in my arm and my purse on my shoulder. When I got to the front of the line, I noticed it was two of my co-workers I couldn't stand. Then one of them asked me my size. I said small. She dug through the box of shirts, and came up with a white blouse with belt loops and a thick black belt. The shirt appeared in mid-air. It was just hanging there. I remember very vividly looking up saying, I LOVE IT!!!!!!!!!!!!!!!!!!!!!! I remember very clearly when I took it. I got such a SAD FEELING! Like a BROKEN HEART! I took the blouse and walked off. I remember as I walked away, thinking they had given me the wrong shirt. I was thinking it's not green like all of the others. I remember walking down a hallway and hearing people talking and laughing. Then I heard water splashing. I thought there was a swimming party going on. I walked into the gym and there was a pool with <u>DOLPHINS</u> in it. They looked like birds. They were BEAUTIFUL, the way they swam back and forth and performed for everyone. Then there was a baby <u>SEAL</u>. I took a double look, because his face was different from the DOLPHINS. As I stood there in amazement, my SOUL LEFT ME AND WENT OVER TO THE BABY SEAL. <u>HE WAS LOST</u>. I remember very clearly feeding him some baby fish. At first I was scared. But once I put my hand in his mouth, and realized he didn't have any teeth, I kept feeding him until he left. HE WAS SO <u>PRECIOUS</u>!!!!!!!!!!! I remember my body was one again. I remember walking around the gym. There were people sitting at tables drinking and laughing. I remember going over to a table to speak to a couple of guy friends and they burst out laughing at me. I remember feeling BAD and walking away. The more I walked, the more upset I became. I remember going back to that line where they were passing out school shirts. I THREW THAT WHITE BLOUSE AND BLACK BELT BACK AT THOSE FEMALES WHO GAVE IT TO ME, AND DEMANDED A GREEN SCHOOL SHIRT! I remember very clearly that same female went through that same box of shirts, balled up a shirt and THREW IT IN MY FACE! I STILL HAD THAT UPSET FEELING! Once again the shirt was A WHITE BLOUSE WITH BIG BELT LOOPS, AND THIS TIME THE BELT WAS IN PLASTIC, AS IF IT WERE BRAND NEW. The other thing that was different was, this time when she through that blouse at me, the background was <u>YELLOW</u>. I held the blouse up, because I thought it went from <u>WHITE</u> to <u>YELLOW</u>. But the blouse was still <u>WHITE</u>. It was the background that was <u>YELLOW</u>. I REMEMBER HEARING A VOICE ASKING ME, IF I GOT IT, AND LOOKED UP AND RESPONDED, YES I GOT IT!! I REMEMBER I ALMOST FORGOT THE BELT THAT CAME WITH THE SHIRT. THE VOICE ASKED AGAIN IF I GOT IT, I LOOKED UP AND SAID YES I GOT IT!! When I woke up I had the STRANGEST feeling. I had such a let go feeling. Then I had a FEELING OF BEING COVERED AND TAKEN CARE OF!!!!!!!!!!!!!!!! I QUICKLY REALIZED I WAS BEING VERY STUBBORN AND VERY HARD HEADED WITH GOD ALMIGHY!! I FELL TO MY KNEES IN FEAR!! I was very hard headed and insisting I go back to work for the School District, mainly for the pay. But GOD was letting my DUMB BEHIND KNOW THAT HE HAD ME COVERED, AND HE HAD SOMETHING ELSE IN STORE FOR ME!!!!!!!!!!!!!!!!!! !!!!!!!!!!!!!!!!!!!!!!!!!!!!!! HE was telling me to GIVE ALL OF MY WORRIES TO HIM AND LET IT GO!!!!!!!!!!!!!! But I can't stop from SMILING when I think about GOD NOT CARING ABOUT MY HARD HEADEDNESS! THAT IS SO NEAT!!!!!!   MY FATHER!! The depression kicked in again. I went to sleep in GOD'S ARMS AGAIN. I HAD DREAM! I was sitting in a bar having a drink, and all of a sudden I DID THE NUMBER TWO! RIGHT THERE ON THAT STOOL! I REMEMBER FEELING EMBARRASSED! I GRABBED A NAPKIN OFF THE BAR AND PICKED IT UP! I REMEMBER PUTTING IT TO MY NOSE AND SMELLING IT. IT WAS GOLD AND BROWN AND IT DID NOT HAVE A SMELL. I THREW IT AWAY AND HOPED NO ONE SAW ME! There were people everywhere. I remember picking up my drink, and I DID THE NUMBER TWO AGAIN! THIS TIME IT WAS TWO LITTLE ONES. I GRABBED ANOTHER NAPKIN, PICKED THEM UP, AND THREW THEM AWAY!!! I LEFT THE BAR!!!!!!!!!!!!!!!!!!!!!!!! When I woke up, I thought to myself, WHAT IN THE HELL JUST HAPPEN!!!! I told my daughter about it and she said, GOD IS TELLING YOU TO LET IT GO! LET GO OF THE STRESS! <u>GOD IS SO REAL</u>!!!!!!!!!!!!!!!

I COULDN'T SHAKE THE FEAR. THAT FEAR WOULD NOT LEAVE ME! Each of those DREAMS GAVE ME STRENGHT!!!! But IT WAS MY MIND!!!!!!! I began to DRAG AGAIN! I HAD A DREAM. There was this old Christmas tree. It was leaning and the branches were bent. THE TREE WAS TIRED AND WORN OUT, AND I FELT THAT PAIN DEEPLY!!!!!!! AS I GOT CLOSER TO THAT TREE, I SAID, THAT'S EXACTLY HOW I FEEL! THE PAIN! Then the scene CHANGED! OUT OF NO WHERE A TALL BEAUTIFUL WHITE CHRISTMAS TREE APPEARED. IT WAS SO TALL AND PRETTY, IT WAS GOING THROUGH THE CEILING!!!!!!!!!!! WHEN I LOOKED UP AT IT I HAD TO BEND BACK!!!! My children were there. The boys were playing on the floor. My daughter and I were standing next to a fire place. I remember she went near the tree and I started fussing. I KEPT SAYING HOW BEAUTIFUL IT WAS!!!!!!!!!!!!!!!!!! I stop looking at it!!!!!!!!!! Then I woke up. I thought about that dream and figured I was transforming in some way. Going from that old bent over tree, to that TALL BEAUTIFULLY DECORATED CHRISTMAS TREE!!!!!!! I pushed on. But the FEAR CAME BACK AGAIN! I HAD A DREAM. In that dream, a shadow took me by the hand and led me to this place. It was like watching a big screen T.V. but the picture was REAL. As I stood there with the shadow, looking ahead, there appeared THE MOST PRESIOUS BABY GIRL!!!!!!!! SEEING HER MADE ME MELT!!!!!! SHE WAS ABOUT TWO OR THREE MONTHS!!!! SHE WAS LYING ON HER STOMACH, AND THEN SHE HELD HER HEAD UP!!!!!! IT WAS WOBBLING AT FIRST, I IMMEDIATELY REACHED OUT TO HOLD HER HEAD UP, BUT THE SHADOW GRABBED MY ARM AND TOLD ME NO!! I OBEYED. THEN SHE HELD HER HEAD UP!!!! The shadow and I stood there looking at the baby girl, with the thick black curly hair, HOLDING HER HEAD UP ALL BY HER SELF!!!!! The shadow and I stood there for a while. Then I woke up. I came to the conclusion, that, that was me, and I was going to be o.k. The PAIN kept coming back. I began to identify it with that little girl who was left in that OLD HOUSE alone, and was SO TERRIFIED OUT OF HER MIND SHE HAD NO CHOICE BUT TO LEAVE!!!!!!! My family had left me alone in that place, and I was SO TIRED AND SORE, I HAD BEEN UP ALL NIGHT!, NO MORE!!! IT WAS THAT SAME FEAR THAT KEPT COMING BACK.

For years, at bedtime, I imagined myself taking GOD'S HEART OUT OF HIS CHEST, CRAWING IN THAT SPACE AND GOING TO SLEEP. NO ONE COULD BOTHER ME THERE. BUT NOW I NEEDED ARMS!!!! I NEEDED SOMEONE TO HOLD ME. I NEEDED SOMEONE TO HUGGED ME AND NOT LET GO! I BEGGED GOD TO PUT HIS ARMS AROUND ME!!! I HAD A DREAM!!! There was this very important person and he was surrounded by security and reporters. He had on a suit with an overcoat. He and the people surrounding him walked through some double doors. I walked up to him, trying to get his attention. I had on a pant suit, with a white collar shirt. The collar on that shirt was high. I had on an overcoat also. The next thing I knew, THAT PERSON GRABBED ME AND WE LAID DOWN TOGETHER! EVERYTHING IN ME MELTED! I DIDN'T WANT IT TO END!, I WANTED TO COMPLEMENT THAT FEELING SO BAD, BUT I KNEW THAT WOULD SPOIL THE MOMENT. I FELT TOO GOOD. IT WAS SUCH A SOOTHING FEELING!!! I HAD TO EXPRESS MY FEELINGS, ALONG WITH A SADDNESS IN MY STOMACH. I remember turning my head and saying, THIS FEELS SO GOOD!!!!!! IT FELT GOOD TO GET THAT OFF MY CHEST, BUT THEN, HE DISAPPEARED INTO THIN AIR!!!!!!!!! Out of no where, this HUGE WINDOW APPEARED. I COULD SEE INTO SPACE. I WAS HURT. I WAS MAD AT MYSELF. I WAS LOOKING FOR HIM!!! HOPPING I WOULD SEE HIM! HE HAD VANISHED THROUGH THAT WINDOW. I remember there were highways everywhere. The cars on the highways were bubbles with people stuffed in them. The cars were going back and fourth. It was exactly like the JETSON'S. I remember what look like air planes flying, but they were floating. I remember pressing myself against the window, hopping HE would come back. Then I woke up.

THANK YOU!!!!!!!!!!!!!!!!!!!!!!!!!!!!!!!!!!!

After that dream, I DROPPED THE THOUGHT OF SEX. It had been on my heart to call my ex. He always called me. He never stopped. The kids thought it was so funny. He would call all day everyday. My phone would only have his number in it. 50 calls. He would come by very unexpectanly, knock on the door, then leave a bottle of wine at the door step. I asked GOD to take him out of my HEART! I knew now, that, he was NOT the answer. My MIND WAS MADE UP. I NEVER WANTED TO SEE HIM AGAIN! I had a dream. In that dream, my ex and I were in his truck. We were arguing. The both of us had what look like walkie talkies in our hand. I remember my ex pulling into a parking lot. I remember him backing into a parking space and I jumped out the truck the moment he parked. I remember walking away from him as he tried to talk to me. I remember looking at the walkie talkie in my hand. I remember putting it in my pocket, walking away, with no intentions of looking back. I remember waking up saying, THANK YOU GOD!!!!!!!

At this time it was getting close to the Presidential Election. Just one more reason to loose my mind. It was NERVE WRECKIING!!!!!!!!!! My daughter had come home from school. She made it clear she wasn't going back. She decided to finish her 30 hours on line. Having one car and having to take her back and forth to work kept me busy. Baby boy was away at Job Corp. When I put him out a couple of years ago, he called me at work wanting to come home and I said no. My HEART HAD HARDEN. He called again and I went and got him. I made it clear there would be NO sitting around my house while I'm at work. He made that decision to leave and do something right. He chose Kansas and stayed for two years. Within those two years, He received certificates in brick laying and cementing. Job Corp. got my son and his new friends a nice job traveling back and forth working on different contracts. I knew if he were home, he would make me forget what was troubling me. All of us fought. The attitudes and tension was THICK. But once again they said it was me! I blew it off as usual, we needed to be together for the Presidential Election. I had a dream. I remember in that dream, I was standing back watching these business people walk back and forth. There were elevators and people were going and coming. A black female appeared. She had on a black sleeveless dress. It was nice. People were walking passed her ignoring her. That made her HOT! She said out loud that SHE WAS HERE TO STAY! Then there was a roll of money sitting on a marble table. It was a roll of five dollar bills. It was a thick roll, but it was clear they were all fives'. Everybody was walking past that roll of MONEY! That female walked over to the table, picked the roll of fives' up, took one and put that roll back on the table. I TOUGHT SHE WAS CRAZY FOR DOING THAT! Then I woke up. I thought about it. I thought the woman was me, but GOD KNEW I WAS GOING KEEP THAT ROLL! (LOL) No joke. I thought a new job was coming my way and GOD was showing me my attitude. I let that dream go. I couldn't make since of it. I had another dream. There were important people in my house. I remember my house wasn't in order, not for those important people. They sat back while I cleaned and rearranged the furniture. The important people asked me for some water. I brought them water on a serving tray. I remember people out of no where started taking the water I had for the important people. I remember being on my knees scrubbing the floor. I remember someone giving me a beige evening gown. I laid it across my arm, while I scrubbed the floor. The important people asked me for water again. I began to get frustrated, because someone kept drinking the water I attempted to take them. The important people came through some double doors still hounding me for water. That group of people consist of, two adult females and two little girls. I looked closer and another female had on the dress, I had across my arm. They requested water again, this time I was PISSED! I stormed into that fancy kitchen, got a silver tray and three huge classes of water. There was another very important person, a male, in another room next to the kitchen. He called me over and asked me, IN A SARCASTIC WAY!, YOU CAN'T GET WATER FOR THE PEOPLE LIKE YOU SUPPOSED TO! I remember walking away with my head down. I remember grabbing the tray with the glasses of water, and out of nowhere, this guy who was supposed to helping me, grabbed one of the glasses of water. I WOKE UP PISSED OFF! I never put that together. The PEOPLE IN THE DREAM IS WHAT FREAKED ME OUT. The Election came. I made plans to bar-b-que. That way my nerves wouldn't be so bad. Being in the kitchen calms me. Preparing food, cooking and cleaning. I WAS NERVOUS! It happened to a white man, it CAN HAPPEN TO A BLACK MAN. BARACK OBAMA WON!!!!!!!!!!!! My children believed it, but I didn't. Every generation should have something SO IMPORTANT HAPPEN IN THEIR LIFE TIME. After the President was Elected, I imagined everybody who had died from the beginning of time were at a PARTY! A CELEBRATION! The DJ was playing Boys to Men's NEW JACK SWING! I ACTUALLY saw them DANCING AND PARTYING! THEY WERE DRESSED AND THEY DANCED THEIR HEARTS OUT! The people who were alive MISSED IT! The holidays kicked in. My cousin Penny called me a couple of times. When I saw her number in my phone, I said something is wrong. My nerves were on edge again. I was coming alone good. I had a dream. In that dream, my daughter was driving a too little car. Her little body was stuffed in that car but she was able to drive it. At first she was going in circles, she was SO HAPPY, then, she burnt rubber. She drove away so fast it was as if I didn't see her. I have never put that one together. Then my son came in my room and gave me a MESSAGE. He had spoken with one of cousin Penny's daughters. That man was dying. He had cancer. I SNAPPED! THAT WAS THE LAST PIECE OF INFORMATION I NEEDED! NOT AT THAT TIME! I WENT OUTSIDE AND TOLD GOD, YOU AIN'T TOLD ME NOTHING! WHAT IS THIS! I WAS TOO SCARED TO HAVE ANY COMMON SENSE! I HAD CUT THEM FOR REAL! MY BROTHERS WOULD CALL BUT I NEVER ANSWERED. THAT WOMAN WOULD

CALL, I SHOW NOUGH WOULDN'T ANSWER! I walked around my own house nervous as HELL! I didn't want to see any of them, and the thought of them thinking I should know about it PISSED ME TOTALLY. My brothers were right there, going back and forth. THAT MADE ME WANT TO THROW UP! My family have always had a way of making me change my mind when I was around them. THAT HOLD THEY HAVE ON ME. EVERY TIME I WOULD TELL MYSELF, I'M NOT GOING TO LET THEM GET TO ME THIS TIME,,,, LOW AND BEHOLD, THEY DID. IT NEVER FAILED! I RAN FROM THAT! IT DROVE MY NERVES TO THE ROOF!, AND I TOOK IT OUT ON BABY BOY FOR TELLING ME, AND I TOOK IT OUT ON MY DAUGHTER FOR NOT STOPPING HIM FROM TELLING ME! They started calling me MAD WOMAN! THEY HATED ME AND I HATED THEM! The bed sweats slowly came. The sleepless nights slowly kicked in. I was literally SCARED! I TOLD GOD I WAS GOING TO KILL WHO EVER KNOCKED ON MY DOOR! I WASN'T GOING TO BED HATING MYSELF, BECAUSE ONCE AGAIN THEY GOT AWAY WITH BULLSHIT! No one came. I was serious about killing them. I thought of so many ways. BEATING THEM DOWN UNTIL THE SKULL AND ALL BONES WERE CRUSHED! That way I would have been tired, crawled in the tub, and off to bed and would have slept like a baby. It's December, my Birthday came. I prayed to GOD PLEASE DON'T LET THAT MAN DIE ON MY BIRTHDAY! I went about my day and had a wonderful time! 12 midnight came and I was relieved. The next day I woke up to text message after text message. He died. My baby brother lost his mind. He was talking to me STUPID!, through the text. He text me five times. I ignored that woman. I ignored that older brother. BUT I GOT BABY BROTHER! Only because he has become one of them and now it was FULL FORCE! THAT WOMAN'S CRAP HAVE RUBBED OFF ON HER OTHER CHILDREN AND THEY DON'T EVEN REALIZE IT! THAT LAST CHILD REALLY THINKS HER FATHER IS DEAD. HE PROBLY IS, BUT IT'S NOT <u>THAT MAN</u>. THAT WOMAN CAN PLANT SOME BAD SEEDS IN A PERSONS' HEAD. <u>I THANK MY HEAVENLY FATHER FOR BLOCKING MY BRAIN!!!!!!!!!!!! AND FOR MAKING ME TO BE DIFFERENT!!!</u> I SHUT ALL OF THEM OUT!!!!! I CHANGED ALL NUMERS! I TOLD BABY BOY IF HE GIVE ME ANOTHER MESSAGE I WAS GOING TO CHOKE THE __ __ __ __ OUT OF HIM! I WENT CRAZY!!!!!! I LOST MY MIND. I didn't know what was going to happen. I knew I was going to SNAP. I made up my mind, if they would have approached me, to leave one somebody alive, so when I ended up in court, I WOULD HAVE MADE SURE THEY WERE FORCED TO TELL THE TRUTH! The day before his funeral I had a dream. Baby boy and I were leaving the house. Baby boy walked in front of me. There was a white van parked in front. All of a sudden, I changed my mind. I told baby boy I'm not going. Baby boy went on. I turned around and there were two people COVERED IN GRASS AFTER ME! I ran in the house slammed the door and put a chair in front of it to lock them out! I ran around the house, I was trying to hide. I wasn't familiar with the house. I ran into a closet and noticed a lot of thick stripe colorful clothes. Then that part of the dream repeated itself. Then I got a strange feeling of being alright. I woke up and had no problem putting that one together. That was that man. He had been asking for me, then he actually wanted me at that funeral. SAD. The thick stripe clothes were the exact clothes hanging in my daughter's closet. It was Christmas, we had gone to Old NAVY. After it was all over, NOTHING SURFACED! NOT ONE MEMORY. I was just nervous, hoping my family would LEAVE ME ALONE! STAY AWAY FROM ME! That nervousness sent me straight to the doctor for hormone pills, when I got there the nurse asked what was wrong and I STARTED CRYING OUT LOUD, I COULDN"T BREATH, I WAS HAVING AN ATTACK! I couldn't sleep AT ALL! Every night my bed was dripping wet! I ran to the library to dig up information about what I was going through, IT WAS MENAPAUSE! The doctor gave me a three month prescription but I only used two. I GOT RELIEF AFTER TAKING THE FIRST PILL. THAT NIGHT I SLEPT LIKE A BABY. I FELT NORMAL AGAIN! I TRIED THE HEALTHY WAY AT FIRST, YOU NEED A PILL! I EAT FRUIT AND VEGETABLES EVERYDAY! I'm curious about the other family members death and how it would affect me. O, well, my son and I were arguing everyday. I began to ask GOD to come and get him! I was serious. I told GOD, I know I would loose my mind, but right now, YOU need to come and get him. I had a dream. In that dream, I was in my house with my oldest son. Someone knocked on the door. I answered. It was that important lady again. She came to pick me and my son up. I remember rushing, moving around the house really fast, trying to find my son something nice to wear. Everything I picked out for him was old and too little. I went from room to room and each time coming up with old too little clothes. The important lady left. I was SO PISSED! I ran to the window remembering I had a car, but it was FLAT LIKE A PANCAKE! THE WHOLE CAR! I ran outside very upset! Then an important man appeared, waved his hand across my car and it was new again. Don't ask me why, but after that dream my baby boy CHANGED! I was really praying to GOD TO COME AND GET HIM. That boy started walking around with an ODOR. It never left. I told my daughter what I had being praying for and she laughed. Now all of a sudden HE CHANGED! That boy got a job and was at work every morning at six am. He was talking different. EVERYTHING ABOUT HIM CHANGED! I LET HIM KNOW HE WILL NEVER REALIZE HOW GOOD HE GOT IT! NEVER! One night we were talking. Baby boy said I wonder if my dad ever think about me. I told him I would make a phone call. I went to bed with that on my mind and my heart. I had a dream. I was in front of my house and there was someone guiding me showing me things, writings on the front wall of the house. The writings kept going and going on the brick wall. The dream kept repeating itself as if to make me understand something. I woke up. I came to conclusion to leave well enough alone. Baby boy never brought it up again and neither did I. I began to ask GOD could I work from home. I was far from being ready to go back to the work force. I had a dream. In that dream, I was in my living room, then I walked into my bedroom. Like MAGIC a desk and filing cabinet appeared. Then the furniture change, as if it was moved, then it went back to the way it was at first. I hopped out of bed, went to target and bought a desk and filing cabinet. My daughter put the desk and cabinet together. I put it in my room. I placed it one way, then, I change it. Then I put it back to the way I had it. I have always known that I was GOD'S PUPPET, but HE JUST KEEP AMAZING ME! HE REALLY CUT FOR ME!!!!!!!!!!!!!!!!!!!!!!!!!!!! I had a dream. I was surrounded by three Doberman pinschers. The one in the middle came towards me. I kicked that dog with everything I had. I kicked him so hard he flew up against a car and died. I remember feeling sorry for the dog after I realized what I had done. Standing in the background was an old lady with a purse on her arm. I recognized her right off it was Mrs. Crabtree. She was just standing back SMILING. I remember thinking to myself saying, SHE IS A STRONG LADY! I never put that dream together. I had another dream. In that dream, there was a familiar person that I knew. She was fat and putting on too little clothes getting ready for a funeral. (The funeral was a feeling) I was standing back viewing what was going on. Then I turned my head and there was an old expensive car. It was high lighted. The next day I thought about that dream, and right when I was about to give up on it my daughter asked me about someone we haven't seen in years. He loved old expensive cars. I take it, he's gone. I change the subject and kept going. I was going through too much. Enough was enough.

I finally made up my mind. It was time for me to SEEK HELP! I told my daughter my decision and she agreed. I talked to GOD and I PRAYED to GOD. I asked him to please help me find the right psychologist and help me PAY FOR IT! I wanted a GOOD ONE. I WANTED SOMEONE FROM CAMBRIDGE. (SOMEONE WHO SPECIALIZED IN GOD AND DREAMS.) I talk to GOD and PRAYED on that decision for a week.

I HAD A D-R-E-A-M!!!!!!!!!!!!!!!!!!!!!!!!!!!!!!!!!!!!!

I went to sleep and there I was in my house. There was a shadow taking me around the house as if it were giving me a tour. We went to the bath room. There was an oval shape tub (exactly like mine) with water in it. I put my hand in the water, it felt good. (This time I wasn't stopped)

The MOMENT WE WALKED OUT OF THE BATH ROOM, THERE WAS A S-T-A-I-R-C-A-S-E. It was in MY FACE!. THE STAIRS WERE BLACK IRON. THE RAILS WERE BLACK IRON WITH BEAUTIFUL DESIGNS ON THE RAILS AND BARS!!!!!!!!!!!!!!!!!!

I REMEMBER SAYIING OUT LOUD, THAT'S NICE!!!!!!!!!!!!!!!!!

THE STAIRS faded in the background but they were still visible. Then I saw a lady looking at the SUN justa TALKING. She began to walk around in circles. I said out loud that she was going to loose her mind early. That was SO CLEAR. Then the shadow took me through the kitchen. I remember saying, girl this is nice, but at the same time I was thinking the kitchen was too little. Then she opened the front door. THERE WAS THE SUN!!!!! IT WAS SO BRIGHT I HAD TO SQINCH!! AND THE VOICE SAID GO TO THE L-I-B-R-A-R-Y!!

I started thinking to myself, saying I've been going to the library.

THE VOICE SAID IT AGAIN!!!!! GO TO THE L-I-B-R-A-R-Y!!!!!

Then a GLASS BOOKCASE APPEARED WITH ABOUT FOUR TO FIVE BOOKS. The bookcase was far away, across a field. It looked like a library. I LOOKED UP AT THE SUN AND SAID O.K.

When I woke up, I THOUGHT ABOUT THAT DREAM!!!!!!!

I actually went and took my but to the library. I sat there and said O.K GOD, NOTHINGS HAPPENING. (I'm so goofy) I checked out some books. I was reading my but off at the time. I FOUND SOME DEFINITIONS. The tub is where I meditate, talk to GOD and READ THE BOOK OF PSALMS. THE STAIRCASE IS MY BRAIN WHERE EVERYTHING IS STORED. (GOD IS AWESOME!!!!!!!!) My kitchen….I love it but it is too small. AND THEN THERE WAS GOD HIMSELF!!!!!!!!!!!!!!!!!!!!!!!!!!!!!!!! THE MAN OF ALL CREATION!

I ran to the store, bought me some journals and I've been writing ever since. THANK YOU, THANK YOU, THANK YOU!!!!!!!!!!!!!!!!!!!!!

I went to San Fransico to visit my SPECIAL ONE! He is doing GREAT!

He was moved around a lot at the beginning, but NOW he is settled in a beautiful home with beautiful people. People who have CONTROL. At the beginning he moved to Houston. Then they shipped him back closer to us. Both places were horrible, but that second one was funny. He got the chance to graduate from High School. I asked someone to take me, which was a mistake. We were late, I forgot my camera, the person I was with forgot their camera, all because they had changed their mind about taking me, but we made it. I cried on the way home. We couldn't take him out to celebrate because it was a very small country town with one red light. My baby walked away from the car with his hand hanging low. GOD THAT WENT THROUGH ME! The second time I went down there to see him, baby boy was with me. My autistic son came running out of that building dressed exactly like HUCKABRY FINN!!!! That boy had on too little jeans, a too little wrinkle shirt, with a STRAW HAT! I LAUGHED FOR A WHILE. I told him, he would have attacked me if I let him leave the house looking like that! We had fun. I took him out to eat. We went shopping and he enjoyed it. Baby boy broke down. I told him to get it together. His brother was going to be fine. After that, he was moved much closer to us, which was only a forty-five minute drive. That was really nice, but through his spells, the people couldn't and wouldn't handle him. When he moved there it was time for his birthday. I had a dream. In that dream, I walked in a house and there were two hands placing a cake on a table. I remembered the cake well. I went out to pick up the cake I ordered and pick up his presents. When I got there, that cake in that woman's hands was the cake scene from my dream. I took a seat. We sang and had some cake, then, I took him out to eat. That's my baby. His stay there didn't last long. I got a phone call. They had already made plans to ship my child to San Fransico. I had no control. I don't have guardianship. The tears came rolling. I knew it would be a very long time before I saw him again. After a year of living in the group home there, those people were ready to send my son to the state school. I asked GOD WHY WANT YOU ANSWER MY PRAYERS WHEN IT COMES TO MY SPECIAL ONE. Before I knew it, a lady that worked for the company where he was living asked the people to give her a chance, and they did. My son is living HIGH ON THE HOGG! That woman has a beautiful four bed room home in a nice neighborhood. She fix grits and eggs for breakfast, chicken and dumplings for lunch and roast and potatoes for dinner. He is very well kept and taken care of. GOD IS COLD! My son has a life, a normal life. They dress up and go everywhere together. That woman actually took my baby on a CRUISE TO MEXICO!!! That is all GOD!

I get upset when I TALK TO GOD AND ASK HIM TO MAKE MY SON NORMAL. It's NOT IN THE PLAN. Right now my son is living better than his mother, brother and sister!!!!!!!!!!

When I got back from San Antonio, I was SO HAPPY. I was So THANKFUL! I had a dream. I was in a hand in the air and it was FUN! The hand began to lower me down and I remember saying HE WANT LET ME FALL. The hand was clear like wind. I jumped down HAPPY LIKE A LITTLE KID! Then there was a line of people who were my friends. I smiled and shook their hands as if I was Miss America. Then I went in my house and some people knocked on the door. I opened the door and let them in. It was the lady who takes care of my son. My son was with her, but he was a baby. There was another lady with a baby. They were in my house and I was supposed to be entertaining them but I left them alone in my house. That was a complicated dream but the things that took place the following week left my mouth wide open. I had another dream. An elderly white woman came up to me and asked what was I wearing (perfume). I said Eternity Moment. The both of us smiled and I woke up. I went to the store that day. I entered the store and went straight to the back and walked right into my dream. There was an elderly white woman discussing perfume, and she began to talk to me. She was so friendly. We talked and laugh and went on.

My car began to act up on me. I have trusted my old mechanic for ten years. He has been trying to get me to let one of his friends look at my car, but that suggestion always rubbed me the wrong way. Well my car wouldn't start one morning, and I've seen a neighbor working on people cars all the time, not to mention baby boy had made friends with the guy the moment we moved here. That man took his time with my car and explained everything to me. What started as a simple problem years ago had spread all over to the other parts of the car, one thing led to another. He replaced quite a few pieces, simple pieces. I paid him and thanked him. But my car started acting up again. Bottom line it needed a Cadillac converter. My old friend didn't know I knew that. I had plans to call him about it, then, I had a dream. In that dream I was being attacked! I was standing back looking at the incident take place. It was WHITE where I was standing. A tall white man in dirty jeans and shirt pushed me down, grabbed my legs and was doing things to me. I was KICKING AND FIGHTING!! That man had my feet up in the air, but I was still KICKING AND FIGHTING. I WAS FIGHTING SO HARD IT WOKE MYSELF UP STILL FIGHTING! I WENT RIGHT BACK INTO THAT SLEEP,

AND MY FRIEND SLUNG ME TO THAT MAN AND HE WAS STILL ATTACKING ME! Then I noticed from where I was standing the man head and his hair. He had a very long hair. But he had a HUGE BALD SPOT IN THE MIDDLE OF HIS HEAD. That was so clear. Doing the attack the both of us was fully dressed. Then I remembered my cell phone was in my pocket. I pulled it out and started to dial a number. I looked up and over in the corner there was my brother standing there in his police uniform. So I figured I was calling the cops. I woke up. I hated that dream. It had me PISSED OFF! I went to see my old friend, who I thought I could depend on. I told him I had finally caught on to his crap. He was still full of lies. He insisted that we go see his friend. I was so uneasy, but I went anyway. I walked right into that dream. We pulled up at this old station and this white man with a very long ponytail came over to us. They both stood there and lied. My new friend had already explained everything to me about the lies my friend had been telling me. Everything. The SUN WAS SHINING BRIGHT! That white man was looking under the hood of my car then he said I'll be back. When he walked away there was that BIG BALD SPOT IN THE BACK OF HIS HEAD. IT HIT ME! I SLAMMED MY HOOD AND LEFT THAT PLACE! I WAS HURT! I TRUSTED THAT MAN AND THAT'S WHAT I GET IN RETURN. I was floored. Then I put it together. I didn't have a reason to call the police so what did my brother stand for in that dream. My brother's name is Tom. My new mechanic name is Tom.

After that incident I shut down. I didn't think. I didn't write in my journals for weeks. I did nothing. I was hurt. I stayed in bed.

Now it was April, Spring. April 10th I had a dream. In that dream there was an electric pencil sharpener. I was looking at the pencil sharpener, but I was confused, I didn't understand. The dream repeated itself. It was like a slide show. The pencil sharpener went away and appeared again. The background was white and the pencil sharpener was silver at the top and purple at the bottom. When I woke up I knew what that meant. GET BACK TO WRITING! I hadn't written anything in two weeks. I said YES SIR CAPTAIN! I have an electric pencil sharpener next to my bed. I use pencils so I can erase. April 14th I had a dream. I saw a little girl sitting in the floor. She was around eleven or twelve. Her hair was black and in two long braids with rubber bands at the end. As I stood there looking at the girl, a woman came up to me and began talking, saying her daughter use to write for a television station.(I want say the name of the station) Then I woke up. I have no clue as to what that meant, but the lady in that dream was one of my favorite teachers I use to assist. She taught at that Middle School my baby boy attended. There were days when I would assist her and was more than happy to. She could read! I started calling her NIKKI GIOVANNI. She taught English, but it was her reading I enjoyed. One day I was having serious problems with my special one and I was in tears. That woman pulled me in a corner and began to sing Yolanda Adams, I OPEN UP MY HEART!! I could have sworn Yolanda had stepped into that woman's body. GOD that felt good. She really cared and tried to help me in every way. When I hear that song, she is all I think about. After I left that school, a year later she left. April 19th. I had a mixture of dreams but I only remember one. Someone gave me an apple. I bit it and it was black inside. I thought it was good at first, then, I realized it was an apple and apples are not black inside. I SPIT IT OUT AND THREW THE APPLE DOWN. I looked at the apple again, it wasn't totally rotten but it was on its way. I had another dream. A guy was sitting next to me, someone I would instantly fall in love with. He was talking to me, then, he put his hand on my thigh. I immediately put my hand on his hand and told him I would die. Then I woke up. I didn't have to think about that one. Prior to those two dreams I was talking to GOD about SEX.

I had begun to read a lot. I never read Edgar Allen Poe, Langston Hughes or the story of KING DAVID!!!!!!!!!!!!!!!!!!!!!!!!!!!!!!!!!!!!!!

I had a ball. Edgar Allen Poe was depressing, but something he said stuck with me. The superior SOUL knows deeply the silent tone of its own self supremacy. The realization that one can only glimpse thru GOD'S EYE! His story took me back. Langston Hughes put fire in me! Something Langston said stuck with me. Good writing comes out of your own LIFE. The only true and lasting art that an artist can produce is that based upon what he knows best. You have to learn to be yourself, natural and <u>UNDECEIVED</u>! As to who you are, calmly and SURELY you. I have no clue why those two people were on my mind. THE STORY OF KING DAVID TURNED ME INTO TINKER BELL!!!!!!!!!!!!!!!!!!!! I've been reading PSALMS for 15 years and never really knew the HOLD STORY!! I LOVE GOD FOR THAT MAN!!!!!!!!!!!!!!! And the guy who wrote and told that story was simply BRILLANT!!!!!!!!!!!!!!!!!! THAT STORY MADE ME FEEL LIKE I COULD F-L-Y!!!!!!!!!!!!!!!!!!!!!!!!!! Now I understand how KING DAVID COULD WRITE SUCH BEAUTIFUL MUSIC!!!!!

One day I was in my room writing in my journal. My daughter ran in my room and told me to come and look. THERE WAS A BIRD NEST AND THE BIRDS WERE BUSY AT WORK PREPARING A HOME FOR THEIR NEW BABIES! IT WAS UNBELIEVABLE! WHY DID THE BIRDS PICK OUR HOUSE! We live in an apartment on the third floor. The birds chose our apartment for their place of SECURITY! I went straight back to my childhood and got a box, placed a towel in it and put paper towels on top of that just in case one of the babies fell they would have a SOFT LANDING. I ran to the pet store to get food to help the parents out with feeding time. To watch the birds in motion was AMAZING! I told my children that was a SIGN FROM HEAVEN!

We were in and out, back and forth and NEVER NOTICED WHAT WAS GOING ON! It was my daughter's friend who made us aware of the nest. The parents guarded that nest like SOLDIERS! The people from the office noticed the nest and wanted to remove it but those birds came after them and I was SO GLAD! I told them to leave them ALONE! And they did. May 26th. The baby birds have hatched! I've never seen something SO BEAUTIFUL! Seeing the baby birds stretch their necks and open their tiny beaks is SO PRECIOUS!

I took a nap that evening and right into a dream. In that dream, my baby boy was a baby again. He kept peeing on himself. I knew the baby would feel better if I put a fresh pamper on him but every time I changed him he peed. In that dream my son went from an infant to a toddler. He peed in his underwear. I cleaned him and got fresh underwear, went into the kitchen and fixed a hot dog. I popped up out of my sleep hungry. I had only been asleep for 15 minutes. I wanted something quick so I fixed a hot dog. As my food was cooking I went into my daughter's room and started picking up stuff off the floor as usual. On the floor was one of my new towels bald up on the floor. Baby boy wasted water on the floor and got my new towel to clean it up. Instead of cleaning my carpet he covered it up. That child................

Time means a lot here on earth. But in dreams there is no time.

May 29th, I went to the store but when I entered the store I realized I had forgotten my grocery list. I ran back to my car and there was an old man lying on the street next to my car. I didn't know what to do. I started talking to him and he responded. I tried to lift him but I couldn't. His daughter who was placing groceries in the trunk and didn't know her dad had fallen. She came running. She asked him what happened and he said his legs just gave out on him. We got him back on his feet and placed him in the car. The precious old man said THANK YOU! I told him GOD HAD HIM COVERED! The man's daughter called me an ANGEL! My insides melted and I turned into Tinker Bell. The one who RUN INTO WALLS! (Just clumsy.) (laughing)

I went home and read MATTEW! I went straight to the question of WHO IS THE GREATEST IN THE KINDOM OF HEAVEN!!!!!!!!

That night I had a dream of being in Best Buy standing at the counter being waited on. As I stood there I heard a <u>WHISPER</u>. You can use your credit card. I repeated what the <u>WHISPER</u> SAID. Then I woke up. My car needed an oil change and I was broke. I was trying hard not use my cards. I took a deep breath and said I have no choice but to use one of my cards. I had another errand to run then I went to Wal-Mart to have the oil changed. They called me over the system to let me know my car was ready. As I stood there I realized I was in my dream. I said THANK YOU FATHER!, and went home. I kept a close eye on the baby birds and noticed these huge birds in the nest and said NO WAY!, could those birds be the babies!, but they were! I made my daughter take pictures of them with her camera phone. She got some good pictures. I watched the birds FLY around in circles at the beginning. Eventually they flew away. Those parents guarded that nest night after night, the children didn't come back. They showed up during the day but eventually they left for good. That hurt. (smiling)

I had a dream. In that dream, I was in a restaurant sitting at a table. A man passed me with a beautiful platter of fried chicken. I tapped him on his elbow complementing how pretty the food looked. I woke up and thought why would GOD show me something I treasure but could not have. I had cut out fried food. It rained all day but my mind was set on going to the fish market. I went to the fish market thinking I was going to walk right into my dream, but it didn't happen. I took my son to work and the man he worked for love fishing. He promised me the next he went fishing, he would cut and clean them and share the fish with me. The following day that man brought me some fresh fish and when he pulled it out I told him how pretty it was. I got home with that fish and the children insisted that I fry it. Normally I would have fixed blacken fish but they wanted fried fish. I fried that fish and there it was my dream on a platter. My GROWN children ate that fish as if they hadn't eaten in years. That baby boy ate standing up! That's a good feeling.

My autistic son was doing very well but I had a quilt trip because I wasn't able to help financially. I thought about his father's Social Security that I never applied for but I was burnt out on that situation and gave it to GOD. I went to sleep with situation weighing on my heart.

I had a dream. I was standing back at a distance. The surroundings were YELLOW. I saw my children's dead grandmother, she was in the kitchen cooking and cleaning. I could here her talking. I saw the children's father he was in the kitchen with her helping her out. They were talking and caring on as if they never passed away. Then I got a strong feeling that I was waiting on him and he stood me up. I got mad and picked up the receiver of a phone and dialed his number. A HUGE YELLOW 1976 ROTARY PHONE APPEARED IN MID AIR! The scene of seeing those people in the kitchen disappeared. It was a circle or hole in the wall that closed up, and there was this old YELLOW phone. I called a number and that phone rang twice, then, I heard a loud noise and REALIZED they had disconnected that phone. It was as if they unplugged it. I got a DEEP FEELING OF DISAPPOINTMENT! My feelings were hurt. Then I woke up. When I put that dream together I realized my children's father and mother were back together again. I stayed in bed all day.

IT IS JUNE 15TH! I HAD A DREAM!!!!

I was sitting in a huge theater. The CURTAINS ARE RED. The SEATS were RED. There was a little girl with me. We were sitting on the second row. I grabbed the little girls hand and as we got up to move I said excuse me to the people we were passing. A familiar person was sitting on the front row in the aisle seat. That familiar person turned and looked at us. I remember saying to him as I held the little girl's hand that I had to GET THE DEVIL OUT OF THIS GIRL! That familiar person LAUGHED HARD! I took the little girl to try and find another seat. As we walked I noticed the RED carpet and RED seats stood out. We went to the top of the theater, at one point it was as if we were on stage. I remember telling the little girl, no that's too close. We took a couple of steps back and there was a row of empty seats that stood out and we sat down looking at the STAGE. The STAGE was PURE WHITE! The floor, the lighting, the area was PURE WHITE, but there was no one on the STAGE, no activity going on. I woke up. That was the strangest dream. The little girl didn't have a head. It was just her body. She had on a ruffle dress with bobby doll socks and black leather shoes, but she didn't have a face or head. She was a little girl, she had to be five or under. I held her hand tight. I thought it was the tacos I had before I went to sleep.

I stepped outside to check on the birds, it was 4 am and they were in the nest sound asleep. The children had come home. The mother guarded them from my neighbor's light post.

I sat on the couch that morning and thought about how GOD is my MOTHER, my FATHER, my T-E-A-C-H-E-R, my GUIDANCE, my PROVIDER, and my SUPPORTER! I sat back in deep thought.

JUNE 25th . I was in the car on my way to the bank. I heard over the radio that Farrah Fawcett passed. My energy left me. I call my daughter and told her I was coming back home. Her death took me back. I have pictures of my hair in that exact FLIP! I didn't finish my errands that day, I went home. My baby boy began to question me about his income tax check. It was June and he had not received it yet. I text my tax man and told him my son had not received his check. He gave me the number to call and see what was going on. In the mean time, we kept texting each other. He made me LAUGH OUT LOUD! I needed to laugh. We were texting each other dirty messages for a while. Then I told him I needed to stop that because I'm not to have sex any more. He didn't care, he just kept texting me. (Thank GOD those messages could be pulled up if needed) Then out of no where there was BAD news about MICHAEL JACKSON! My son came running and said momma MICHAEL HAD A HEART ATTACK! I TOLD HIM TO QUIT PLAYING WITH ME! I RAN TO THE T.V. and stayed there! I PRAYED HARD!!!!!!!!!!!! I JUST KNEW GOD WAS NOT GOING TO ALLOW HIM TO DIE! I JUST KNEW IT!!!!!!!!!! The news kept going back and forth. I'm sitting on the floor rocking! NERVES SHATTERED! I STAYED ON MY KNEES IN FRONT OF THE T.V. My friend kept texting me as if NOTHING was going on IMPORTANT! THAT REALLY ROCKED MY NERVES!!!!

As I began to text him back and tell him about Michael, I CAUGHT MYSELF!!!!!! I KNEW HE WOULD SAY SOMETHING THAT WOULD HAVE RUN ME H-O-T!!!!!!!!!!! Something very NEGATIVE! THEN THE NEWS CAME! I KEPT TELLING MYSELF IT IS NOT TRUE!, IT IS NOT TRUE!!!!!!!!!!!!!!!!!!!!!!!!!!! I PRAYED THAT MICHAEL HAD FINALLY GOT THE MESSAGE ABOUT PEOPLE AND DECICED TO DISAPPEAR! As I tried to get up to get my phone and call my daughter it was hard. I called my daughter to tell her MICHAEL HAD PASSED, AND I CRIED AS IF I HAD LOST ALL OF MY CHILDREN AT ONE TIME!!!!!!!!!!!!!!!!!!!!!!!! I DON'T KNOW WHAT HIT ME!!!!!!!!!!!!!!!!!!! I FELL IN THE FLOOR CRYING MY HEART OUT!!!!! MY BABY BOY CAME RUNNING!!! HE TRIED TO HOLD AND COMFORT ME BUT THERE WAS NOTHING HE COULD DO!!!!!!!!!!!! He started crying. He couldn't STAND SEEING HIS MOTHER IN SO MUCH PAIN!!!!!!!!!!!!!!!!!! I CRIED SO MUCH I MADE MYSELF SICK!!!!!!!!!! Every time I thought I was through CRYING MORE TEARS SURFACED!!!!!!! Through all of that my friend kept texting me, but by this time he had become VERY IGNORANT AND VERY SARCASTIC!!!!!!!!!!!!!! I cut my phone OFF and placed it in a drawer. I TRULY HATE HIM!!!!!!! HE TURNED OUT TO BE A PUNK __ __ __ __ __! I HATE THAT MAN! I had to get myself together. I had to pick my daughter up from work and SHE KNEW THE STATE OF MIIND I WAS IN! SHE HAD SEEN IT MANY TIIMES BEFORE!!! I crawled in bed with my journals and began to write. It HIT ME! THAT DREAM OF THOSE RED CURTAINS AND SEATS IN THAT THEATER! GOD KNEW I WAS GOING TO GET IN TOUCH WITH THAT PERSON ON THAT DAY! GOD KNEW THAT WE WERE GOING TO BE TALKING DIRTY! GOD KNEW!!! !!!!!

THAT LITTLE GIRL WITH NO HEAD WAS ME! TELLING THAT PERSON THAT I HAD TO GET THE DEVIL OUT OF THAT CHILD! THAT WAS ALL ME DOING SOMETHING I WAS N-O-T SUPPOSED TO BE DOING! MOVING TO ANOTHER SEAT IN THAT THEATER WAS ME GETTING AWAY FROM THAT PIECE OF __ __ __ __! SO I COULD FOCUS ON WHAT WAS GOING ON , ON T.V. (GOD. GOD. GOD. GOD. GOD. GOD. GOD. GOD. GOD!!!!)

JUNE 26th. I WAS SICK AND THERE WAS NO GETTING OUT OF BED!!!!!! WHEN I FOCUSED AND NOTICED THE STAGE MICHAEL WAS ON AND THOSE THICK R-E-D C-U-R-T-A-I-N-S I BALD UP UNDER THE COVER AND DIED! GOD HOW CAN A PERSON HAVE SO MANY TEARSSSSSSSSSSSSSSSSS!!!!!!!!!!!!!!!! WHAT WAS I GOING TO DO! NOT SEEING MICHAEL ANYMORE WAS AN IMPOSSIBLE THOUGHT!!!!!!!!!!!!!!!!!!!!!!! I have NEVER EVER paid the NEGATIVE press any attention! I KNOW PEOPLE!!!!!!!!!!!!!!!!!!!! I KNOW ENOUGH TO STAY THE HELL AWAY!!!!!!!!!!!!!!!!!!!! I STAYED IN BED. I GAVE IN TO THAT PAIN. TRYING TO GO AGAINST IT WAS A JOKE! I ROLLED WITH THE MOTIONS!!!!!!!!!!!!!!!! I KNEW WHAT IT TOOK TO GET IT OUT OF MY SYSTEM, LET THE MOTIONS FLOW!!!!!!!!!!!! I TALKED TO GOD AND I QUESTIONED GOD! My children DID EVERYTHING TO MAKE ME LAUGH AND IT WORKED!!!!!!!!!!!!! BUT IT HURT!!!! IT HURTS TO LAUGH WHEN YOU ARE IN PAIN!!!!!!!!!!! MICHAEL'S MUSIC!!!!!

LISTENING TO THE PEOPLE PLAY HIS MUSIC OVER AND OVER AGAIN GOT ME OUT OF BED! BEFORE I KNEW IT I WAS D-A-N-C-I-N-G MY BUT OFF!! I DANCED AND I DANCED AND I DANCED!!!!!!!!!!!!!!!!!!!!!!!! MY BABY BOY JOINED ME!!!!!!!!!!!!!!!!!!!! WE H-A-D F-U-N!!!!!!!!!! I didn't have to make it clear to my children that they needed to sleep in my room. THEY ALREADY KNEW. THEY KNOW THAT I'M SUPER SCARY!!!!!!!!!!!!!!!! It was the weekend. The children were at work. I was home alone. I was in the bath room talking out loud to GOD asking HIM to come stay with me because I couldn't do it alone. My BEDROOM DOOR SLAMMED SHUT!!!!!!!! IT MADE A LOUD NOICE!!!! I STOPPED BREATHIING! I LOOKED AT THE BATHROOM DOOR AND IT WAS ALREADY CLOSED. NOW MY HAND IS TREMBLING TOO MUCH TO OPEN THE BATHROOM DOOR. I FINALLY GOT MYSELF OUT OF THERE, TRIMBLING LIKE DON KNOTTS. I CHECKED THE WINDOWS. THEY WERE CLOSED. THERE WASN'T A STRONG ENOUGH WIND TO MAKE THAT DOOR SLAM THE WAY IT DID!!!! I WENT OUTSIDE ON THE BALCONY UNTIL IT WAS TIME TO PICK MY KIDS UP FROM WORK. While I sat there I told GOD, YOU GON MAKE ME JUMP!!!!!!!! !!!

I HAD A DREAM!!!!!! In that dream, I was standing in this room alone. There was a night light. There was a door. The door opened and a man and two children came through it. The man walked up to me, with that walk, and he was in my face! He began to try to talk to me but the little girl was eaves dropping. She was very nosy, the way children are. The man turned around and made her leave. She went and stood next to the little boy who was standing at that door. The man got back in my face and HIS LIPS WOULD NOT STOP MOVING BUT NOTHING WAS COMING OUT. I KEPT TRYING TO MAKE SENSE OF WHAT HE WAS TRYING SO HARD TO TELL ME BUT NO SOUND WAS COMING OUT OF HIS MOUTH. WE STOOD THERE FOR A LONG TIME. MY HEAD WAS GOING FROM SIDE TO SIDE TRYING HARD TO UNDERSTAND. I REMEMBER SAYING WHAT ARE YOU TRYING TO TELL ME. HE WOULD STEP BACK AND THEN HE WAS IN MY FACE AGAIN. I WOKE UP AT 4:30 am that morning. I never made sense of that dream, but that person was TRYING HARD TO TELL ME SOMETHING. IT WAS HIS LIPS. THEY WOULDN" STOP MOVING. HE GOT CLOSER TO ME BUT NO SOUND EVER CAME OUT OF HIS MOUTH. After that dream I told the kids I was to sleep in my room alone. We always got a kick out of sleeping on the floor, ESPECIALLY TO WATCH THE ONE AND ONLY MICHAEL MYERS MY MAIN MAN! But when someone else die, THEY ARE GOING TO SLEEP WITH THEIR MOTHER!!!

It was Sunday, and BET was coming on. I asked the kids to stay home and watch it with me. Baby boy was off that day but my daughter had to work. The moment I dropped her off she called me right back and said mother I don't have to work today. I flew to go and pick her up. I put some meat on the grill that day trying hard to make myself very tired. BET came on and we DANCED OUR ASS OFF! Then we watched every one of MICHAEL'S videos over and over again.

His MUSIC WORKED WONDERS BUT HE WAS GONE.

My emotions were on A ROLLERCOASTER!

That night I had a dream. I was giving my children a tour of this house we were in. There were two ladies and a baby boy. We began to clean up and take out the trash. There were people outside and I asked them how often was the trash picked up and they said once a week. I got upset and thought that was strange. I woke up. That day the Foster mother called me crying. She was TIRED OF MY SON AND HIS WAYS. SHE REALLY NEEDED TO TALK. I TOLD HER TO SEND HIS BEHIND BACK TO THE GROUP HOME! SHE SAID NO. SHE COULDN'T DO THAT. I TOLD HER GOD HAD CONTROL OF WHATEVER WAS TAKING PLACE. I MADE IT CLEAR I WAS ON HER SIDE WHATEVER HER DECISION TURNED OUT TO BE. I don't understand why GOD WILL NOT ANSWER MY PRAYER WHEN IT COMES TO THAT CHILD. When he was younger I was cleaning his room and pulled the curtains back and my son had written on the window glass with a crayon. It said GOD PLEASE HELP ME. When I read that my SOUL left me alone. All I could do was sit and think about was happening and WHY.

In the mean time I constantly wrote in my journals. All that was on my mind was Michael's passing. I kept my T.V. on the news. I never changed the station. I wanted to know everything that was going on about Michael. I began to write about racism. I wrote something pertaining to it slowly fading away. After I wrote that I got sick to my stomach, ran to the bathroom and stuck my face in the toilet but nothing came up. I knew what it was. I immediately ERASED what I wrote. Then I had a dream.

In that dream I was in bed and heard people outside arguing and getting ready to fight. I ran to the window, opened the blinds and looked out the window, but I couldn't see out of my left eye. A fight broke out and I told my son let's go and help the person that was being jumped but I couldn't see out of my left eye. My son ran down the stairs and I was right behind him. I went to my car to get my crow bar. My son vanished and I was alone but I had my crow bar. I ran towards a big female, getting ready to hit her but she came on to me strong, so I stopped and took a couple of steps backwards. I couldn't see out of my left eye and everything was blurry. There were some people around me and I asked them to take me home. I told them I couldn't see. I ended up feeling my way back home. I had to climb a wall to get home, but I made it in the house. When I got home I still couldn't see and that had me scared. Then I woke up. I had fallen to sleep very early. When I woke up it was 10 pm. I got up thinking about that dream and was glad to have my eye sight again. I started cleaning up. I told my son to take out the trash but someone was out on the parking blowing a horn. My son ran to the window and it was one of his friends who had a new car. I ran to the window to see the car. My son ran outside and down the steps. I was right behind him. I was fussing at him about the trash but they drove off. I finished cleaning and decided to take the trash out. I grabbed my car keys because I'm use to driving to the trash can. I told myself to stop being lazy and walk to the trash can. It was a quiet and beautiful night. It is so peaceful where I live. I grabbed the trash and headed down the steps. I G-O-T WEAK! I turned around and thought about getting in the car after all but I thought that was just laziness. I went forward and said GOD TAKE CARE OF ME. I'M JUST WALKING TO THE TRASH DUMPSTER.

There was a group of white kids sitting on their balcony. They were in their early twenties. They were drinking and laughing. I got a good look. We were the only people outside. This town shuts down at 10 pm every night. I was walking in the street, then, I got on the sidewalk right where their balcony started. As soon as I passed them, the word NIGGER came out of their mouth. Then the only guy that with that group of girls started calling at me as if I were a DOG! I looked back to make sure they were talking to me and they were. MY SPIRIT LEFT ME! I rushed to that trash can. I walked HARD on that same sidewalk but OF COURSE THEY TOOK THEIR __ __ __ __ __ in the house. (One of the females work in the rent office.) After I passed that balcony and noticed they were gone MY HEAD DROPPED! MY SPIRIT WAS HURT! I walked with my head down not paying any attention as to where I was going. As I got close to home I heard a sound that scared the crap out of me! I jumped (scary) and looked up it was a woman with a hospital uniform on and a head rag on her head. She was a big woman. It hit me right away that I was in that dream. As much as I have experienced I still want the world to be a nice place. That's why I couldn't see out of my left eye. I got in the house and I wanted to cry so bad but nothing would come out. Which made the HATERED WORST! Baby boy came back home and I told them about it. HE WAS READY TO GO!!!!!!!!!!!!!!! Something in me died. I remembered the fight in my dream. I told my children let's go bed. I made baby boy promise me not to leave my house and he didn't. He is very well known for knocking people OUT! He made a name for himself, but I reminded him that people don't FIGHT because they can't.

They shoot to kill. I went in my room and TOLD GOD I WOULD NEVER MAKE THAT MISTAKE AGAIN! RACISM IS FRESHER THAT EVER. I believe nothing was going to happen to me that night, I just needed a wake call and GOD GAVE ME THAT WAKE UP CALL! When I go to the office to pay my rent I just look at that little girl. My eyes tell her I know it was you. She can't face me. <u>EVERYTHING STARTS AT HOME</u>!!!!!!!!!!!!!!!!!!!!!!!!!!

The next day I began to think about a football. I have always had a crush on a couple of players. I worked HARD at trying to erase that but a football player was on my mind. So to try and erase those thoughts I began to read and came across a paragraph: A diamond can't be polished without friction, nor a person perfected without trials. Your confidence now to reach a dream is more POWERFUL than ANYTHING MAN-MADE. I dwelled on that for a long time, trying to forget what I was thinking about.

I fell asleep and had a dream. I'm sitting back watching these football players play football. That was the biggest picture I had ever seen and everything was so clear. There was a player with the number 88 on his jersey, he had the ball in his hand getting ready to throw the ball but another player with the number 1 was blocking the player with number 88 and all I could see was one 8. That player who had on the number 1 jersey would never move out of the way. I said he keep blocking the other number on that 88 jersey. I woke up. I begged GOD to forgive me for dwelling on some football player. It was summer. Football nor the players were on my mind. I don't know where that came from.

July 5th.

Steve McNair was shot and killed. His number was 9.

I already couldn't use my legs and that just weakened them more.

Now I'm really in knots waiting on the HOMECOMING OF MICHAEL. I'm nervous. I'm tired of crying but I had NO CONTROL. I kept asking GOD WHY WANT YOU JUST TAKE ME WITH YOU!

I HAD A DREAM!!!!!!!!!!!!!!!! I was standing at a BUS STOP. The BUS came and I got on. The BUS DRIVER seemed to be very FAMILIAR. I had a strange FEELING about that BUS DRIVER. I wanted to say YOU FINALLY CAME TO SEE ME. THAT FEELING WAS STRONG. I looked around and there were passengers. It was quite a few. I looked around at everyone. The bus took a couple of turns. As the BUS DRIVER made those turns I clearly remember thinking I'll never remember how to get back. I didn't know where I was going. All I know is those turns through me off. I remember thinking that everyone on the bus worked together and the job provided the BUS for their employees because it is a nice thing to do. Then the BUS stopped. A passenger stood up on the bus and got off. When the passenger stood up, I turned to look at him and had a strong feeling of not liking him. When he got off the BUS I had a strong feeling of relief thinking I don't have to see him anymore. He was BLACK with ponytails. The BUS stopped again, this time I got off. I ended up in a house. Someone else was with me but it wasn't clear. I walk into a room and grabbed the remote to turn that weird shaped television on. It was silver and tall and skinny, slim. That was very strange. I turned that television on and the television took a SPIN and fell to the floor on its BACK! I remember looking at the television with my mouth wide open, thinking, WHY DID THAT HAPPEN! Then I woke up.

July 6th

I grabbed a book I had on dreams because the dreams were driving me crazy, I NEEDED AN EXPLANTION. WHEN I READ ABOUT THE B-U-S D-R-I-V-E-R I WENT THROUGH THE ROOF!!!!!!!(Roger rabbit) Everything I looked up made me happy as HELL! I couldn't find the definition about that passenger I was uncomfortable about. I ran and told baby boy about that dream and got him to read the definitions. We looked at each other and smiled. My daughter was still sleep so I didn't wake her. My daughter finally woke up and we decided to go get some take out. I was in no mood to COOK. Before we left I wanted to tell my daughter about MY DREAM! As I began to tell my daughter about my DREAM, baby boy got mad, upset and very impatient. He was ready to go. THAT PISSED ME TO THE HIGHEST! I was so mad I scared the living daylights out of that boy. He didn't open his mouth once while we were in the car. I told him GOD was going to tear his behind up for cutting me short. I sat there and told my daughter about the DREAM. I took my time. We got something to eat. I took that BOY to pay his phone bill. Then he had the COURAGE to ask me to drop him off at the barber shop. I started loud talking his but, and it hit me. Take him and drop him off. We needed some time apart. I went home, stormed in the house. I stayed close to the television trying to keep up with what was going on. I began to write in my journals. I was writing anything down. I couldn't think and my DREAMS were pouring in. I couldn't make sense of nothing. I talked to GOD. I imagined myself in his arms and rocked myself to sleep.

JULY 7th!

I woke up, put my coffee on and grabbed my journals. It was 6:50 am.

I wrote, That nervous, shaky FEELING is worst than ever. Crying makes me weak. I remember well now how I taught myself not to cry. I learned when I didn't cry, I was strong. I acted out the exact way victims act out, but LOVE NEVER LEFT ME. Now how could that have happen. (<u>I'm sitting on the floor writing and talking to myself the same way I did as a child after I was SAVED</u>)

When I wrote the sentence about LOVE NOT LEAVING ME, and asked

myself how could that have happen, I WROTE GOD

Then I slowly began to draw. A couple of pages before this particular page I had begun to draw and it eased my SOUL. I kept DRAWING. I took my time. Then I began to like my art. I kept at it. I was GONE! I sat there and KEPT WORKING ON MY LITTLE MASTER PIECE!! I DREW SO LONG MY HAND BEGAN TO ACHE. I SLOWLY BEGAN TO COME OUT OF IT, AND WHEN I FELT THAT I WENT RIGHT BACK INTO MY DRAWING!!! I GOT TIRED AGAIN!!!!! I FELT MYSELF COMING OUT OF THAT Z-O-N-E! EVERY TIME I BEGAN TO COME OUT OF THAT ZONE, THE PAIN WAS SITTING BESIDE ME WAITING FOR ME TO COME BACK! I GOT TIRED OF FIGHTING IT. I PUT THE PENCIL DOWN. I CAME BACK FROM WHERE EVER I WAS AND NOTICED MY PICTURE!

I D-I-S-A-P-P-E-A-R-E-D!!!!!!!!!!!!!!!! THE EXACT SAME WAY I DID AS A CHILD!!!!!! I DISAPPEARED!!!!!!

After leaving my grandmothers house and going back with that family I would stay in my room ALONE! I had tones of paper and plenty of pencils and in that room I worked SO HARD AT TEACHIING MYSELF how to WRITE AND READ!!! I W-O-R-K-E-D H-A-R-D!

I work so hard I would FORGET WHERE I WAS!!! I WOULD FORGET ABOUT BEING HUNGRY!!!!!!!! When that woman would call me to come and eat I simply said I wasn't hungry. NOT IN THAT WORLD I LIVED IN.

I ERASED WHAT HAPPENED TO ME THOSE THREE YEARS!
MY PENCIL AND PAPER T-O-O-K ME A-W-A-Y!!!!!!!!!!!!!!!!
I WORKED SO HARD!!!!!!!!!!!!!!!!!!!!!!!!!!!!!!!!!!
AND THE THOUGHT OF SOMEBODY HELPING ME DROVE
ME CRAZY!!!!!!!!!!!!!!!!!!!!!!!!!! I HATED WHEN I WAS DISTURB!!!

I HATED REALITY !!!!!!!!!!!!!!!

I wrote my alphabets and my name until my hand fell OFF!
I don't know how I learned to read.
I WAS SO BEHIND, I WASN'T SUPPOSED GO TO THE SECOND
GRADE AFTER FINALLY GETTING OUT OF THAT HOUSE BUT I
DID AND I TALKED TO GOD AND ASKED HIM NOT TO LEAVE
ME BEHIND ANYMORE!!
 I HAD MICHAEL'S PICTURES EVERYWHERE!!!!!
I MADE SURE I KISSED THOSE PICTURES BEFORE I WENT TO
BED. SITTING ON THAT FLOOR TEACHING MYSELF TO WRITE
TOOK ME TO ANOTHER WORLD AND I LOVED IT!!! IN THAT
OTHER WORLD THERE WERE NO PROBLEMS AT ALL!!!!!!!!!!!!!!!!
!!!
I never stayed after school for tutoring. No teacher ever worked with me on
a one to one basis. I HATED THE THOUGHT!!!!!!!!!!!!!!!!!!!
In the first grade I was placed in group three and I DIED!!!!!! LORD I DI
ED!!!
In the first grade when I would get my report card I couldn't wait to show that
woman. I couldn't read so I HAD NO IDEA THERE WERE NO GRADES
ON IT. ALL MY REPORT CARD SAID WAS:
SHE NEEDS HELP
SHE NEEDS HELP
SHE NEEDS HELP
SHE NEEDS HELP
SHE NEEDS HELP
SHE NEEDS HELP
THAT WHOLE YEAR.
I KEPT THAT REPORT CARD FOREVER.
IT WASN'T UNTIL MY DAUGHTER FOUND IT, AND I TOLD
HER I LOVE MY REPORT CARD AND SHE ASKED ME WHY?
I NEVER PAID ATTENTION TO THOSE WORDS UNTIL
THEN!!!!

I RIPPED MY REPORT CARD UP THAT I THOUGHT WAS GOOD ALL THOSE YEARS. I BEGAN TO UNDERSTAND WHY I CHOKED UP WHEN I TRIED TO READ TO MY DAUGHTER.

BUT I READ TO MY BOYS LIKE A CHAMP!!!!!!!!!!!!!!!!!!

I'VE BEEN RUNNING FROM REALITY ALL MY LIFE. BUT GOD ALMIGHTY HAD ME! HE HAD ME IN THE PALM OF HIS HANDS THE WHOLE TIME.

THAT PICTURE IN MY JOURNAL IS MY <u>MASTER PIECE.</u>

G-O-D H-A-S C-U-R-E-D M-E!!!!!!!!!!!!!!!!!!!!!!!!!!!!!!!!!!!!

GOD PUSHED ME TO HAVE A BREAK THROUGH!!!!!!!!!!!!!!!!

GOD PUSHED ME TO GO BACK AND REMEMBER ALL! NO MORE BITS AND PIECES, ALL! EVERYTHING!!!!!!!!!!!!!!!!!

GOD GAVE ME MY ANSWER!!!

YOU CAN'T GET AN ANWSER WITHOUT A QUESTION!!!!!!!

THE TEARS

I don't how I got myself together for Michael's HOMECOMING but I did. And there it was. THE TWIST. The family changed their minds and thought it would be best if his body was at the celebration. GOD HAD ALREADY SHOWED ME! In that dream GOD was the BUS DRIVER! HE IS ALL I HAVE AND ALL I'VE EVER DEPENDED ON!!! That person who stood up and got off the bus was my baby boy. He wore his hair in those ponytails when he was in the seventh grade. That was GOD'S way of telling me my child's problem. Mentally he is still in the seventh grade. And I hate it. That's when my ex left for good. My baby boy running me hot and getting off the BUS. Here on earth it went according as planned. The television set was in some way Michael's body. GOD IS AWESOME!!!!!!!!!!!!!!!!!!!!!!

YES GOD WORKS IN MYSTERIOUS WAYS, AND I WOULDN'T HAVE IT ANY OTHER WAY!!!!!!!!!!!!!!!

ALL OF MY LIFE, MY SADDNESS HAVE ALWAYS BEEN DOUBLED!!!

IT HAD TO BE FOR A SOME UNKNOWN REASON!!!!!!!

I just accepted Luther Vandross being in HEAVEN laid back in a lounge chair kicking it!!!!!!!!!!!!!!!!!!!!!!!! Now Michael.

When I play Luther's POWER OF LOVE (<u>THAT KING DAVID WROTE</u>) I imagine Fred Astaire and Gregory Hines DANCING THEIR HEARTS OUT HAVING THE TIME OF THEIR LIVES!!!!!!!!!!!!!!!!!!!!! I'M NOT READY FOR MICHAEL TO BE THERE. GOD ALMIGHTY HAS HIS WAY OF DEALING WITH ME.

When I listen to Luther's <u>NEVER TOO MUCH</u>! I IMAGINE THE UNIVERSE SURROUNDING GOD AS HE SIT ON HIS THRONE ENJOYING HIS PEOPLE PRASING HIM!!!!!!!! KING DAVID IS PLAYING ALL INSTRUMENTS!!!!!!!!!! AFTER ALL OF THIS TIME KING DAVID IS STILL TRYING TO PLEASE GOD!!!!!!!!!!!!!!!!!!!!!!!!!!!!

When I listen to Luther's <u>STOP TO LOVE</u>!!!!!!!!!!!!!!!!

I IMAGINED THE UNIVERSE SURROUNDING GOD AS HE SIT ON HIS THRONE PATTING HIS FEET AND HANDS!!!!! KING DAVID HAS ASKED JIMMY HINDRICKS TO JOIN HIM ON THE GUITAR! THE PEOPLE FINALLY GOT THE MESSAGE AND GOD IS VERY PLEASED!!!!!

THE UNIVERSE IS THE CHOIR !!!!!!!!!!!!!!!!!!!!

When I listen to Luther's <u>POWER OF LOVE</u>!!!!!!!

FRED ASTAIRE AND GREGORY HINES TAKE OVER THE DANCE FLOOR, BUT THIS TIME GOD IS UP OFF THE THRONE TO JOIN THE TWO!!!!!!!!!!!!!!!!!!!!!!!!!

THIS TIME THE CARTOON CHARACTERS HAVE JOINED IN TO CELEBRATE GOD ALMIGHTY!!!!!!!

THE UNIVERSE IS SINGING ITS HEART OUT!!!!!!!!!!

When I listen to Luther's <u>DON'T WANT TO BE A FOOL</u>!!

I IMAGINE SAUL TAKING OVER, FRONT AND CENTER!

AND HE IS SINGING TO GOD WITH ALL HIS HEART AND SOUL!!!

JONATHAN HAS JOINED KING DAVID ON THE INSTRUMENTS AND THE BOTH OF THEM ARE SO PROUD OF SAUL, AND SO IS GOD!!!!!!!!!!!!!!!!!!!!!!!!!!!! THE UNIVERSE IS THE CHOIR!!!!!!!!!!!!!!!!!!!!!!!!!!!!!!!!!!

Of course LUTHER IS DOING WHAT HE DOES BEST!!!

BUT THE MOMENT <u>DON'T WANT TO BE A FOOL</u> COMES ON, LUTHER TAKES A STEP BACK AND LET SAUL HAVE IT!!!!!!!!!!!!!!!! !!!!!!!!!!!!!!!!!!!!!!!!!!!

<u>MY IMAGINATION</u>!!!!!!!!!!!!!!!!!!!!!!!!!!!!!

I stayed in the bed. My children knew not to bother me at all. I was in a knot and I STAYED THERE. The thought of eating or drinking water made me want to throw up. I feel so close to GOD WHEN I'M IN MY BED. July 7th I didn't have the strength to even TALK TO <u>MY GOD</u>.

I HAD A DREAM.

In the dream I was back in High School. There were large groups of people. They were in the hall, then, disappeared into class. I was alone in the hallway. I ended up in a classroom standing in front of a Teachers' desk. The Teacher gave me a hand full of ORANGE PILLS AND SOME TYPE OF CRYSTAL substance. My hand was full. The CRYSTAL was pretty, it was piled high. I took both, the pills and the CRYSTAL. There was one pill that stood out. It was broken in half and sitting on top of the stack of pills in my hand. I didn't take all of it. After I swallowed the pill and the CRYSTAL, I went back to the Teacher to find out what I had taken, but the dream switched. Class was dismissed, and I ended up with a girlfriend I could depend on. But she and another friend had other plans. They were going out to some event or party. I saw myself changing clothes. I put on a lime green pant suit, but I clearly remembered I had worn that outfit to a previous event and I didn't want to wear the same thing again. I changed my mind about going out with them. I didn't want to wear the same thing and I didn't have any money. I walked up to my friend and told her I wanted to go home. That's when my old neighborhood popped up. I remember very clearly my friends were mad at my decision. I remember thinking where I lived was far away, out of the way in which they were going, but she took me home anyway. Then I woke up. I have no clue of the meaning. I just remember being sad in that dream.

I had begun to keep track of my BREAK THROUGH. I thought something MAJOR was going to happen to me if I ever got to the CORE of my problem. July 8th, nothing happened. July 9th, nothing happened, July 10th, nothing happened to me. I'm still just as off as I have always been. Nothing is DIFFERTENT. I HAVE NO IDEA OF WHAT I THOUGHT WOULD HAPPENED TO ME. Could it have been I was MORE worried about that family than I was myself, I THINK THAT'S IT. Now I remember. I thought I would loose my mind. I thought I would go back to being that little girl, but this time I would STAY THERE. That's what I was so afraid of.

When Michael's magazines hit the news stand I ran and bought as many as I could. As I stood in line to pay for them I actually turned around to see if Mrs. Crabtree was walking down the aisle shopping for groceries. I couldn't help but to SMILE. When I got home with MY magazines it was too much for me. I crawled back in bed and stayed there. Normally when I have been in the bed too long my body would ache. Not this time. I was wilth GOD. THE CLOSER, THE BETTER.

July 12th .

My children knew what would get me out of bed. The BIRDS HAD MORE BABIES!!!!! That got me up, and moving around. Watching that mother do whatever it takes to protect her babies was inspiring. I kept the egg shells. The momma bird had six babies and none of them died. This time I saw the babies fly on their first try. I thought I had to run under them to catch them, GOD IS COLD!!!!!!!!!!!!!!!!!!!!!!!!!!!!!!!!!!!!!

While I was in bed, I caught a good movie, Beyond the Sea. I hadn't seen a movie like that since Young at Heart. I enjoyed it. I watched it twice. It's the story.

July 13th .

I had a dream last night. It's not very clear but I was getting ready to go somewhere and it seems as if I missed out. Before I knew it my mind was made up and I insisted on doing whatever it was anyway. Then a SOLDIER APPEARED. He WALKED WITH A HIGH STEP! He was DRESSED EXACTLY LIKE THE SOLDIERS WHO GUARD THE PALACE! THE TALL HAT, THE SUIT, THE MARCH! I REMEMER THE SOLDIER, HE WAS VERY CLEAR!!!

HE APPEARED AT THE END OF MY DREAM, right before I woke up.

July 16th. 3:54 pm

I've been constantly reading and I RAN INTO MY PROBLEM!

ANS- Automatic Nervous System.

Anxiety and Fear

A combination of ABUSE AND DEPRESSION MAKES THE BODY MOST REACTIVE TO STRESS.

These STRESS REACTIONS EXHAUST THE BODY. WOMEN WHO WERE ABUSED AS CHILDREN ARE APPARENTLY CARRYING A H-I-S-T-O-R-I-C BURDEN THAT MAKES CURRENT BURDEDS ALL THE MORE UNBEARABLE.

JULY 17th . 2:12 pm

I HAD A DREAM!!

In that DREAM, I saw my baby boy sitting ALONE. He was wearing his UNIFORM, which is an ORANGE SHIRT and BLACK PANTS. He was LOOKING SO SAD. I asked him WHAT'S WRONG ? HE SAID MOMMA THEY JUMPED ME! THEN DROPPED HIS HEAD IN PAIN AND SADDNESS!!

THAT HURT ME SO!!!

I WOKE UP! I KNOW FOR A FACT I WAS IN GOD'S RIGHT HAND BECAUSE I LAYED MY HEAD DOWN IN SADDNESS AND WENT BACK TO SLEEP.

July 21st 1: 17 pm.

I had a dream, It's not clear but I was in a place where people were moving things, like furniture. I left with an attitude, BAD attitude. Someone said I missed out. I replied in ANGER, MISSED OUT ON STORAGE! Then a plastic doll appeared. It had the sweetest FACE, with precious EYES. It had its HANDS together as if to be PRAYING. It caught my attention and I STARED at the doll. I REMEMBER THINKING THAT'S MINE! Then I woke up.

July 30th 2:57 am.

I had a dream.

I was HIGH IN THE SKY. I had a perfect view of a tall building. I was looking down on the tall building. The top of the building had GIGANTIC LETTERS. THEY READ

G O D.

THEN A VOICE SAID UNDER NEW MANAGEMENT.

Then I ended up inside the building. There was construction going on. The place was newly remodeled. I REMEMBER THINKING HOW NICE IT WAS. The building had a lot of rooms and people. The rooms were made of glass. I could see straight through them. I walked and turned a corner. I passed this black female, pretty, very well dressed, professional. She had a big smile on her face as if she was happy to see me. It was if I knew her but I couldn't recall where I knew her from or her name. I walked passed her and had a STRONG SENSE that she was happy to see me. I felt SO WELCOME as I walked past her. I walked in a waiting room. There was a little girl lying in someone's arms. I grabbed her hand and said to her I thought you weren't coming back. THEN I WOKE UP.

119

July 31st .

Last night I heard THE BIRDS SCREAMING!!!!!!!!!!!!!!! as I was cleaning the kitchen. I RAN TO THE DOOR TO SEE WHAT WAS WRONG!!!!!!!!! SYLVESTER AND HIS FRIEND HAD SHOWED UP AND THEY WERE MESSING WITH MY BABIES!! I TRIED TO KILL EM!! But they were HEALTHY cats. I knew they belonged to someone so I just chased them away with my BROOM!!!!!! That was straight out of a cartoon. IT WAS TOO PRECIOUS!!!!!!!!!!!!!!!!!!

August 3rd 8:02 am.

I had a dream last night.

In the dream I walked into a room and there were a group of women. I noticed one was someone from my childhood. I called her first and last name, then, we hugged each other. I was happy to see her. I asked her how was she doing and she told me she had cancer. I grabbed her hand and told her she was not going to die. I told her that twice as I held her hand. Then I TOOK OFF RUNNING TO MY CAR AND IT WAS ONLY A FRAME OF A CAR WITH THREE TIRES AND THE KEYS IN THE IGNITION. I COULD SEE STRAIGHT THROUGH THE CAR! I WAS UPSET! I WENT BACK INTO THE PLACE WHERE THE WOMEN WERE AND TOLD THEM MY CAR WAS TOWED AWAY! I WAS UPSET AND COMPLAINING! I TOLD THAT CHILDHOOD FRIEND I HAD MY OWN PROBLEMS! I SAID OUT LOUD, I PARK THERE ALL THE TIME, SO WHY DID THEY TOW MY CAR AWAY! THEN I REMEMBERED THAT THE KEYS WERE STILL IN THE IGNITION, WHICH MADE ME REALIZE THAT THE CAR WASN'T TOWED, BUT I COULD SEE STRAIGHT THROUGH THE CAR. THERE WAS ONLY A FRAME. I REALIZED THE KEYS WERE STILL THERE WHICH MEANT I COULD STILL DRIVE IT. I WANTED SO BAD TO LEAVE AND GET AWAY FROM THAT PLACE! THE NEXT THING I KNEW I WAS IN THE CAR! THE KEYS WERE GOLD. (My keys are silver)

THE CAR WAS WHOLE AGAIN! I WAS IN MY CAR. AS I DROVE TO GET AWAY, MY CAR BEGAN TO SHUT DOWN! I GOT VERY NERVOUS BECAUSE THERE WAS A CAR BEHIND ME AND I KNEW IT WAS GOING TO CRASH INTO MY CAR! I TRIED TO START THE CAR WITHOUT PUTTING IT IN PARK! THAT'S HOW NERVOUS I WAS! I PUT THE CAR IN PARK, I LOOKED

INTO THE REARVIEW MIRROW TO SEE IF THE CAR BEHIND ME WAS GETTING CLOSE, AND IT WAS! ONCE I PUT THE CAR IN PARK IT STARTED IMMEDIATELY! I BEGAN TO DRIVE OFF! I IMMEDIATELY PULLED INTO THE RIGHT LANE TO AVOID THE CAR BEHIND ME! AS THE CAR WAS ABOUT TO HIT ME, IT TOOK A SHARP TURN TO THE LEFT TO AVOID HITTING ME, AND RAN HEAD ON INTO ANTHER CAR THAT HAD TO BE GOING THE WRONG WAY! IT WAS A HEAD ON COLLISION! THE CAR THAT AVOIDED HITTING ME FROM THE BACK WAS TOTALLY CRUSHED, SMASHED!!!!!!!!!!! I HAD A STRONG FEELING THAT THE TWO PEOPLE IN THAT CAR DIED ON THE SPOT! I IMMEDIATELY MADE A U-TURN AND BURNT RUBBER!!!!!!!! I REMEMBER CLEARLY TRYING TO HURRY UP AND GET AWAY!!!!!! I DIDN'T WANT TO BE THE BLAME FOR THE CRASH AND THE DEATH OF THOSE PEOPLE!

I REMEMBER GETTING HOME TRYING TO HIDE MY CAR ON THE PARKING LOT WHERE I LIVE! I REMEMBER SAYING I DIDN"T KILL THOSE PEOPLE, BUT DEEP DOWN INSIDE I KNEW I HAD!!!!!!!!!!!

Family members were trying to get in touch with me.

MY GOD IS COLD!!!

August 3rd 3:12 pm.
I had another DREAM.
In that DREAM the children and I were in my grandmother's house. My oldest son was a toddler. We were playing chase. He chased me around the house. I ran and jumped on the couch, he ran and jumped on the couch. I ran and jumped in the bed, he ran behind me and jumped in the bed. He was so tickled. THEN I HEARD A NOICE! IT WAS A ROAR! IT WAS SCARY! IT MADE ME NERVOUS! I PUT THE KIDS IN THE BED!!!!
I TIPPED AROUND THE HOUSE AND THERE IT WAS!!
A LOIN!!!!!!!!!!!!!!!!!!!!!!!!!!!!!!!!!!
I DID WHAT I HAVE ALWAYS IMAGINED I WOULD DO
FAINT!!!!!!!!! I PASSED OUT!!!!!!!! I KNEW THERE WAS NO GETTING AWAY!!!!!!!!!! I REMEMBER PASSING OUT ON THE BED WHERE MY CHILDREN WERE!!!!!!

I TRIED TO GET UP TO PROTECT THEM BUT I WAS TOO WE AK!!

I REMEMBER WAKING UP IN THAT BED!! I REMEMBER BEING TOO SCARED TO LEAVE THE BED, BUT I HEARD VOICES, PEOPLE TALKING!!!!!!!! I GOT UP, PEAKED OUT OF THE BEDROOM DOOR AND NOTICED PEOPLE IN THE KITCHEN FIXING FOOD, AND PEOPLE WALKING IN THE HALLWAY!!! I ASKED THEM ABOUT THE LION THAT WAS IN THE HOUSE, THEY SAID THEY HADN'T SEEN IT!!!!! I THOUGHT OH

__ __ __ __! THEN I HURRIED TO CLOSE ME AND THE CHILDREN OFF!!!!!!! THE ROOM WE WERE IN WAS HUGE!!! I CLOSED ONE DOOR. RAN TO THE OTHER SIDE OF THE ROOM, THERE WAS NO DOOR. I WAS SO SCARED!!! OUT OF THE BLUE, I GRABBED THE WALL AND A GATE APPEARED!!!!! I PULLED IT SHUT!!!! THEN I RAN TO THE OTHER SIDE OF THE ROOM, AND THERE WAS NO DOOR!!! THAT'S WHEN I REALIZED IN THE DREAM THAT I WAS IN MY GRANDMOTHERS HOUSE!!! I WANTED THAT LAST ENTRANCE CLOSED. THEN I NOTICED A TALL BROWN CHEST WITH A LOT OF DRAWERS. I GRABBED IT AND BLOCKED THE ENTRANCE!!!! NIGHT CAME! I WAS STILL SCARED! I REMEMBER PEAKING OUT OF THE WINDOW SCARED!

I REMEMBER BEING ASKED TO ATTEND A PARTY BUT I SAID NO. I WOULDN'T LEAVE THE ROOM!!!! I WONDERED IF I HAD MISSED SOMETHING. SOMEONE TOLD ME AN IMPORTANT PERSON WAS AT THE PARTY I MISSED. I REMEMBER BEING UPSET, THEN I WOKE UP.

That was also family related.

I asked GOD was I doing a good job with my writing, I HAD A DREAM!

In that dream, I was sitting in my room and looked at my desk. It was covered with paper. Within a blink of an eye, I was standing over my desk. A PINK STICKY PAD APPEARED ON TOP OF THE STACK OF PAPERS! I WOKE UP WITH A SMILE!!!!!!! THE COLOR OF PINK IS LOVE!!!!!!!!!!!!! I HAVE STICKY PADS FALLING OFF THE CEILING!!!!!!!!

August 4th 9:05 am.

I had a dream.

In that dream, I had a newborn baby GIRL. I HELD HER IN MY RIGHT ARM. THERE WERE TWO LADIES WITH ME. THEY WERE THERE TO TAKE ME TO WORK. I KEPT COMING UP WITH EXCUSES NOT TO GO. I WAS PACKING THE BABY BAG WITH THE THINGS SHE WOULD NEED. I CLEARLY REMEMBER NOT WANTING TO GO TO WORK! (The feeling was so strong) I DIDN'T WANT TO GO BECAUSE OF MY BABY GIRL. I PICKED HER UP AND SHE WAS SOAKING WET. I TOOK HER PAMPER OFF AND SENSED THERE WERE NO MORE PAMPERS. I SEARCHED UNTIL I FOUND ONE. I ASKED ONE OF THE LADIES TO CALL THE JOB AND TELL THEM WE WERE GOING TO BE LATE BECAUSE WE HAD TO STOP AND PICK UP SOME PAMPERS. THE WOMAN CALLED THE JOB AND TOLD THEM WE WERE GOING TO BE LATE. I PUT THE FRESH PAMPER ON THE BABY AND LAID HER DOWN. I BEGAN TO PACK HER BAG AGAIN BUT I WAS TRULY PROCRASTINATING. I DIDN'T WANT TO LEAVE MY BABY. I DID NOT WANT TO GO TO WORK. THE LADIES WERE TRYING TO GET ME TO HURRY, WHICH IRRITATED ME, IT WENT THROUGH MY SKIN. THE BABY BEGAN TO CRY. I PICKED HER UP, I KNEW SHE WAS HUNGRY. I GRABBED HER BOTTLE AND BEGAN TO FEED HER, BUT NOTICED THE MILK WASN'T FRESH, SO I GRABBED A BOTTLE OUT OF THE BAG I WAS PACKING AND NOTICED SOMETHING WAS WRONG WITH THAT BOTTLE. THE MILK IN THAT BOTTLE WASN'T FRESH EITHER. SO I TOLD THE LADIES TO CALL THE JOB AND TELL THEM WE WERE GOING TO BE REALLY LATE. THEY TOOK A DEEP BREATH AS TO BE TIRED OF MY EXCUSES. I REMEMBER CLEARLY HOLDING MY BABY AND LOVING HER. FINALLY I WAS READY TO GO. AS WE BEGAN TO LEAVE THE TWO LADIES WERE IN HEAD OF ME, I WAS LAST. AS I WALKED THROUGH THE LIVING ROOM HEADED FOR THE DOOR, I NOTICED THERE WERE FLOWERES, FRESH FLOWERS, NEW FLOWERS, A BUNCH OF THEM. I TOOK ANOTHER STEP BACK AND LOOKED BACK, THE FLOWERS SEPARTED, AND THEN A COUCH OR BED APPEARED. I WOKE UP. THE TWO

LADIES WERE INVISABLE, I NEVER SAW THEM, BUT THEY WERE THERE.

I don't want to go back out there.

August 6th 7 am.
I had a dream last night.
In that dream, I was sitting looking at a painting that was in front of me. The painting was a picture of the SKY. The SKY was light blue, with white puffy CLOUDS. BEAUTIFUL!!!!!
I noticed the stand the painting was on. The stand had three legs. That's what made it obvious it was a painting.

August 12th 6:30 pm.
I was in the store when baby boy called me and told me the people who run the apartments had someone two knock THE BIRD NEST DOWN!!!!!!!!!!!!!!!!!!!!!!!!!!! They have been trying to sneak around me and REMOVE THE NEST, so the COWARDS waited until I was gone to KNOCK IT DOWN!!!
CRUSHED IT!!!!!!!!!!!!!!!!!! (PEOPLE.)
I ENJOYED THE SIX BABIES THAT WERE BORN!!
IT WAS EVEN BETTER TO SEE THEM FLY!!!!!!!!!!!
THANK YOU GOD!!!

August 20th 6:15 pm.
I had a dream.
In that dream, I was standing in the MIRROW combing my hair, curling my hair with curling irons. I took a good look in the MIRROW, and it was me. I thought to myself, I'm curling my hair. Then I woke up.
I rarely wear my down and when I do you can rest assure it's not curled. I have no clue.

August 30th 4:41 pm.
I had a dream. In that dream, I was bare foot and I clearly remember stepping on a piece of wood and the wood broke off in my FOOT AND IT HURT BAD!!! IT WAS A THICK PIECE OF WOOD! I remember sitting down, taking a look at my FOOT and noticed the pieces of WOOD AND BLOOD. I was asleep but I CLEARLY REMEMBER HOLDING MY FOOT UP IN THE AIR DUE TO THE PAIN. I HELD MY RIGHT LEG UP SO

LONG IT WOKE ME UP OUT OF THAT SLEEP. I remember thinking I got to get this out of my foot. I MADE AN ATTEMPT TO GET UP AND GET A PAIR OF TWIZERS BUT I WAS ASLEEP And COULDN'T GET UP. I remember looking at my foot twice, I was IN PAIN, my FOOT was HURTING!!!!! BUT I COULDN'T MOVE. IN MY SLEEP I HELD MY RIGHT FOOT SIDEWAYS SO NOTHING WOULD TOUCH THE WOOD IN MY FOOT AND MAKE THE PAIN WORST. I kept thinking when I wake up, the first thing I was going to do is get that wood out of my foot. Finally I woke up HOLDING MY FOOT IN THE AIR!!!!! THAT WAS VERY REAL, BUT I HAVE NO CLUE AS TO WHAT IT MEANT.

September 20th

I had a dream this morning.

In that dream, I saw a female on her hands and knees, scrubbing the floor with a long skinning brush. I remember thinking that person is hurting bad deep down inside. I remember thinking that person was lost. I have no clue.

SEPTEMBER 24th 7:55 am.

I HAD A DREAM LAST NIGHT.

I WAS IN THIS PLACE WITH OTHER PEOPLE BUT NO ONE WAS FAMILIAR. THEN I RAN INTO THAT MAN THAT FATHERED ME. I ASKED HIM FOR SOME MONEY AS I ALWAYS HAVE, AND HE PULLED OUT TWO ONES AND A FIVE! I WAS HOT!!!!!!!!!!!!!!!!

I WAS YELLING AT HIM AND HE TURNED THE MONEY OVER. THERE WAS A ONE HUNDRED DOLLAR BILL ALONG WITH THE FIVE AND TWO ONES!!!!!!!

HE MADE ME PAY CLOSE ATTENTION TO THE ONE HUNDRED DOLLAR BILL. IT HAD A STAMP ON IT.

WHEN I NOTICED THAT MONEY AND THAT STAMP, EVERYTHING IN ME MELTED!!!!!!!!!!!!!!!!!!!!!! THAT MAN HAD TAKEN A SEAT. I WENT STRAIGHT TO HIM AND LAID MY HEAD IN HIS LAP!!!!!!!!!!!!!!!!!!!!!!!!!!!!!!

THAT FEELING, THAT FEELING, THAT FEELING, THAT FEELING!!

I LAID MY HEAD IN HIS LAP AS IF TO SAY I'M SORRY! I REMEMBER THINKING AS I LAID THERE, HE HAD NEVER DONE THAT FOR NOBODY BUT ME!!!!!!!!!!!

THEN I REMEMBER THINKING THOSE FAMILY WERE GOING TO BE UPSET. I WOKE UP.

I have a clue but I'm not sure.

Later that day my daughter and I were headed for the store, it had been raining all day, but by now it had stopped. As we were driving through the apartments, my daughter said LOOK IN THE SKY! THERE WERE TWO BEAUTIFUL RAINBOWS, AND IN THE MIDDLE IT WAS AQUA GREEN, VERY LIGHT, THAT WAS THE MOST BEAUTIFUL SCEN E!!!!!!!!!!!!!!!!!!!!!!!!!!!!!!!!!!!!!

I DROVE VERY SLOW, I WOULDN'T HAVE MISSED THAT FOR THE WORLD!!!!!!!!!!!!!!!!!!!!!!!!!!!!!!!!!!!!

AS I DROVE, IT ACTUALLY FELT LIKE WE WERE GOING DOWN THE YELLOW BRICK ROAD, AND I TOLD MY DAUGHTER THAT!!!!!!!!!!!!! YOU SHOULD HAVE SEEN THE SMILE ON HER FACE!!!!!!!!!!!!!!!!

SHE WAS FIVE AGAIN!!!!!!!!!!!! SHE BELIEVE!!!!!!!!

IT GOT EVEN BETTER!!!!!!!!!!!!!! MY DAUGHTER STAYED IN THE CAR WHILE I RAN IN THE STORE, AND WHEN I WALKED OUT OF THAT STORE, THE RAINBOW HAD SWITCHED POSTION AND IN THE MIDDLE OF IT WAS   P---I---N---K!!!!!!!!!!!!!!!!!!!!!!!!!!!!!

I BELIEVE THAT WAS FOR ME!!!!!!!!!!!!!!!!!!!!!!!!!

I BELIEVE!!

GOD IS SO AWESOME!!

SEPTEMBER 25th 1:15 am

I HAD A DREAM!!

I WAS BACK INSIDE THE SCHOOL BUILDING WHERE I USE TO WORK. I NOTICED PEOPLE EVERYWHERE. THERE APPEARED A WHITE MAN, A TEACHER. IT WAS LEONARDO DECAPRIO. HIS HAIR WAS IN A PONYTAIL. I REMEMBER THINKING HE IS SO OUT OF PLACE. HE DON'T BELONG HERE. WE WERE FACE TO FACE. I CLEARLY REMEMBER LOOKING INTO HIS EYES. HE TURNED AND WALKED INTO A CLASSROOM.

I REMEMBER SAYING THEY ARE GOING TO KILL HIM.

I REMEMBER BEING SCARED FOR HIM, AND VERY WILLING TO TAKE UP FOR HIM.

THEN I TURNED TO MY LEFT AND THERE WAS ONE OF MY OLD FRIENDS FROM HIGH SCHOOL, A MALE. HE WAS VERY WELL DRESSED. HE HAD ON A NICE SUIT STANDING THERE SMILING. I WAS HAPPY TO SEE HIM AS USUAL. THEN TO MY RIGHT, A BATHROOM APPEARED. THE TOILETS WERE STOPPED UP. I REMEMBER THE JANITOR SAYING SOMETHING IS WRONG WITH THIS WATER, I KNOW NO ONE IS SITTING ON THESE TOILETS. I LOOKED AT THE TOILETS FROM WHERE I WAS STANDING AND NOTICED THE WATER IN THE TOILETS WERE BROWN. MY THOUGHT WAS, I KNEW THEY WERE NASTY. THEN I ENDED UP IN MY OLD NEIGHBORHOOD, AND I GOT A FEELING OF HATE, EMBARRASSMENT AND SHAME, I DIDN'T WANT TO BE THERE. I REMEMBER CLEARLY SAYING, WHY CAN'T I HAVE A HOUSE. I WAS WALKING AROUND FUSSING AND COMPLAINING, QUESTIONING OUT LOUD WHY CAN'T I HAVE A HOUSE! I WAS VERY UPSET AND HATED WHERE I WAS. THEN I ENDED UP IN THE SCHOOL AGAIN, AND MY FRIEND WAS STILL STANDING THERE SMILING, WAITING ON ME. WE BEGAN TO TALK AGAIN. I'M STILL TRYING TO AVOID GETTING TOGETHER WITH HIM, DUE TO THE SECRETS FROM MY PAST, THAT I DON'T CARE TO TALK ABOUT, NOT TO MENTION, I'M NOT DOING AS WELL AS HE IS. THEN I ASKED HIM ABOUT HIS BEST FRIEND I WAS DATING. I REMEMBER I GOT VERY NERVOUS WHEN I ASKED HIM ABOUT HIS FRIEND. HE SMILED AND SAID, LET ME GIVE HIM A CALL. HE PULLED OUT HIS CELL PHONE. I BEGAN TO TRY AND RUN. THEN THERE WAS A LOUD NOICE AND IT BECAME PITCH BLACK. THE WHOLE SCENE TOOK PLACE IN THE HALLWAY, AND I WAS STILL THERE IN THE HALLWAY. THEN THERE WAS THUNDER!!!!!!!!!!!!

I SAID OUT LOUD HE IS MAD!!!!!!!!!!!!!!!!!!!!!!!!!!! I SAID IT AGAIN. HE IS MAD!!!!!!!!!!!!!!!!!!!!!!!!!!!!!!!!!!

MY FRIEND DISAPPEARED. STRONG WINDS CAME!

THE SCHOOL BUILDING TURNED INTO A MUSEUM OR AQUARIUM. IT WAS DARK, THEN TWO HUGE WINDOWS

APPEARED, ON EACH SIDE OF ME. I ACTUALLY SAW THE SKY ON THE GROUND, THEY TOUCHED!!!

THE CLOUDS WERE DARK!!!!!THE CLOUDS ON MY LEFT BEGAN TO RISE, THAT'S WHEN I BEGAN TO TRY AND MAKE SENSE OF WHAT I SAW. THE CLOUDS ON MY LEFT WERE SHAPED LIKE COTTON BALLS, AND WERE IN THE SHAPE OF A <u>W-I-S-H-B-O-N-E</u>!!!!!!!!!!!!!

AS I TRIED TO MAKE SINCE OF IT, I KEPT SAYING THAT LOOK LIKE A WISH BONE. (I have raised my children on grabbing the wish bone and making a wish) I'M STANDING IN THE HALLWAY THE WHOLE TIME TERRIFED!!!! IT GOT DARKER!!! I REMEMBER SAYING HE LEFT ME!!!! I REMEMBER GIVING INTO DEATH, THINKING NO ONE CAN SURVIVE WATER. I WAS TOO SCARED TO TURN TO MY RIGHT, BUT I DID WITH MY EYES CLOSED!!!!!!! I OPENED MY EYES AND I COULD SEE UNDER WATER. I COULD SEE THE BOTTOM OF THE SEA!!!!!!!!! I SAW EVERYTHING THAT LIVED IN THE WATER. I SAW A BIG FISH AS IF IT WERE COMING TOWARDS ME. I CLOSED MY EYES. I WAS FRIEGHTEN!!!! I OPENED MY EYES AGAIN AND THERE WAS THIS HUGE GIGANTIC SEAWEED SWAYING BACK AND FORTH. IT WAS HUGE!!!!!!!!!!!!!

I THOUGHT IT WAS AN OCTOPUS AT FIRST, BUT SOMETHING MADE ME KEEP STARING AT IT, I WAS FORCED TO LOOK! THAT'S WHEN I NOTICED IT WAS A SEAWEED.(A BIG WET TREE!!!!!!!!) THE THUNDER CAME AGAIN, AND I KNEW THAT WAS IT!!!!!!! THE WATER CAME! I GAVE IN. I WAS TOTALLY HELPLESS AND SO TERRIFED!!!!!!!!!!

I KNEW THAT WAS GOD!!!!!!!!!!!!!!!!!!! AND I KNEW I WAS DEAD!!!!!!!!!!!!!! THE SEA TOOK OVER!!!!!!!!!!!!!!

I REMEMBER THINKING HARD, HE WOULD SAVE ME, BUT THEN I REMEMBERED HE WAS TOTALLY ANGRY!!!!!!!!!!!!!!!!!!!!!!!!!!!!!!!

THEN IT WAS OVER!!!!!!!!!!!!!!!!!!!! I REMEMBER CLEARLY FEELING MYSELF WAKE UP, BUT I DIDN'T WANT TO!!!!!!!!! I ASKED WHY!!!!!!!!!!!!!! I WAS GASPING FOR BREATH!!!!!!! THE WATER WAS CALM, BUT I WAS STUCK TO A WALRUS!!!!!!!!!!!!

I TRIED VERY HARD NOT TO LOOK, BUT I WAS STUCK TO THIS SUPER HUGE WALRUS!!!! I WAS CRYING, I WAS TRYING TO

DISCONNECT MYSELF BUT I COULDN'T, I LOOKED DOWN AND I DID NOT HAVE LEGS!!!!!!!! FROM MY STOMACH DOWN, THE BOTTON HALF OF MY BODY WAS GONE!!!!!!!!!!! I COULDN'T USE MY ARMS, THEY WERE STUCK TO MY BODY!!!

I WRIGGLED, I TURNED AND WAS TWISTING HARD TO DISCONNECT MYSELF FROM THAT DEAD WALRUS!!!!!

THE BOTTOM HALF OF MY BODY WAS GONE, AND MY ARMS WERE USELESS, IT WAS JUST MY ELBOWS AND UP!!!!!!!!!!! I FINALLY GOT THE COURAGE TO LOOK OUT AND ABOUT, THE SEA HAD NO ENDING AND IT WAS TOTALLY CALM!!!!!!!!!! !!!!!!!!!!!!!!!!!!!!!!!!!!! I TRIED HARD NOT TO LOOK AT THAT WALRUS AGAIN BUT I HAD NO CHOICE, I WAS STUCK FOR LIFE, ON A DESSERTED BEACH!!!!!

10:30 am

I JUST REMEMBERED THE BEGINNING OF THAT DREAM!!!!!!!!!!!

A TALL BLACK MAN APPEARED. I LOOKED UP AT HIM, BUT I DIDN'T SEE HIS FACE. I NOTICED HIS SHIRT, IT DIDN'T HAVE SLEEVES. I NOTICED HIS PANTS WERE BLACK JEANS WITH WHITE STITCHING. I WAS WAITING ON HIM IN A STAIRWAY. HE WALKED THROUGH A DOOR AND TOOK ME BY THE HAND. MY FOREHEAD CAME TO HIS WAIST. I HAD A STRONG FEELING OF REALLY BEING CRAZY ABOUT HIM!!!!

MY FOREHEAD BUMPED HIS ARM AND THAT FEEING WENT THROUGH ME!!!!!!!!!!!!!!!! WHEN HE REACHED OUT FOR MY HAND I NOTICED HIS HAND, MAINLY HIS FINGERNAILS. THEY WERE VERY WELL KEPT!!! HIS FINGERNAILS WERE CLEAN!!!!!!!!!!! WE WENT DOWN A FLIGHT OF STAIRS, AND THAT WAS FUN!!!!!!!!!!! !!!

THEN WE WALKED THROUGH A CROWD OF PEOPLE AND IT FELT SO RIGHT!!!!!!!!!!!!!!!!!!!!!!!!! THEN HE OPENED ANOTHER DOOR, AND I WENT THROUGH IT. THEN HE DISAPPEARED!!!!!!!! THAT'S WHEN I ENDED UP IN THE SCHOOL BUILDING, STANDING IN THE MIDDLE OF THE HALLWAY ALONE.

IF PEOPLE COULD SEE THE SMILE ON MY FACE!!!!!!

Every time I was out in public and someone was TRULY friendly or nice to me, I made it a habit to tell them;

MAKE A WISH AND GOD WILL MAKE IT COME TRUE!

(I don't know much, but I think that's what GOD meant when he said GIVE HIM YOUR UNDIVIDED ATTENTION)

Printed in the United States
by Baker & Taylor Publisher Services